This Time Forever

USA Today Bestselling Author

Denise Devine

An Inspirational Romance

Wild Prairie Rose Books

This Time Forever

Print Edition

Copyright 2014 by Denise Devine

www.deniseannettedevine.com

ISBN: 978-0-9915956-2-4

Published in the United States of America

Wild Prairie Rose Books

Editors: L. Ness and L.F. Nies

Cover Design by Christopher Edmund

Want to stay in touch with me?

Sign up for my newsletter at https://eepurl.com/csOJZL and receive a *free novella*. You'll be the first to know about my new releases, sales, and special events.

———————————◆———————————

Want to find more authors who write sweet romance?

Join my reader group - Happily Ever After Stories. If you like sweet romance and want to be part of a great group that has lots of fun and fantastic parties, visit us at https://www.facebook.com/groups/HEAstories/.

Chapter 1

Libby Cunningham had risked heartbreak in the past, but not like this. Never before had she come so close to finding the child her father forced her to give up for adoption almost sixteen years ago. Years spent praying and trusting God for a breakthrough had led to disappointment again and again—but not tonight. This time her heart possessed an unexplainable peace, giving her renewed hope. Had God finally answered her plea?

Then she saw the girl.

"That can't be my daughter," Libby murmured as she watched a teenager ascend the stairs of a crowded bleacher at the River's Edge High football game. "That young lady has someone else's genes."

Medley Grant reached over and squeezed her hand. "Lib, Lib, you've got to keep an open mind. I warned you that Amber might not be what you expected."

The crowd roared and Amber MacKenzie pivoted, gazing down at the play in progress. Towering floodlights cast a silvery sheen upon the tall, slender girl wearing a coral sweater and hip-hugging jeans. Waist-length hair hugged her shoulders and arms like a luxurious black shawl.

Libby studied every detail of the girl that she could glean from a distance, desperate to find some connection. "I expected to see something of myself in her," she confessed. Instead, she'd come to a dead end, once again facing the reality that the odds of finding her daughter didn't lean in her favor. "She doesn't resemble me at all."

"Yes, she does!" Medley looked up and stared at the girl, perusing Amber with a smile of approval. "She reminds me precisely of you at that age."

On the field, River's Edge cheerleaders led the raucous crowd into a frenzy of school spirit. Clad in maroon skirts and gold sweaters, they swung matching pom-poms and kicked their legs high. "Push 'em back, push 'em back, w-a-y-y-y back! G-o-o-o Otters!" Behind them, both teams joined arms in their respective huddles, discussing their next plays.

Libby ignored the game and the crush of boisterous spectators seated elbow to elbow on the hard, metal bleachers. The crisp, September evening provided perfect weather for football, but she and her cousin never intended to spend their time watching the game. They were here on a mission—to find Amber MacKenzie. Ever since the girl walked into Medley's salon last week to get a trim, Medley had pressured Libby to attend this event and observe Amber for herself.

Libby twisted at the waist, her gaze sliding from Amber back to her cousin. "What do you see that I don't? I'm blonde and fair. She's so...totally like her father."

Medley paused, holding a couple of kernels of popcorn to her burgundy-tinted lips. "She inherited Cash MacKenzie's looks, but I see other ways you two are exactly alike. That day she came into the salon, I noticed aspects about her that reminded me of you. She has your tall, slender frame. You both frown the same way when you're reading. Oh, and another thing," Medley paused to sip her soda, "Amber's voice..." Medley's fine, penciled brows arched. "She sounds exactly like you."

"I wish I knew for sure." Libby sighed and looked away, not wanting Medley to see her doubt. A couple of similar attributes didn't prove a thing. "If she's almost sixteen she could be mine. If she's younger, then she's his daughter by someone else."

Even though it happened long ago, the thought of Cash MacKenzie marrying so soon after he'd severed all ties with her still touched a nerve. How could he have forgotten her so easily? Had he been seeing someone else all along? That could explain why he'd turned his back on her when she needed him the most...

She stared hard at Amber, wishing with all her heart this girl could be *the one*. For a moment, she dared to entertain the possibility.

"All these years I've believed total strangers adopted my baby," she declared. "If Amber *is* my child and her biological father raised her..." Libby's throat tightened as a simple question hovered in her mind. How did Cash end up with Amber? The only answer possible proved difficult to bear. The people closest to her, the ones she'd trusted, had deceived her.

Amber reached the top row. Squeezing past several people, she slowly made her way to her seat.

"There's Cash." Medley nudged Libby in the ribs. "Wow. The years have been good to him, haven't they?"

The mere mention of his name made Libby tense. Ignoring the comment, she focused straight ahead and pretended to watch the game, but the players on the field quickly melded into a blur as the ploy failed and painful memories ambushed her. The past clouded her thoughts as she recalled the wayward, motherless girl of sixteen who thought she'd grasped the chance to have everything she'd ever wanted—the love of her life and a family of her own. Instead, she'd ended up lonely and alone, rejected by Cash MacKenzie, the only man she'd ever loved or trusted. She didn't want to glance in his direction much less take inventory of his seasoned good looks. It took years to get over him, even longer to forgive him for what he'd done—and left undone.

Medley's gentle nudge brought Libby's attention back to the

present. She expelled an unhappy sigh. "What's *he* doing here? You said Amber planned to come with a friend."

"That's what Amber told me," Medley chirped in her bird-like voice. She looked like a nosegay of fall chrysanthemums in her gold Ann Taylor sweater and dark green slacks. Her chin-length flip of auburn hair glistened with burgundy highlights. "Maybe her friend canceled."

Libby cut Medley a sidewise glance. "Or maybe you secretly arranged this little reunion."

"Don't be ridiculous!" Medley's quick laugh pierced the air. "When have I ever tried to match you up with a man?" Her heavy lashes fluttered. "Well, not this time. Honestly, I didn't know he'd be here." She leaned close. "But I did Google him on the Internet the other day." A mischievous smile turned up the corners of her full lips. "He's not married, you know."

"Cash MacKenzie's personal life is of no interest to me." Libby pointed a warning finger at her. "So, don't even *think* of hatching a scheme to get us together!"

"Aren't you even curious about him?" Medley gazed up at Cash like an adoring groupie. "Like I said, he's still a hunk." She held out a small set of binoculars. "See for yourself."

Libby pushed the binoculars away. "No thanks." Medley's cheerful persistence grated on her nerves, but her cousin had no way of knowing how deeply Cash had wounded her. She didn't see any purpose in discussing the unpleasant details of her past, so she let it go.

"What about Amber?" Medley's jade eyes twinkled. "You've waited so long. Don't you want to gaze upon your own daughter? You'll adore her once you meet her."

"Meet her?" Libby shot her cousin an annoyed look. "On what basis? I have absolutely no proof she's my child."

"She *is* your daughter. I knew it the moment I saw her." Medley

8

grabbed Libby's hand and slapped the binoculars into her palm. "Here. Satisfy your curiosity, once and for all."

Libby debated only a moment. Then she gingerly tugged on the visor of her maroon and gold cap and leaned back to see past the shoulders of the mountainous man sitting to her right. She lifted the silver, palm-sized spyglasses and peered into the stands.

Amber MacKenzie sat tall and straight like a porcelain doll. Heavy lashes hooded her cocoa eyes as she scanned the crowd instead of watching the game. Nothing in either the girl's manner or her features convinced Libby they were mother and daughter.

Someone bumped her elbow, shifting the binoculars sharply to the left. Her hand froze as a tall, broad-shouldered man wearing jeans and a long-sleeved denim shirt popped into view. The front hung open, revealing a gold T-shirt stretched across a wide, muscular chest. Cash MacKenzie, the man who'd shattered her teenage heart looked exactly as she remembered him, only more handsome and more mature. A little voice in the back of her mind warned her to look away, but curiosity held her. At thirty-five, he still had thick, onyx hair. His dark eyes still held the bold, piercing look of a man who planned to conquer the world but now reflected wisdom and confidence as well. He leaned toward his daughter and spoke into her ear. Amber responded with stony silence, her bow-shaped lips pursed into a defiant pout.

Cash kept his expression calm and appeared to accept the rejection, but Libby sensed his tension as he looked away.

The chill between father and daughter continued, vacillating between clipped words and taut silence. Libby watched for several minutes, caught up in the drama of their little family spat. Something in Amber's stubborn expression bothered Libby, giving her the unshakable feeling the girl's unhappiness ran deeper than mere teenage growing pains. She seemed troubled...

Libby sensed someone watching her. She shifted the binoculars and found herself staring straight into Cash's visual line of fire. For a moment she floundered, stunned as his dark, piercing gaze seared through her.

A scene flashed through her mind, sweeping her back to a sultry, starry night. Cash's sinewy arms encircled her waist, his lips softly brushing hers as he whispered, "I'll always love you..."

Liar!

A hollow feeling seeped through her, displacing her peace with emptiness, as though the bottom had just dropped out of her soul. She ducked her head and spun around, using the bulky man next to her as a shield.

Stop this nonsense, she chided herself, aware that her emotions were getting out of hand. *You don't love him anymore. You'd be crazy to love him still—after what he did to you!*

"I need popcorn," she blurted to get her mind off the subject and thrust her fingers into the red and white box, almost knocking it out of Medley's hands.

"Touchdown!" Coronets and drums blasted out the school song.

Medley sprang to her feet with the thundering crowd as they gave the team a standing ovation. Libby followed, using the distraction to keep her mind off the most unsettling moment she'd experienced in a long time. She snatched the popcorn box from Medley and stuffed a handful into her mouth. Did Cash recognize her? "I hope not," she worried aloud.

Medley cupped one ear with her hand. "What?"

"Nothing," Libby shouted over the cheering and clapping. "Nothing that—"

"What? Did you say 'who's that?' I don't know, but he sure is trying hard to get Amber's attention."

Medley motioned toward an attractive young man at the base of the bleachers, standing off to one side. The tall youth wore low-rise, faded jeans and, despite the cool evening, a rust-colored tank top that showed off his lean, muscular build. Thick, walnut brown hair hung in loose waves about his shoulders. Libby lifted the binoculars once again and watched him make signals with his thumb and forefinger. She shifted her focus to Amber, who discreetly signaled back.

The crowd returned to their seats. Libby sat down and observed the teenage instant messaging in progress, curious about the secret conversation. Were they simply flirting, or being cautious because Cash disapproved of their friendship? That could explain why they weren't exchanging text messages or why the boy didn't simply climb the bleachers to talk to her.

Loud booing swelled among the crowd. The man next to Libby jumped out of his seat and blocked her view as he shook his fist, loudly disagreeing with the ref's call. She turned back to the activity on the field, but her thoughts only intensified on Amber and the pain of not finding her child. Despair crept into her heart, draining her hope. Why bother to stay any longer when the answer seemed clear? She'd reached another dead-end.

Libby glanced into the stands and saw Cash sitting alone, talking on his cell phone. She nudged Medley. "Amber is gone. So is her...um...friend."

Medley scooped up her designer handbag. "Yeah," she responded in a tone that sounded more like a question. "I saw them sneak off together while you were daydreaming. Want to take a walk and get a closer look at her?"

Libby slung the strap of her purse over her shoulder and stood. "Amber MacKenzie's social life is none of my business." She checked the time on her cell phone, noting that she should be going over last-minute details of a pre-nuptial dinner scheduled for tomorrow night. Her job as an event planner for a local restaurant didn't run itself. "Let's go. There's only a minute left of the fourth quarter and River's Edge is ahead by fourteen points." She looked up, scrutinizing Cash McKenzie once more. "This game is over."

They squeezed past a half-dozen people, made their way down the crowded stands, and headed toward the school parking lot.

Libby surveyed seemingly endless rows of vehicles. "Do you remember where we parked?"

Medley gestured toward the farthest corner. "Over there." However, once they reached *over there* they still couldn't find Medley's car.

"What's the deal here?" Gripping her hands on her almost non-existent hips, Medley stopped and looked around. "How hard can it be to find a blue Focus?"

They wandered through more rows, looking for Medley's car.

Medley suddenly grabbed Libby by the forearm. "Don't look now, but Amber and her friend are right over..." She nodded toward the driver's side of a red Grand Am. "...there."

Libby craned her neck to see them.

"Don't stare! You'll give us away!"

Curious, Libby looked anyway. Amber stood in a semi-circle with five other teens, sharing a cigarette. The boy in the rust-colored tank top stood next to her, his muscular arm draped possessively around her shoulders as he gazed intently into her eyes.

Libby knew that look. It meant trouble.

Suddenly Cash appeared out of nowhere and strode toward his daughter, his expression grim, hands clenched at his sides. He grasped her by the arm and pulled her away from the boy.

"The restrooms are over there," he said to Amber and pointed across the lot. "What are you doing here?"

Crimson, Amber glanced at the other teens. "I'm talking to my friends, Dad! Go away!" She tried to hide the cigarette behind her back, but Cash grabbed her hand and tossed the butt to the damp ground. He splayed her fingers, exposing a large class ring. Shaking his head, he slipped it off her hand.

"Don't!" Amber grabbed at it to get it back.

Cash held up the ring in the boy's face. "Is this yours?"

The teen reciprocated with an arrogant shrug.

"Take it back. She's too young for you."

"Stop it!" Tears pooled in Amber's eyes. "Leave Brian alone!"

Scowling, Brian snatched his ring back.

Cash rebounded with a stern look. "Smoking, ditching homework, skipping school—my daughter never did any of those things until she started hanging out with *you*."

Brian cut Amber a sideways glance then stared back at Cash. "If you say so."

Cash let the statement go unchallenged and turned his back to the group. "C'mon, we're going home," he said tersely to Amber. Their gazes locked—hers rife with defiance and resentment, his burdened with disappointment and pain.

As he turned to go, he glanced across the trunk of the car and met Libby's gaze. Jolting to a stop, he blinked and did a double-take, his mouth gaping as though he couldn't believe what he saw—or, more accurately, *whom*.

Libby froze, but her heart pounded so hard she feared everyone could hear it. She never meant for Cash to see her, much less realize that she'd witnessed the entire episode at his expense.

"Oh-oh. Time to go," Medley whispered.

Libby barely heard the words but knew she needed to get out of there. She needed to escape from *him*, a living reminder of the most tragic event of her life. Without a word, she turned and swiftly walked away, leaving Cash MacKenzie to stare after her.

*   *   *

Cash drove out of the parking lot in an emotional daze. His hands steered, his foot accelerated and worked the brakes, but his heart shifted his thoughts into instant replay mode, reviewing the scene back at school.

"You embarrassed me, Dad! You made me look stupid!"

He vaguely heard the sobbing accusation. It sounded like Amber, but thoughts churned in his mind so hard he couldn't concentrate on anything other than navigating his pickup.

"You look fine," he mumbled, barely aware he'd replied.

Libby...

He still couldn't believe it. Had their paths crossed accidentally or had she deliberately planned this encounter?

Her tall, slender image loomed in his mind like a permanent screensaver in Technicolor. She looked the same, yet different. She still wore her blonde hair long and sleek. And she still looked good in jeans and a blue blazer—the color of her eyes. Yet, something about her made him pause. Besides the passage of time, what made her seem different? He stared at the road ahead, wondering why it mattered. After all, she had turned her back on him and Amber long ago. He thought the years had erased the hurt over the betrayal they'd suffered, but it still lived in his heart. He clutched his gut. Now it had affected his stomach, too.

"I'll never be able to face my friends again! Tomorrow everyone in school will be talking about me. And laughing!"

"We'll discuss it when we get home," he muttered.

So... Why show up now? What did Libby want? An accusing little voice whispering from a far corner of his mind suggested what he already suspected; she'd come back to reclaim her daughter. She meant to take Amber away from him. The possibility made his stomach burn like acid.

He reached into his shirt pocket and pulled out a roll of antacids, popping two into his mouth, chewing them like candy. The pain in his stomach flared. He devoured two more. His stomach couldn't take any more bad news. Amber's obsessive crush on a kid with a bad attitude had him tied in knots. Libby Cunningham's intrusion could destroy his family.

What's going on, Lord? You've already pushed me into a season of testing with Amber. Do you expect me to deal with Libby Cunningham, too? Why are all of these things happening at once? What are you trying to do, turn me inside out?

"I'm never going to school again! Ever!"

Amber's shouting finally broke through his thoughts. He cut her a sideways glance. If she hugged the door any closer, she'd be in the street.

"You're the worst dad in the world," she spat with a loud sob. Tears streamed down her cheeks. "I hate you! I hate you! I'm going to run away!"

Cash turned into his driveway and shut off the engine. At any other time, he would have bridled at Amber's behavior and grounded her on the spot. Today, however, her tantrum seemed tame compared to what he'd just experienced. Gripping the steering wheel with one hand and clutching the keys—still in the ignition—with the other hand, he tipped his head back, closed his eyes, and expelled a deep groan. He had a bad feeling his life would never be the same again.

Suddenly, he became aware of an odd silence in the truck. Pushing aside his troubled thoughts, he looked sideways at Amber. She sat smeared to the door, glowering at him with the tenacity of a cornered wolverine.

"You haven't heard a word I've said!" She rounded out the claim with an exaggerated sniff and swiped the back of her hand across her cheek. Thick, wet lashes fringed her large brown eyes. It reminded him of how she looked as a young child. She had once been so sweet, so trusting and carefree. He wanted his little girl back. Where had she gone?

Amber continued to stare at him as if his reticence garnered suspicion. "H-how come you're not yelling at me for smoking and sneaking off with Brian?"

He couldn't imagine how to explain what he'd just been through, so he stayed silent.

She sat up straight and placed her hand on the door latch, frowning in confusion. "What's the matter with you, Dad? Ever since we got into the truck, you've been acting strange. Spaced out—like you've been struck by lightning or something." She squinted, giving him a curious once-over, as though trying to catch something she'd previously missed. "Are you okay?"

Struck by lightning? Or the divine hand of God? Deep in his heart, Cash knew God had put him on notice today and the pain in his gut told him he'd better pay attention because neither Libby Cunningham nor his indigestion planned to go away. Or God, for that matter. But what God wanted from him he wouldn't give—couldn't give. All these years he'd believed he'd forgiven Libby for deserting him and their child. Seeing her today made him realize he'd neither forgiven nor forgotten what she'd done.

Man, did he have a mess on his hands. He had problems with Amber, Libby, and now, God, too. He reached into his pocket, hunting for his antacids. The way things were going, he figured he'd soon be buying them by the case.

*   *   *

"I know you meant well, Medley, but we've checked her out and she's not my daughter. So, let's put it behind us and move on. Okay?" Libby paced the ivory carpet of Medley's living room, making a futile attempt to walk off her frustration.

Medley emerged from the kitchen with two orange mugs of French roast and set them on the coffee table next to a tin of chocolate-dipped biscotti. She collapsed onto her white leather sofa with a satisfied sigh and kicked off her dark green shoes. "Sit down, Libby." She patted the cushion next to her.

Medley's condominium looked like an IKEA showroom with leather furniture, glass, and wood bookcases, and brass table lamps, all in the modern, simplistic styling that described her outlook on nearly everything. "Let's have some Starbucks and discuss our next move."

Libby walked over to the window instead, lifted the curtain, and stared down at the tree-lined street. The burgeoning fall colors in Minneapolis provided a mosaic of scarlet, orange, and gold under the glow of city streetlights.

"I appreciate your wanting to help find my daughter, I really do, but we struck out this time and I don't see the point in talking about it anymore. We gave it our best shot. Unfortunately, it didn't turn out as we'd hoped it would." Her sigh formed a misty spot on the glass. "I'm tired and I have a busy day at work tomorrow. I need to go home."

Home meant the lonely, six-bedroom monstrosity overlooking Lake Harriet that she'd inherited from her late father, former U.S. Senator, Franklin Cunningham.

"What you really need is to lighten up." Medley pursed her lips as she pulled the cover off the tin. "You can't be tense when you talk to Cash; otherwise you may not be able to convince him that the best situation for Amber is to have both her parents involved in her life."

Libby let the curtain fall and spun away from the window. "Medley, I'm not going to put myself through embarrassing agony and call him begging for non-existent information." The stress of another defeat had taken its toll. She swallowed hard, fighting a catch in her throat. "Didn't you notice when they were arguing how much alike they looked? It's obvious she's not mine!"

"Of course, she is!" Medley's quick smile asserted that she believed it without a doubt.

"How can you be so sure? She doesn't possess a single characteristic that resembles me."

"Lib, Lib, you're just upset because so much is at stake. It's natural to be apprehensive." Medley offered her a steaming mug. "You've dreamed of this moment for years."

Libby walked back to the sofa and sat down. She accepted the coffee and took a sip. The rich, hot liquid soothed her throat but did nothing for her morale.

"Cash didn't appreciate our intrusion. We both saw the shock on his face. Even if, by a remote chance, Amber is my daughter, I can't imagine him welcoming me into her life."

"He knows what's best for her. He'll do the right thing." Medley set her mug on the coffee table. "You want to know the truth, don't you? So, you can put this behind you and get on with your life?"

"You know I do."

Medley picked up her cell phone and placed it in Libby's free hand. "Then stop being so stubborn about this. Swallow your doubts and make the call. For Amber's sake as well as your own, confront him and get it over with."

Libby's hand shook so hard she could barely set her mug down. She held the gold bling case in her quaking palm and stared at it as unbearable pain filled her heart. She dreaded the thought of having her hopes destroyed again—like so many times in the past. Now that she had observed Amber, the mirror image of Cash MacKenzie, would today be any different?

Medley produced a business card from her handbag. "He owns a construction company. Amber dug this out of her backpack when I said I wanted to remodel the kitchen." She placed it on the coffee table and pushed it toward Libby. "Come on, Lib. Do it."

Libby's heart raced as she tentatively punched in the number and waited. She held her breath and listened to one ring, then another. She'd almost given up when he finally answered.

"MacKenzie here." Cash's telephone voice had a deep, masculine note, precisely as she remembered it. The sting of his abandonment gripped her heart with fresh intensity, as though it had happened yesterday.

The assault on her confidence startled her and she nearly dropped the phone. Her mind suddenly went blank. She squeezed her eyes shut, reluctant to expose the deepest part of her to someone who hadn't cared back then and wouldn't now.

Holy Spirit, please, she prayed, *I need Your help! Give me the right words to say to him!*

Medley gave her a gentle nudge, pressuring her to speak.

She took a deep breath and opened her eyes. "Hello, Cash."

Chapter 2

Cash sat in the den, perched on the edge of a pillow-back sofa with his cell phone in one hand and a mouth-watering slice of pepperoni pizza in the other. He'd intended to devour a large bite when the call came. Now he'd lost his appetite.

He tossed the pizza back into the box and picked up the television remote, hitting the mute button.

Her cousin's name appeared on his Caller ID screen, but he knew Medley Grant didn't have any reason to call him. No, it had to be *her*.

"Who is this?" he demanded, forcing her to make the first move.

"It's Libby...Libby Cunningham."

The sound of her voice, so gentle and feminine, so...sincere, threw him off guard. He hadn't expected that. Was it an act? Wary, he pressed on. "What do you want?"

"I'd like to talk to you about Amber."

The quiet determination in her delivery tripped an alarm in his heart, putting his defenses on 'fight or flight' alert. Given the stakes, he chose to fight and braced himself for a confrontation. "What's done is done. The past speaks for itself. There is nothing to talk about—"

"We should have had this conversation years ago, Cash." She sounded prepared. "Let's talk now."

He released a taut sigh and stared at the congealing pizza on the coffee table. If given the choice he'd put her off forever, but he knew she'd keep pursuing him. "All right," he said brusquely. Might as well duke it out tonight and settle the situation. He picked up the remote again and hit the power button. The screen went black. "What do you want?"

"The truth. Is she mine?"

The question surprised him at first. Then it angered him. He sprung from the sofa and began pacing the room. After years of silence, why had she chosen to show up now demanding answers? Her timing seemed too convenient to be accidental. Did she know about his problems with Amber? Moreover, did she expect to use them as an excuse to draw Amber into a relationship with her? Libby's interference, he feared, would distract Amber, confuse her and possibly pull her even farther away from him.

"I've got to know," Libby insisted, disrupting his internal monologue. "Is she my daughter?"

He crossed the room and peered through the doorway to make sure Amber hadn't overheard him talking. The house remained quiet except for faint notes of music wafting from her bedroom at the top of the stairs on the second floor. Relieved, he shut the door. "You gave birth to her," he replied soberly as he leaned against it, "but, no. *She's mine.*" There. That set her straight.

He heard her gasp. Awkwardness pervaded the ensuing silence.

"Oh," she whispered, her voice trembling with shock. "I...I didn't expect..."

It took a moment to sink in that he'd made her cry. "I didn't mean to be so blunt," he declared, wondering if the tears were real, "but I'm skeptical about your intentions. Amber doesn't hear from you once in her entire life and now suddenly you're a phone call away. *Why?*"

"After they took her away from me, I had no way to find out what happened to her," she responded. "Now that I've found her, I intend to make up for lost time."

Though she didn't sound threatening, he heard between the lines. Things were about to change—with or without his cooperation. Fear and dread clouded his judgment.

"No, you're not," he countered in a low, level voice. "Look, I don't know where you've been for almost sixteen years or why you've decided to surface now, but I suggest you go back to where you came from and leave us alone. You have no right to interfere."

"I'd never do that. All I want is what's best for Amber."

"Then stay out of her life. You've been out of the picture since her birth and as far as I'm concerned, that's where you belong. Goodbye."

"Wait! I still don't understand how or why you—"

"That's all I have to say," Cash interrupted, losing patience again. "*Good night.*"

"You can hang up on me, Cash, but I'm not going away. You have something I've literally dreamed about finding for almost half my life—*my child!*" She spoke with so much force he pulled the phone away from his ear. "Please, I want to know more about Amber," she continued in a softer tone. "I need to know more! You're right. It's late and we're both tired. Meet me tomorrow for coffee. There's so much I'm anxious to ask—"

"*No.*"

An ominous silence settled over the moment. Cash knew he should hang up, but something made him hold on.

"I don't understand," she said at last. "You admit that Amber is my child, but you're not willing to talk to me about her?"

"That's right."

"Why?"

"I just told you."

"You didn't tell me anything," she insisted, "except that you're afraid to adjust."

"I'm not the one who might have difficulty adjusting."

"You mean, Amber's going through a difficult stage."

"I mean, she's no different than any other girl her age."

"In other words," Libby said smoothly, "it's about a boy."

He didn't answer at first. What could he say? She'd witnessed that unfortunate scene in the school parking lot tonight. She knew the score. "I'm handling it," he said finally.

"Cash, if my daughter is having issues, I want to know about them."

"What happened tonight is between Amber and me—"

"Listen, I know what you're thinking," Libby argued softly, "and I don't agree, but that's a discussion for another time. All I'm asking is to meet with you and talk about the important things I've missed in my daughter's life. Just you and I. Amber doesn't have to know."

Cash debated the idea. Every shred of instinct he possessed made him want to shout "Forget it!" but that still, small voice coming from his conscience argued that she wouldn't give up until she got some answers. She had the right to know about her daughter, that he understood. But she didn't have the right to interfere. Amber belonged legally to him—lock, stock, and curling iron.

"All right," he said after a moment. "Meet me at Sandhill Nature Center tomorrow morning at nine sharp. I drive a red Dodge pickup."

"I'll be there!" Excitement and surprise rang in her voice.

Cash shut off his cell phone and set it on the table then picked up the pizza box and headed for the kitchen. On his way out of the den, he paused in the doorway and gazed up the stairs to the partially closed door of Amber's bedroom. He'd have a talk with Libby and set her straight, once and for all. He couldn't tell if her feelings for Amber were genuine, but one thing he knew for sure; he'd never allow her to hurt Amber the way she'd hurt him.

Ever.

*   *   *

Libby arrived early at Sandhill Nature Center. She needed time to strengthen herself in the Lord and calm the jitters in her stomach before meeting Cash. Why had he insisted they meet at Sandhill? The last time she and Cash secretly met there, they were still in high school. They'd ambled along the walking trail, holding hands and trading kisses...

She drove into a large, sloped parking lot surrounded by towering trees cloaked in a patchwork of gold, scarlet, and orange. She'd expected to be the first to arrive but saw right away that God had other plans.

Cash MacKenzie stood next to his glossy red pickup, poured into faded jeans, a gray T-shirt, and wire-rimmed sunglasses. He leaned against the tailgate, soaking up the golden rays of the late September sun with ankles crossed and his solid, muscular arms folded across broad his chest. The mere thought of him being relaxed and confident with so much at stake unnerved her.

"Dear God, please give me the strength to get through this," she whispered breathlessly as she glided her white BMW into the space next to his. This meeting could turn out to be the most important conversation of her life. Her knees wobbled as she opened the car door and climbed out.

This is not good, she thought, gripping the doorframe to steady herself.

Cash pushed himself away from the tailgate. "You're early," he stated with an air of authority in his deep, throaty voice. He reached the car and rested his hand next to hers.

Her fingers clenched the top of the doorframe, her palms moistening. He stood taller, wider in the shoulders than she remembered. The rich, spicy scent of his aftershave surrounded him like invisible armor. He stood too close, towering over her as though he meant for his mere presence to intimidate her. Mustering courage, she straightened her five-foot-ten-inch frame and looked up. "So are you."

He nodded in reply, but his silence made it clear he didn't want to be there. Libby gripped the door tighter and stared at her reflection in his sunglasses, forcing herself to appear calm while her bravado nose-dived. Perhaps this would be the *shortest* conversation of her life.

He surprised her, though, and stood aside, gesturing with a sweep of his hand for her to lead the way. She let go of the door and stepped from the car, willing her knees not to buckle as he shut it behind her. They walked in silence through the parking lot to the heavy, cedar gates leading into a wooded area. Cash swung open the gate and stood aside, allowing Libby to enter first. They walked together along a paved, curving walkway toward the interpretive center. A large group of schoolchildren chattered in joyful disorder as they crowded around the entrance to the square, one-story complex, waiting for a park naturalist to guide them on a nature tour.

Cash cut a sharp left and guided Libby past the main building and outdoor amphitheater along the perimeter trail, a walking path that circled the entire Sandhill natural area. They continued in silence through a dense forest of cottonwoods, aspens, and maples, passing an occasional jogger, until the blacktopped path turned to crushed limestone. A gentle breeze whispered through the trees, showering them with colorful leaves. Birds chorused overhead. Suddenly she knew why Cash insisted they meet here. Sandhill Nature Center's secluded trails provided the perfect public place for a very private conversation. She cut him a pointed, sideways glance. Did he plan to talk soon or walk off his bad mood first?

"Let's cut to the chase. What do you want?" he said suddenly as if reading her thoughts.

His abruptness startled her. "To—to meet Amber."

He halted in his tracks. "Why?"

"Because she's my daughter and she needs me."

His jaw tensed. "I don't agree. She's *my* daughter and all these years we've managed fine—without you."

Libby shoved her fists into the pockets of her black blazer. She'd spent years learning to forgive him. Ironically, it only took a few words from him to resurrect the hurt and anger she'd worked so hard to bury. "I'm not trying to interfere! I simply want to be involved in my daughter's life."

"Is that so?"

She flinched at the bitterness in his retort.

"Then where were you when she cut her first tooth? Where were you on her first day of school? Or the day she flew off her bike and cried her little heart out while getting stitches under her chin? You should have been there!"

His accusation pierced her heart, but she pressed on, determined to win his cooperation.

"I understand how you must feel, but please don't judge me before you hear all the facts, Cash. I may not have been with her, but she has always been with me. She's always on my mind." *And in my heart*, Libby thought as a familiar ache swelled deep inside her. "Over the years, every time I came home

25

to visit my dad and I saw a little blonde girl about Amber's age, I wondered if I had looked into the face of my own child. You have no idea what I've suffered, coping with the reality of someone else raising my baby, tucking her into bed every night."

Cash yanked his sunglasses off. "What gives you the right to miraculously appear after all these years and barge into our lives?" He glared at her. "Who do you think you are?"

His indignation stung. She pursed her lips, ready to fire off a dozen reasons, but stopped short when she saw the dark circles lining his deep-set cocoa eyes. *Didn't he sleep last night, either?* She glanced at his hand and saw the sunglasses tremble. *Did he fear her as much as she feared him?*

"I'm her mother," she replied, projecting a new level of resolve. "I love her. I always have!"

Cash shoved the sunglasses into his T-shirt pocket. Gripping his hands on his waistband, he stepped close, staring down at her, his rock-hard gaze loaded with mistrust. "If you care so much, why did you give her up in the first place?"

Libby blinked in disbelief. The butterflies in her stomach settled, hardening into cement cocoons. "You know why," she countered swiftly, her tone matching the fire inflaming her cheeks. "I was only sixteen and totally alone because everyone I trusted turned against me." She jabbed her index finger into the center of his solid chest. "...including you."

He pushed her hand away. "That's not—"

"You promised to stand by me, but instead you took the coward's way out." She jabbed him again. "Don't deny it! You abandoned me, Cash. You dropped out of sight and left me to deal with my father on my own!"

"Don't!" Her stomach did a strange little dance as his long fingers wrapped around her narrow wrists. Confusion flickered in his eyes. For a moment neither spoke. Then he dropped her hands and moved away, shoving his fists behind him. "I'm no coward and you know it."

"Oh, really?" She fired back. Deep in her heart, a fervent voice whispered to let it go, but she ignored the warning. She'd harbored this little speech for years. She had to let it out. "Then where were *you* when I needed you the most? You certainly weren't by my side as you promised! My father nearly had a heart attack when he found out what I—" she raised her palms, "—what *we* had done. He blamed himself, saying he'd failed me because he'd never remarried after my mother died. He never got over the fact that his little girl had gone all the way with a boy and ended up in trouble."

Terror flickered in Cash's eyes, suggesting that he held the same fear concerning Amber. Reaching into his jean pocket, he pulled out a roll of antacids. He peeled off several and popped them into his mouth like peanuts.

"My grandmother took a different view," Libby continued. "She condemned me, claiming that my reckless indiscretion held the potential to cause embarrassment and permanent damage to Dad's political career. She convinced him that a private adoption would solve everything. Amber would have a normal family life with..." Libby almost choked on the irony. "...two parents and our family's reputation would stay intact. They made the decision and ordered me to sign consent forms, terminating my parental rights. I begged them to let me keep her, but my grandmother insisted I do the *right* thing and give up my baby."

Her mouth tasted salty as she swallowed back harsh memories. "Adoption may have been the right decision for them, but I've struggled with guilt and regret ever since for caving under their pressure."

"A touching story, but I'm not impressed," Cash retorted, stone-faced. "The senator must have rewarded you well for turning your back on your child. What did he offer you? A new car? A trip to Europe?"

Libby gasped at his callous assumption. "He didn't discuss the process with me or even ask about my feelings. My actions hurt him so deeply he barely spoke to me after that."

Cash stared hard at her. "The way I figure it, you both wanted Amber out of the way. Her existence caused embarrassment for a senator who touted *family values* and having a baby in your care put a crimp in your social life."

"That's not true!"

"Isn't it? Then why didn't your father acknowledge your mistake, apologize to his supporters and simply move on instead of covering it up?"

An elderly couple wearing green hiking suits and matching sun visors appeared on the trail. Self-conscious, Libby folded her arms into a tight bow and spun away. From the corner of her eye, she saw Cash follow suit. They stood back to back, cooling their tempers as the couple passed by.

Libby looked away to avoid their curious glances. As the crunch of their footfalls on the gravel faded, she whirled around. "The truth is, I don't know why he covered it up. What difference does it make, anyway? We can't control what our parents do; neither can we go back and change the past."

He refused to answer, his silence communicating his true feelings about the matter.

"You've never forgiven me for giving her up, have you?"

He stood silent for a moment, as though carefully choosing his next words. "How do you think I felt when I found out that you'd put our daughter up for adoption? What I find hard to forgive is why you—and your father— deliberately chose to exclude me from the process." A muscle in his jaw tightened. "Let's get out of here." He walked away, approaching a fork in the path, taking the one that led back into the sunshine and a large cattail marsh.

Libby watched him go, disappointed in his reaction, though she understood how he felt. She hadn't forgiven herself, either. Would Amber?

She went after him, taking two steps to each of his long strides. They approached the floating boardwalk, a one-hundred-fifty-foot dock that carved a path through the cattails to the other side of the marsh.

"I didn't let you know because I couldn't reach you. Cash, you didn't even bother to tell me goodbye." Libby's black shoes tapped on the metal planks as she hurried past a maple with a crown of bright scarlet. Oddly enough, the bottom half of the tree remained green. "You just disappeared. Why? Why did you break my heart like that?"

Cash stared straight ahead. "I had no choice."

"That's an excuse, not an explanation."

"It's the truth. When the senator found out about your condition," he cut her a sideways glance, "he dispatched two of his aides to my parents' home. They ordered me to stay away from you and warned if I didn't, the senator would press charges."

"Is that all?" She glanced across a small patch of sparkling blue water and fought the urge to push him off the dock. Perhaps a good dousing would bring him to his senses! "Since when did you let my father tell you what to do? You were well aware in those days that he disapproved of you, yet you'd never allowed his opinions to sway you before."

Cash shook his head, squinting in the bright sun. "Once my parents became involved, everything changed. My mother held me solely responsible for what happened and made me apologize for the grief I'd caused our family. After all, by that time I'd turned eighteen, but all along I'd always known what we were doing could have dire consequences." Guilt shadowed his face. "I shouldn't have—"

"Neither of us should have," Libby cut in. "Grandma Cunningham accused me of the same thing. She made me feel so ashamed and unworthy that I couldn't face my father any longer. I agreed to go to a private Christian home for unwed mothers to spare my dad any further hurt and humiliation than I'd already caused. I spent the loneliest, most miserable months of my life there, waiting to hear from you."

"You're not the only one who ended up lonely and depressed." Cash shrugged. "I had no knowledge of your whereabouts or how you were getting along. After the incident with the senator, my parents refused to even talk about the situation, much less acknowledge my feelings."

"You could have gotten word to me somehow—if you'd cared enough."

"I tried. I called Medley's house but her mother said she'd gone to New York for the summer. I checked with your friends, but no one knew what had happened to you." Cash eyed her suspiciously. "Then again, you knew my phone number. Why didn't you contact me?"

"I did! I called you a dozen times and couldn't get past your mother. After that, I wrote to you almost every week, explaining the situation and begging you to call me. You should have written back and told me to leave you alone. It would've hurt, but at least I'd have had closure."

Disbelief clouded his face. "I never received any letters from you."

His answer surprised her, causing her to pull back. "Then your mother obviously intercepted them."

He looked stunned for a moment then answered with a cynical snort. "My mother's a decent person. She wouldn't do that."

"How did you obtain custody of Amber?"

"I got Amber the old-fashioned way—with a lot of earnest prayers and a good lawyer. Forgive my skepticism, but I find it hard to believe you didn't know I had adopted her. I've never tried to hide her from you or your family."

"They took her away two days after I gave birth. I had no way of knowing where she went or who adopted her," Libby said, drawing deep breaths. The walk proved to be good exercise, but the discussion had generated more stress than she'd bargained for. "A couple of days after I left the hospital, Grandma Cunningham had my things packed and shipped me to a private school in Seattle to uphold the 'good girl' image that she and Dad had constructed for the public. Eventually, I grew up and accepted the fact that you'd...moved on. I didn't decide to come back to Minnesota permanently until they'd both passed away. Once I relocated back here and got settled into Dad's house, I avoided every place I could possibly run into you."

Granted, the likelihood of crossing paths with one person out of several million across the seven-county metro area proved small, but she hadn't taken any chances. "I've never gone back to your old neighborhood."

Cash slipped his sunglasses back on. "After the senator threatened me, I rarely went back to yours, either."

They came to the end of the boardwalk and connected with the perimeter trail once again. Libby saw the park entrance up ahead. The end of their walk loomed in the distance and probably their conversation as well. All the questions she'd planned to ask him, but didn't get a chance to voice could wait, except one.

"I want to meet my daughter," she announced when they reached the white and brown facade of the Interpretive Center. The place was deserted now. "Will you arrange it?"

Cash wheeled around. "Then what? Do you plan to see her again?"

"Of course," she replied, taken aback.

"Why?"

His constant interrogation taxed her patience, but she kept her temper, knowing it wouldn't help her cause to agitate him further. "I want to be part of her life, Cash. The world is a very different place than what we experienced growing up. She needs me now more than ever."

His brows drew together above the sunglasses. "What guarantee do I have that you'll live up to your promises?"

"You have my word as her mother."

"That's not enough."

Libby's heart sank. "I don't understand."

"She's a person. Not a toy for you to play with as long as your interest lasts."

"I wouldn't use her like that," Libby replied softly, hurt that he'd believe her capable of such a thing. "Give me a chance, Cash. I've been living for this day since I lost Amber. Now that God has brought us together again, I won't let you keep us apart."

His lips pressed into a hard line. "I trusted you with our daughter once and you proved you couldn't handle the responsibility." Wariness threaded his voice. "I'm sorry, but I'm not willing to take that chance a second time."

He turned and stalked out of the park, once again abandoning her; once again breaking her heart.

*   *   *

Still shaking from his encounter with Libby Cunningham, Cash drove onto the job site and slammed on the brakes, parking next to a white, monster-sized pickup. Clouds of sand billowed around his Dodge Ram, covering both vehicles with fine grit. He glanced across the lot at his current construction project and inhaled a deep breath, hoping the serene quality of his surroundings would calm him down.

The forty-acre subdivision with rolling hills and dense hardwood forest would be a beautiful place to live once the custom-built homes were finished. The project bordered a sprawling wildlife refuge managed by the State of Minnesota. More lakes than he could count on both hands were scattered within the community.

A flatbed truck sat next to the framework of a future four-thousand-square-foot home. The truck's boom lifted a truss, mounting it atop the building's frame.

Ping! Ping! Ping!

A chorus of nail guns echoed as Cash's jeans and T-shirt-clad crew worked like bees around a hive. Somewhere on the lot, a stereo screamed music louder than an outdoor concert.

Cash usually handled the company's finances and left the project management to his partner, Todd Trisco. Not this time, however. The serene, pristine beauty of this northern suburb of Minneapolis had not only caught his eye but had captured his heart as well. Each time he came to work he experienced a deep calm, as though he belonged here. Every day he grew more attached to the idea of him and Amber living out here in the country, enjoying a quiet, peaceful life...

His mood began to lighten when suddenly Libby Cunningham's face popped into his head, exploding his thoughts into confusion. Visitation with Amber?

"Over my dead body," he muttered then took it back. What if God sided with Libby? He didn't want to prophesy his own demise!

A horn blast nearly blew him out of the truck. Todd Trisco's black Hummer came to a sliding stop, narrowly missing a dumpster full of scrap materials.

Todd hopped out of his vehicle. "Well? How'd it go?"

Cash slid out of his truck, slammed the door, and looked across the Hummer's shiny hood to a six-feet-four-inch, blue-eyed Norseman wearing a sky-blue tank top over a golden tan. "She says she wants to be involved in Amber's life."

Todd straightened his broad, freckled shoulders and tossed a lock of fine, blond hair off his forehead. "Yeah, I figured that. Are you gonna set it up?"

"Negative." Cash walked between the two vehicles and met Todd at the back of the Hummer.

Todd opened the rear hatch. Before he could catch it, a galvanized minnow bucket tumbled out and bounced on the ground. "Why not?"

"I can't trust her."

"Maybe she's changed, Cash." He grabbed the bucket, shoved it back into the Hummer, and wiped his hands on his jeans. "Or maybe you've been wrong about her all along." He ducked under the hatch and leaned inside the vehicle, crammed tight with fishing gear. "Have a heart for the little lady, would ya?" he said as he pried open a cooler.

Cash's palms glistened with sweat. He hadn't expected a lecture from his partner, the one person he thought would truly understand.

"What about Amber's heart? She gave Amber away. What guarantee do I have that she won't reel in the kid's affection then lose interest in her again?"

Todd held out a cup of ice water, complete with large cubes. "You need to chill."

Cash shook his head, half expecting to see a few minnows floating between the ice.

Todd helped himself. "She's the girl's mother," he said after taking several huge gulps. "She deserves at least a chance. Besides..." He downed the last of the water. "She's gonna get what she wants. So, why not just cooperate and avoid all the hassle?" He held out one palm. "You know it's a losing battle."

Cash couldn't believe it. "Whose side are you on, anyway?"

"Yours. Amber's." Todd looked around and shrugged as though his logic needed no defense. "Everybody's." He poured the ice on the ground and pitched the cup into the dumpster. "Pardon me, but someone needs to point out common sense here. You're not gonna stop a mother from seeing her daughter. I mean, once she tells Amber that you're trying to keep them apart, it's all over but the support payments for you, my friend."

"Yeah, well, I lose more than my paycheck if Amber decides she wants to live with her mother."

"Don't worry about it." Todd grinned broadly. "You're her pa, King Big Heart. Princess Clothes Horse knows who's holding the gold card. She's not gonna leave all that."

Cash leaned against the Hummer and folded his arms. "Gee, thanks. I feel better knowing I have the appeal of Fort Knox."

"She's a teenager. What can I say? Her life revolves around two things—how she looks and whom she impresses. Come on. You know we were the same way at that age." Todd glanced at his reflection in a tinted window and smoothed his shoulder-length locks. "You also know that no matter how she acts, she loves you." He sobered. "She's been raised by the best. If her mother isn't sincere, Amber will sense it right away."

"Yeah, but—" Cash leaned his head back and sighed. "That's exactly what I want to protect her from. I don't want to risk the chance of Amber getting hurt."

"Hey." Todd's wide, work-roughened hand reached out and squeezed Cash's shoulder. "You're always lecturing me to trust the Lord whenever I have a major problem with a woman. For once, take your own advice. Okay? Call her and set up a time for Amber to meet her. Invite her out for dinner or something. Make this situation easier on yourself—and Amber. Trust me; everything will work out for the best."

"I need some time to think about it," Cash said, resisting the tug on his conscience to stop judging Libby. "I'll take that water now."

Todd leaned inside the Hummer again and rummaged through coils of nylon fishing line, boxes of tackle, and an assortment of fishing reels to retrieve the green, reusable shopping bag that he always kept filled with Styrofoam cups. "What happened exactly?"

Cash stared at his Nikes. "I lost it."

"Whoa." Todd halted. "That doesn't sound like you."

Cash looked up. "She upset me so much I couldn't be civil. Yet, she scared me so much I could hardly breathe. They're a great deal alike, you know—the stubbornness, the defiance. Amber exhibits the same rebellious traits her mother possessed at that age. It terrifies me."

He gazed at the cloudless sky and wondered about Libby's letters. Had she honestly tried to contact him or had she conveniently made up that story just to elicit sympathy? He'd considered calling his mother in Florida to question her about it but decided against the idea. His family didn't need to know about

Libby or his problems with Amber.

Todd slammed the lid on the cooler. "Did you ask her?"

"Ask her what?"

Todd held out a cup of water. "You know; if she had a husband and other children."

Cash nearly dropped the cup. "*NO*."

"Why not?"

"Because it's none of my business. Besides, I really don't care."

Todd chuckled, showing off a perfect set of gleaming teeth. "Oh, yeah? Then why'd you get a haircut this morning?"

Cash looked him square in the eye. "I needed one."

Todd's blue eyes twinkled. "You double-shaved, too."

Heat surged into Cash's face. He knew where Todd intended to take this conversation and he didn't care for it one bit. "Knock it *off*, Trisco. I don't need a matchmaker."

Todd grinned from ear to ear, like a kid who'd gotten the last ice cream cone on a sweltering day. "I think you need a counseling session with Dr. Phil. You're still in love with the woman, aren't you?"

"Give me a break." Cash frowned at him then checked the water in his cup to make sure it didn't accidentally contain any live bait. "I don't even know her anymore."

Todd's grin changed into an aggravating, know-it-all smirk. "Then why is your face getting red? Is it really your daughter's heart you don't trust her with, or *yours*?"

"That's enough." Cash pushed himself away from the Hummer. "If we weren't best friends, I'd—"

"You'd what? Throw a punch at me for getting too close to the truth?" Todd shoved one hand behind his back and pointed at his chin with the other. "Go ahead, bro. Take your best shot if it'll make you feel better."

Cash tossed the cup and folded his arms to keep his temper in check.

35

"Don't be ridiculous."

Todd stared back, his smirk changing into a stern look. "Then get over yourself, MacKenzie. Either let go of the past or deal with it because it's not going away. Neither is *she*."

Cash looked away, more irritated with himself than Todd. He *had* let go. Unfortunately, the pain of his past wouldn't let go of *him*.

Chapter 3

"He called!"

With one hand on her cell phone and the other navigating the steering wheel, Libby sat in rush-hour gridlock on the Hennepin Avenue suspension bridge. Down below swirled the swift waters of the Mississippi River, separating downtown Minneapolis from residential neighborhoods.

"Cash invited me to dinner!" She could barely contain the happiness that bubbled from her soul into her voice. "I'm going to finally meet Amber."

"That's wonderful!" Medley laughed, sounding almost as excited as Libby. "When?"

"I'm on my way to meet them at the Nicollet Island Inn."

"See? Cash simply needed time to think it over. I knew if you were patient he'd come around," Medley stated in her usual know-it-all tone. "Romans 8:28 says so."

"Right," Libby replied, too keyed up about tonight to recall that verse. Her mind kept replaying the brief message Cash had left on her voicemail. He'd sounded tense, as though he already had second thoughts about the evening. After the way he'd acted a week ago at Sandhill Nature Center, she never expected him to undergo a change of heart. She'd called him every day, always getting his voicemail, never receiving a call back. He took her by surprise when he finally responded. She returned his call and left another message, confirming she'd be there.

"Traffic is moving again. Talk to you later." After disconnecting the call, she tossed her phone into her purse and stepped on the gas. Nicollet Island loomed just ahead on the Mississippi, close to the residential side of the river. Listed on the National Register of Historic Places, the island provided a small-town atmosphere in the heart of a big city. Oval-shaped, Nicollet Island's footprint was small enough to walk from end to end but large enough to include residences, a school, a hotel, and a large park.

The gray limestone building known as Nicollet Island Inn stood in full view on the east end of the island, flanked by the rolling lawns and tall cottonwoods of Nicollet Island Park. Libby exited the bridge and turned her BMW onto Wilder Street. She rounded the inn's tree-lined parking area and drove in. Once parked, she scanned the vehicles in the small, square lot. Cash's red pickup didn't appear among them. Panic surged inside her. Maybe he'd never gotten around to checking his messages. Maybe he'd meant next Friday. Maybe he'd changed his mind!

"Stop expecting the worst," she scolded herself. "He's here."

Nervous but excited, she threw open the door and climbed out of the car. A neon pumpkin of a harvest moon loomed over the city skyline. Stars glittered like diamonds across a navy sky. She inhaled the brisk evening air and raised her hands in praise. "What a beautiful night. Thank you, God, for making my dream come true!"

Golden light from the inn beckoned her as she hurried with giddy anticipation toward the canopied entrance. An oak door with beveled glass opened up to a windowed entryway. Her heels tapped on the marble floor of the dark-paneled lobby as she passed under the chandelier and approached the maître d'.

"Good evening and welcome to the Nicollet Island Inn." He smiled. "May I take your coat?"

"Yes, thank you," Libby replied to the red-haired man dressed in a black suit and crisp white shirt.

He slipped her black satin trench coat off her shoulders. "May I have your reservation?"

"I'm meeting the MacKenzie party at seven."

"They're waiting for you. Right this way, please."

She followed him into a dining room of dark wood, cream linen, soft lighting, and a wall of windows overlooking the river. The hum of conversation and tinkling of silverware on fine china blended with soft strains of classical music.

She saw the MacKenzies first, seated across the crowded venue at a table with an excellent view of the river. Cash sat on the left, looking as dashing and confident as ever in a brown tweed sport coat. Amber sat opposite him, outfitted in a long, red tunic, black leggings, and black leather boots. Their glistening onyx hair, cocoa eyes, and matching profiles caused Libby to swallow back a twinge of doubt. How could Amber be her child and not possess any resemblance to her?

Her stomach tumbled with uncertainty as she nervously followed the maître d'. What would she say to Amber? Could she even eat? Her heart missed a beat when they turned in her direction. Both stood as she approached their table. Amber's wide-eyed gaze met Libby's with open fascination and curiosity. Cash smiled, but the guarded look in his eyes indicated that their conversation at Sandhill and his doubts about her sincerity toward Amber brewed fresh in his mind.

Libby forced a smile in return then regretted it as her heart fluttered wildly at their tense exchange. The harsh words he'd flung at her that day still haunted her. Could they put their differences on hold and simply enjoy a meal together for Amber's sake? She'd been so ecstatic about meeting her daughter that the thought hadn't occurred to her before.

"Hello, Cash," she offered first, determined not to let their personal issues cast a cloud over the evening. "Thank you for inviting me."

"Thank you for accepting," he replied in a businesslike tone, not explaining why he'd changed his mind. For a moment, neither spoke. As they stood face-to-face, behaving like civil adults for Amber's sake, Libby sensed the discomfort between them building into an invisible wall.

The maître d' silently retreated.

"Amber," Cash suddenly turned to their daughter, "this is your mother,

Lib—" He cut himself off as if taking a mental step backward. "Olivia Cunningham."

Amber responded with a tentative smile and held out a velvety red rose. "For you," she said innocently.

"It's beautiful. Thank you!" Libby accepted the flower and threw her arms around her daughter, swallowing back tears of joy. *My baby! I'm finally holding my baby again!* "This is the happiest day of my life. I've waited *so* long to see you again."

"Me, too," Amber offered shyly as she accepted Libby's embrace.

They pulled apart and stood holding hands, studying each other. Amber stared in awe as her gaze roamed over Libby's blonde hair and blue silk dress. "I've always wondered what you'd look like," she said boldly. "I never imagined you'd be so...pretty." She looked at Cash, her eyes filled with unanswered questions.

Cash cleared his throat and responded with a quick nod as he pulled out the chair next to Amber. "Olivia..."

Olivia? The persistent formality in his voice prompted Libby to turn around. For an instant, he looked vulnerable—worried—as his dark-eyed gaze burned into hers. Did he have second thoughts about this meeting? Or did he harbor guilt for not arranging it years ago?

He blinked and the guarded look returned. Without a word, he slid the chair back farther. She sat down, laid the rose next to her plate, and clutched her menu. He gently pushed her chair forward.

Amber frowned in puzzlement as her gaze shifted from one parent to the other, taking in their uneasy, awkward exchange. She looked confused and uncomfortable.

Libby winced, wondering how much Cash had told her about their past. Or had he refused to discuss it at all?

Thankfully, a tall youth wearing a white shirt and black slacks approached carrying a silver water pitcher. He set the pitcher on the table and bowed. "The honored guest has arrived."

Amber burst into a smile at the striking, dark-haired teen. "This is Matt."

Stars twinkled in her eyes. "He's our server *and* captain of the varsity basketball team."

Thank you, Matt, Libby thought with an inward sigh of relief as she watched Amber's face glow. Cash, however, didn't share Libby's enthusiasm. He silently took his seat, keenly observing the teens' exchange.

Matt ignored Cash's disapproval and gave Libby a gleaming, mega-watt smile as he filled her water glass. "Welcome to the Inn. Would you care for a beverage?"

"I'll have an iced tea with lemon, please."

Cash ordered a club soda with a twist of lime. Amber requested a cherry Coke. As Matt walked away from their table, an awkward silence replaced the energy his mere presence had generated.

"This is my first visit here," Libby said in an attempt to revive the conversation. She gazed over the top of her menu and caught Cash studying her. His curious, pointed stare made her nervous, but at the same time, a flicker of recognition in his eyes gave her pause. Did sitting across the table from her bring back poignant memories from the past for him, too? She stared back, still forcing a smile, resolved not to let thoughts of the youthful love they had once shared affect her evening. "What do you suggest?"

"I'm having scallops," Amber offered and sipped her water.

"I prefer the walleye." Cash straightened and laid down his menu. "However, the salmon is excellent, too."

Matt returned with their beverages and suggested an appetizer. Amber scrunched her nose at the idea, prompting him to announce the daily featured item. He took their dinner order and departed, once again leaving a conversational vacuum in his wake.

"He seems like a nice young man," Libby remarked after a few moments, hoping to find mutual ground with Amber.

Amber beamed and whisked her long cape of ebony hair past her shoulders. "Matt has been nominated for Homecoming King this year! My friend, Brian Hanson, asked me to the dance, but..." Her smile tightened into a resentful pout. "Dad said *no.*"

Cash's jaw tensed. "We've been through this a dozen times, honey. He's too old for you."

"All my girlfriends are going out with older boys." Amber folded her arms and glared at him. "I'm never going to have any fun!" She turned to Libby. "How old were you when you and Dad hooked up?"

Hooked up? Mortified, Libby's face burned as an involuntary flush raced up her neck to the crown of her head. How had the discussion turned to their past so quickly? That conversation needed to take place, but not tonight, and definitely not here. Afraid she'd say too much or the wrong thing, she looked to Cash to gauge his reaction.

Let me handle this, reflected in his eyes.

"Our past has nothing to do with this." Cash sat rigidly, his fingers gripping the edge of the table. "We'll talk about that at another time."

As if on cue, Matt appeared with salads and warm herbed rolls. No one returned his smiles or conversation this time. Taking on a bewildered frown, he placed the food on the table and withdrew.

Amber leaned forward. "Let's pray." She held out her hands, one to each parent. The action surprised Libby until she remembered Cash's family always prayed that way. Cash, on the other hand, hesitated as though he hadn't expected the tradition to follow them to the restaurant.

"Dad?"

Amber's prompting embarrassed him into action. He extended his hand to Libby.

She understood his reluctance. The last time they'd experienced such closeness they were young and foolishly in love. She didn't want a reminder of the past any more than he did, but neither did she want Amber to suspect their discomfort. She gingerly slipped her fingers into his broad palm and looked away, willing herself to ignore the awkwardness of the situation. Instead, the gentle strength of his grasp caught her off guard, startling her. Self-conscious, she tried to pull back, but he held on. Their gazes locked as his long fingers slowly closed, enveloping her hand in his.

From the corner of her eye, she saw Amber's puzzled gaze switch from one parent to the other, taking in every detail. Libby quickly bowed her head. Cash said a brief prayer, though she barely listened to the words. The roughened palm in her left hand and petal-soft fingers in her right hand distracted her so much she could hardly breathe. Here they sat, praying like a model family, yet in reality, they barely knew each other. The moment filled Libby with such an aching sense of loneliness she fought back the urge to cry. She wanted so desperately to experience what they took for granted.

"Amen," they said in unison and raised their heads. Cash dropped her hand and pulled back as though touching her caused him uncertainty and pain. Why? Did their past haunt him more than he let on?

"So," Libby directed to Amber, forcing herself to sound cheerful as she started on her salad. "How do you like school?"

"It's okay." Amber shrugged and picked up her salad fork. "I like stuff that goes on after school better."

"Really? What kind of...stuff?"

"Football games and ski trips," Amber replied as she picked the sliced onions out of her salad. "I'd rather be with my friends than listening to some boring teacher. I hate sitting in class." She focused on Libby for a few moments then glanced at Cash as if testing their reactions. When no one responded, she helped herself to a dinner roll.

Amber's preoccupation with her food disheartened Libby. She forged ahead, however, determined to engage her daughter in conversation. "You're in tenth grade, right? What's your best subject?"

Amber paused. "Lunch."

Okay... Libby thought. *I've covered boys, school, and activities without success. Now what?*

A burst of Caribbean music echoed under the table. Amber reached down and pulled a cell phone out of her purse. She smiled as she held the phone to her ear. "Hey, what's up?"

"Not now." Cash shot her a stern look. "You know we don't take calls during dinner, and besides, it's disrespectful to your guest."

"But...it's Jenny," Amber argued defensively, her voice dropping to a whine. "She just called to find out about—"

Cash's face turned to stone. "Turn that thing *off*."

"I'll call you back," Amber snapped into the phone. "Dad's flippin' out. Okay, bye." She stabbed the phone with her index finger to disconnect the call.

Libby struggled to keep the conversation going through dinner. Amber sulked over the canceled phone call, barely answering Libby's questions. Cash offered little discourse, putting most of his energy into consuming his walleye. The dismal mood permeating the evening confused and upset her.

Libby's salmon looked as delicious as he'd suggested, but she barely tasted it. Frustration had ruined her appetite.

Midway through the meal, she attempted to engage Amber in friendly conversation again.

"Do you like to shop?"

Amber's somber countenance brightened. "Sure. Who doesn't?"

Libby smiled with renewed hope. "Then perhaps we should take a trip to the Mall of America some Saturday. Do some power-shopping!"

"I guess so." Amber gave her a bored look. "I mean, I go there all the time with my friends."

Libby kept smiling, but Amber's indifference began to drain her energy. "Great," she answered with dwindling enthusiasm. "You can show me around. I've only been there once."

"Get out!" Amber stared in amazement. "Are you serious?"

Libby put down her fork. "I love to shop, but I don't have time for it anymore. I'm usually working."

"Where do you work?"

"Stefano's Restaurant and Event Center."

Amber grabbed her soda. "Are you a server, like Matt?"

"No, I'm an event coordinator." Amber's bewildered expression spurred her on. "Stefano's has private rooms for entertaining. During the week, I deal mostly with business meetings and seminars, but weekends are booked solid with family events—like wedding receptions, anniversary celebrations, and showers. As a matter of fact, I've got a groom's dinner booked tonight." She checked the time on her cell phone, noting that her staff would be serving the guests Chicken Marsala and Fettuccine Alfredo right now.

"Weddings are so cool," Amber cooed. "Someday I want a huge one with a harpist and six bridesmaids."

Cash's face turned the color of Libby's rose. Making a strangled sound, he grabbed for his water glass, looking like he'd just swallowed a brick.

Amber rolled her eyes but ignored him. Her face grew serious. "Are you married?"

Cash ceased gulping, his hand frozen to the glass in mid-air.

Libby's gaze alternated between father and daughter. Their sudden interest in her personal life took her off guard. "No, I'm not."

A strange, expectant silence hovered around the table.

Amber's eyes widened. "Are you...like...divorced?"

"No..." Libby blotted her lips with her napkin, anxious to change the subject. "I don't have much time for dating. My job keeps me extremely busy."

Amber pointed an accusing finger at Cash. "So does his!"

The arrow hit its target. Cash flinched and looked away, as though mortified that his daughter would broadcast the current condition of his social life. The conversation abruptly ceased as Matt appeared out of nowhere and cleared the table.

After he left, Amber's phone suddenly rang. She scrambled for it and checked the caller's I.D.

"I told you to turn that off." Cash thrust out his hand. "Give it to me."

"But Dad, it's Jenny again. I promised—"

"*Now...*"

Smiling, Matt approached their table with a silver coffee thermos and a tray of sugary delicacies.

Amber dropped the phone like a hot coal in the center of the table and shoved back her chair.

"Would you, ah..." Baffled, Matt's gaze followed her as she stomped away. "...care for one of our featured desserts?"

Cash sat like a steel post, glowering with fury and humiliation.

"No, thank you." Libby turned over her cup and then stared helplessly at Amber's retreating form. "Just coffee."

Cash remained silent until Matt walked away and then shook his head. "I'm sorry you had to go through this. I don't know what you expected, but at least now you know what you're up against. She's been acting like this since she started hanging around with that...*that kid*, Brian Hanson. Honestly, I don't know what's gotten into her."

Libby clutched her coffee cup to keep her hands from shaking. "I'm not sure what I expected, either, but I've always held out hope meeting her would fill the emptiness that's been in my heart since the day they took her away from me." Her eyes swam with tears at the hollow feeling gnawing inside her. She took a sip of the hot, rich coffee to wash away the salty taste in her mouth. "I want so much for us to at least be friends, but it's obvious she won't forgive me for—"

"What's done is done," Cash said softly. "She'll get over it."

"If she hasn't come to terms with it by now," Libby's voice broke, "I don't see how she ever will."

"She's still got a lot of growing up to do." He reached across the table and wrapped his strong fingers around hers. "Just—" He faltered as their gazes met and held. "Give her time."

Her heart vaulted to her throat at the tenderness in his touch. She pulled from his grasp.

She suddenly couldn't breathe. Grabbing her purse, Libby shoved back her chair. "I need a moment alone." Her four-inch heels clicked a staccato beat on the wood floor as she bolted across the room with as much grace as one could in her state of mind.

Once outside, she leaned against the canopy support, gasping for breath. Her heart raced as though she'd run ten miles. What just happened back there?

She'd made a fool of herself, that's what! First, trying to buddy-up to Amber and then literally crying to Cash for sympathy—as if that could remedy the mistakes of her past!

After a couple of minutes, the crisp air began to cool her down, settling her nerves. She smoothed her hair and walked back into the inn, only to find Cash standing in the reception area, holding her coat and her rose. Amber stood next to him, sullenly staring at the floor. Her eyes looked puffy, her cheeks stained from crying.

"Thank you," Libby managed to say as Cash helped her don her wrap. She glanced up and saw the same cool detachment in his eyes that he'd shown her when she first arrived for dinner.

They left the inn in silence.

"Thank you for inviting me tonight," she said once they'd reached her car.

"Thank you for coming," Cash replied politely, but offered nothing more.

Though it appeared futile, Libby's heart wouldn't allow her to leave without one final effort to reach out to Amber with uncompromising love. She dug into her purse and pulled out a business card. "This contains both my work and cell numbers. Call me—any time you need help with homework or if you just want to talk, okay? I'll always be here for you."

Amber nodded and took the card.

Libby wrapped her arms around her daughter and willed herself not to break down again. "I love you so much. You're in my prayers every night." She let go of Amber and stepped back. Amber's big brown eyes filled with confusion as her arms dropped to her sides.

"Goodnight," Libby said to them. "Have a safe trip home."

"You, too," Cash replied and opened the car door for her. He hesitated briefly, as though he wanted to say something else, but instead went silent.

She slid in and swallowed hard as he shut the door. Through blurred eyes, she watched them disappear into the night. Cash's strained relationship with their daughter puzzled her, but Amber's behavior toward her tonight reflected what Libby had always feared. The girl would never forgive her for the mistakes of her youth. Libby couldn't forgive herself, so why should her daughter?

Suddenly Romans 8:28 flashed through her mind.

"And we know that in all things God works for the good of those who love Him..." she said aloud in the chilly darkness of her car.

Discouraged and depressed, she leaned her head on the steering wheel and sobbed aloud. How could rejection by her only child work into something good?

Her dream had turned into a nightmare.

*   *   *

The brisk evening air seemed warm to Cash compared to the chill between him and Amber as they walked to their home on the other end of the island. They traveled in silence along Merriam Street, past the monolithic silhouette of the Nicollet Island Park Pavilion and sloping parklands until Merriam curved and became West Island Avenue.

Overhead, vehicles zoomed across the Hennepin Avenue Bridge. On their left, the Mississippi echoed a deep roar as the swirling current rushed downstream and tumbled over St. Anthony Falls, a block or so away.

"I'm disappointed in you." Cash stuffed his hands into his trouser pockets. "Your behavior tonight was rude. Inexcusable."

Amber increased her pace and sped ahead with her arms swinging, her hair rippling behind her like a flowing veil.

He hated the silent treatment from women, especially Amber. He'd never figured out how, but it always gave them the upper hand. Amber's wall of silence bothered him even more, as though he continued to fail the lifetime test of fatherhood.

"I'm talking to you, young lady."

"Maybe I'm disappointed in you, too," she shouted without turning around. "Your manners were worse than mine."

He caught up with her in a couple of strides. "I make no apology for correcting you in front of Olivia. You hurt her feelings and embarrassed me. You owe me an explanation."

She cut him a sideways glare. Her cheeks glistened with tears in the moonlight. "Like, I'm surprised either one of you even noticed. You were staring at each other all night and ignoring me. I mean, you were practically burning holes through each other!"

He pulled a roll of antacids from the pocket of his sports coat and peeled back the foil. "I don't know what you're talking about."

"Yes, you do! You said we were having dinner together so I could meet her, but you made her so nervous she couldn't talk."

"I did not." He palmed a couple of tablets and buried the roll back in his pocket. "I purposely stayed in the background so as not to interfere. And if you remember correctly, she asked you a number of questions. You shut her down every time."

Amber grabbed a stick off the ground and threw it into the bushes. "Yeah, and every time she asked me something, she looked at you to see if you were listening." She whirled around, confronting him directly. "I think she was more interested in meeting with *you* than me."

"That's nonsense. All Olivia wants is to get to know you."

"Why?" Amber started walking again. "And why do you keep calling her Olivia? Her card says, *Libby* Cunningham."

Cash stared off in the distance, uncomfortable with the question. "The Libby I knew doesn't exist anymore."

"Why?" Amber's acid tone instantly turned curious. "What happened to her?"

He thought about it for a moment. "She's changed."

"How?"

"Amber..." He let the word hang, taking a time-out to get his attitude under control. He didn't want to discuss the past; he didn't see the point, even if she did. "Her behavior isn't the issue here. Yours is."

"Oh, yeah?" she retorted, raising her voice again. "What about yours? You didn't care about anyone's feelings when you yelled at me for talking to Jenny."

"You know the rules. I don't take business calls during dinner and you don't socialize with other kids."

"Jenny's my best friend, Dad." She sped ahead again, shouting back at him. "She just wanted to know what Libby was like and if we were having a good time. I guess you let everyone know the truth, didn't you?"

The way Amber said "didn't you" made him sound like a real jerk. He didn't mean to come across that way, but he didn't want to give Libby the impression that he couldn't handle raising a teenager on his own, especially one with an attitude like Amber had recently cultivated.

He stared at the back of her head. "I'm still waiting for your apology."

Amber spun around and began walking backward. "What about yours?" She looked hurt and insulted. "You spent the whole time staring at her and yelling at me. She kept talking to me and watching you. Both of you made me feel like I didn't belong there."

"That's not true, Amber. Of course, you belonged there." He reached out and placed his hand on her arm. "We arranged this evening expressly for your benefit."

She pushed it away. "You were only there *because* of me—your worst mistake. I wish I'd never been born!" She took off running, her shoes tapping on the asphalt.

Laden with guilt, Cash watched as she sprinted across the railroad tracks and ran the last half-block to the front porch of their home. Never once in almost sixteen years had he thought of her as a mistake, only as his most cherished blessing.

You did the right thing and it backfired in your face. Some father you are. After what happened tonight, even Libby must think you're a total failure.

Cash shoved his hands in his pockets and trudged along, his morale dropping faster than water rushing over the falls. From the way Amber acted tonight, it looked as though he and Libby had both failed. Amber's rejection of Libby brought her no closer to her mother and possibly pushed her farther away from him as well—as far apart as he and Libby would always be.

It made him feel like the loneliest man in the world.

Chapter 4

Libby sat at her computer, proofreading a contract when the phone rang. Could it be Amber? Or, could it be Cash calling to apologize for Friday night's 'family' debacle and to set up another event? For the past five days, both thoughts had raced through her head every time she heard a phone ringing. However, since Friday, every caller had turned out to be someone else.

Discouraged, she glanced up. The clock above her wall calendar read 4:55 pm Ardelle Johnson called Stefano's about this time nearly every day to review the specifications of her daughter's wedding reception. The thought of enduring another session of review, demands, and negotiation made Libby close her eyes, and take a deep breath, willing her frazzled nerves to even out.

Her weekly banquet meeting with the executive chef and the general manager to review next week's bookings had lasted nearly three hours. Afterward, she returned to her office to find her computer's mailbox full of numerous 'High Importance' emails from clients. Typically, Wednesday's schedule kept her at the restaurant until late, but today she didn't feel up to the task. Amber's rejection and Cash's lack of enthusiasm at Nicollet Island Inn last weekend still weighed heavily on her mind, ruining her ability to concentrate.

The phone rang again, interrupting her solo pity party. Stretched to her limit of patience, she grabbed the receiver. "This is Libby," she said in a tight voice. "May I help you?"

"Well, *this* is Ardelle Johnson," said the caller in a disdainful tone. "I've been reading over my contract and I've found several errors."

The click-clack of spiked pumps on the oak floor outside Libby's office alerted her to someone's approach. Expecting it to be a client, she spun in her chair to acknowledge the person, only to bump a ceramic mug with her elbow, spilling black coffee across her desk. "Oh, no!" She jumped up in time to avoid getting her gray suit drenched.

"Oh, yes!" Ardelle declared. "The contract specifically states the flower arrangements will be delivered by noon. The problem is that you fail to specify the color scheme. How would you know if you received the wrong ones?"

"Well...ah..." Libby backed away as the dark liquid ran over the edge, dripping onto the expensive rug under her desk and chair. In the process, the phone's spiral cord caught the edges of several client folders and dragged the entire stack across the desk. Before she could catch them, they slid to the floor. Contracts and menu cards were scattered across her small office. "What colors did you order?"

A petite redhead in a gold sweater and matching skirt appeared in the doorway clutching a scrap of paper. Her prominent green eyes widened even more as she took stock of the carnage. With a sympathetic wince, she dropped the note in Libby's in-box and grabbed a bundle of cloth napkins piled on a nearby chair, proceeding to tear off the shrink-wrap. She pulled out a couple and tossed them on the floor to sop up the mess.

"The success of this event is your responsibility," Ardelle snapped. "If I'm not happy, I guarantee you won't be, either! So, I suggest you call the florist this instant and find out!"

Libby glanced at the note and saw 'Amber' scrawled across it. She snatched up the piece of paper and caught her breath as she skimmed the writing. Her daughter had called!

"Yes, of course," she blurted, interrupting Ardelle's rant. "You're absolutely right. Thank you for bringing it to my attention. I'll take care of it. Talk to you later."

She disconnected the call and began punching the numbers on the note. "Brianna, when did this call come in?"

"About five minutes ago. You were on another line so I picked it up." Libby's assistant dropped the sopping brown napkins into an empty trash basket and proceeded to scoop up the scattered files. "She sounded disappointed that you weren't available."

Disappointed? A glimmer of hope lifted Libby's mood.

She stood aside from her desk, extending the phone cord as far as it would stretch in an effort to get out of Brianna's way. "Thanks, Bree, for taking care of my mess," she said gratefully, pausing with her hand over the receiver. "You're a sweetie."

Amber answered on the second ring.

"Hi, Amber! It's Libby." She drew in a nervous breath, wondering if she should say the word *Mom* in front of Brianna then changed her mind.

Not today, she thought. Not until Amber had accepted her as one.

She tried to conceal her excitement, but her voice quivered, giving her away. "I just received your message."

"Hi." Amber's soft, tentative reply gave her pause.

Brianna piled the folders and the scattered contents on top of Libby's printer then picked up the wastebasket full of soiled napkins and left the room.

"I'm so glad you called." Libby rested her hip against a dry corner of her desk, making a futile effort to relax. "You've been on my mind all day," she injected warmly, attempting to fill the awkward silence on Amber's end of the line. *Something's wrong*, she thought. "How are you?"

"Okay, I guess. Um...I was wondering..."

Amber's hesitation set off an alarm in Libby's heart. She waited, hoping her patience encouraged the teen to continue.

"Could you give me a ride home from school? I usually walk, but it's storming outside."

Yes!

"I think so." Libby's reply sounded calm, though her heart jumped for joy. "Where's your father? Is he aware that you stayed after school?"

"He's not answering his phone. He must be at the gym. When he works out he usually leaves it in his locker." She paused. "I-I hope you don't mind. I mean, I think it would be cool to cruise around in your Beamer."

Libby almost laughed at the comment but managed to keep her voice even. "What time shall I pick you up?"

"Um...like right now?"

She surveyed the disorganized mess on her desk and the coffee stains on her wool and silk Turkish rug. A voice in her head reminded her that she had work to do on Ardelle's contract and an office to clean, but she pushed the thought aside. "Okay. If the freeway isn't jammed, I'll be there in about fifteen minutes."

"Do you need directions?"

"I know where River's Edge High is."

"All right," Amber replied, sounding relieved. "I'll wait inside the entrance."

Libby hung up and glowed with joy as she grabbed her purse and shut her office door. She didn't know if Amber truly needed a ride home or simply used the weather as an excuse to let her friends see her 'cruising' in a cool car. It didn't matter. Libby had vowed to Amber, in front of Cash, that she'd be there when Amber needed her. Today she intended to prove it.

*   *   *

Bone-chilling rain pummeled Libby's white BMW as she pulled up to the entrance of River's Edge High School on Nicollet Island. She peered through the passenger window, hoping to see Amber standing inside the glass doors, but the entrance looked empty. She waited a few moments, contemplating a run into the school to find the girl. Suddenly a tall, slender form emerged, dashing toward the car. She reached over and pushed open the passenger door. Amber scrambled into the car and slammed it shut. Her maroon and gold backpack hit the floor with a heavy thud.

"I'm soaked!" Amber's white tank top dripped water all over the light blue leather seat. Goosebumps covered her bare arms. A wide band of tanned flesh exposed her navel and separated her low-rise jeans from the skimpy, flimsy top.

The low, scooped neckline exposed two inches of rounded cleavage.

Libby turned up the heat. "Where's your jacket?"

Amber shivered. Rain-soaked hair hung past her waist in thick ropes. "I f-forgot it at home."

Come again? Libby reached into the back seat and grabbed her stadium blanket. "Here, this will warm you up."

As Amber huddled under the blanket, Libby wondered if Cash allowed her to wear such revealing clothes; or did she simply change once he left for work?

Libby stepped on the gas. "Which way do I turn?" She knew the address from the business card Medley had given her but couldn't remember which side of the island Amber lived on.

"Go straight," Amber said. "This road connects with Eastman. Take Eastman to West Island Avenue and turn right."

Amber's phone began to blare with rock music in her backpack. She pulled it out, read the number, and shut it off.

Libby took that as an encouraging sign. "Did you have practice after school?"

Amber cut her a sideways glance. "No." She pulled the blanket up to her neck and stared ahead.

Here we go again. Now, what do I do?

A rumble in her stomach reminded Libby that she'd neglected to eat lunch today because she was too busy preparing for her meeting.

"Hey, there's a MacDonald's about ten minutes away. Are you hungry? Shall we stop for a burger and fries?"

A spark of hunger flickered in Amber's eyes then quickly faded. "I love Chicken McNuggets, but I'd better go home. Got a lot of homework today."

Libby came to a stop sign and turned right. Up ahead a freight train snaked across West Island Avenue. She pulled up to the cross-arms and gazed down the tracks. A chain of slow-moving boxcars extended across the river on a long railroad bridge.

"Oh, great!" Amber shifted impatiently in her seat. "We could be stuck here for at least ten minutes."

Libby smiled inwardly. *Thank you, Lord, for the time-out.*

Now, if she could only get her daughter to open up! She shifted the car into park and settled in her seat. Racking her brain, she frantically searched for some subject to ignite Amber's interest. She glanced at Amber's hand and saw a name penned across the back in a graffiti-like style. The homemade tattoo of a boy's name brought back old memories.

"Nice artwork," Libby declared and pointed at Amber's ink. "Who's Brian?"

Self-conscious, Amber buried her hand under the blanket. "He...he's a friend," she replied shyly.

"Is he cute?"

"Yeah..."

"Really? What's he like?"

Amber studied her for a moment as if weighing her sincerity. "He makes me laugh."

"Is he a server at the Nicollet Island Inn?"

"N-o-o-o!" Amber's cheeks brightened as a giggle escaped her lips. "He works at a music store and he's like, s-o-o-o cool!"

"I suppose you sit next to him in every class."

Amber shook her head. "He's a senior."

"Oh," Libby replied softly, remembering Cash's lecture at dinner last Friday night about older boys being off-limits.

The atmosphere abruptly chilled. She sensed the girl withdrawing and she panicked, wondering how to salvage her error. A thought unexpectedly composed in her mind.

Love is patient, love is kind...

She reached over and brushed a strand of damp hair from Amber's face. "I'd like to meet him someday. I'm sure I'd like him, too."

"Really?" Amber's eyes widened with surprise. "Dad doesn't. He made me give Brian's ring back."

"I'm sure it's not personal," Libby said, avoiding taking sides. "Your dad is concerned about you. That's all."

Amber shifted in her seat, facing her. "Brian's going to be eighteen this Friday and I can't go to his birthday party." Her dark eyes flashed with resentment. "All of my friends are going to be there. It's not fair!"

The caboose rolled by. A few seconds later, the cross-arms lifted. Libby shifted into drive and drove across the tracks.

"Perhaps we could have our own little celebration that night," she offered. "Why don't we have a sleep-over at my house? We could order pizza, watch a movie, and nuke some popcorn. I have more than enough room. I could talk to Cash about it. Would you like that?"

Amber stubbornly shook her head. "I want to go to *Brian's* party."

Disappointed, Libby stopped in front of a white, two-story house with forest green trim. Amber's abrupt reply had trampled on her heart, but she kept it to herself, determined not to let the defeat get her down.

She peered through the windshield. "The rain seems to be letting up, but it's still pretty wet out there. Do you want to keep the blanket on?"

"I'll be all right without it." Amber peeled off the purple and gold coverlet and reached for her backpack. "Thanks for the ride home. Your Beamer is *cool*." She hauled the heavy bag onto her lap and hesitated. "I-I'm sorry about this weekend. I didn't mean to be rude, but I just *have* to be with Brian on his birthday." She placed her fingers on the door handle. "The sleep-over sounds like fun, though. If you want to plan it for another weekend, I guess that would be okay."

Really? Libby smiled, realizing she'd finally begun to gain Amber's trust. She started to reply, but before she could suggest a date, Cash's red pickup rumbled to a stop behind them. Curious, she glanced at the side mirror as he jumped out of the cab and slammed the door. Wearing a black leather jacket and jeans, he strode toward the car with swift, purposeful strides. He stared straight ahead, his jaw rigidly set.

She'd never seen him so upset and wondered what had set him off. Did she do something wrong? She looked away, not wanting Amber to see her sudden apprehension.

Amber must have sensed something, however, because she immediately twisted around, peered out the back window, and let out a horrified gasp. She grabbed the blanket and pulled it snugly around her. "I'll call you later, okay?"

Before Libby could answer, Amber threw open her door and bolted from the car.

Cash stood outside Libby's BMW in the mist, white-knuckled hands gripping his hips as his gaze followed Amber's hasty retreat.

She lowered the window and shivered as a gust of chilly, damp air assaulted her. "Is something wrong?"

"Amber," Cash bellowed over the top of the car, "go to your room. We'll talk when I'm finished here."

Bending slightly at the waist, he met Libby's questioning gaze with a grim stare. "Yes, something is very wrong, but you and I are going to change that—right now."

*　　*　　*

Cash marched around Libby's car to the front passenger door, jerked it open, and crawled in, settling in on a heated, butter-soft leather seat. "What are you doing here?"

She had the audacity to appear baffled.

"I gave Amber a ride home from school." She stared at him, looking wide-eyed and clueless. "It's obvious she couldn't walk in this storm."

"She should have called me! I was less than a mile away."

Despite the warmth in Libby's luxurious car, he saw her shiver in her gray wool suit and peach blouse.

"She did," Libby protested, "but you didn't answer your phone. She assumed you were working out at the gym."

He had intended to be firm, though fair about the situation, but her feigned innocence disturbed him even more. "Then why didn't she leave me a message?"

When Libby shook her head to indicate that she didn't know, he leaned close to give her the answer. "She didn't want me to know she had detention again." A tantalizing whiff of Libby's perfume invaded his nostrils. The fragrance distracted him for a moment. He pulled back a couple of inches. "She talked you into picking her up instead." He exhaled a tense sigh, unhappy about what he had to say next. "You two figured you'd race home before I found out."

Libby's jaw dropped. Her hand flew to her throat and clutched a gold cross necklace. "No! Cash, I—I didn't realize she had to stay after for that. I thought she needed a ride home from an after-school activity."

Just because he'd invited her to dinner to get to know Amber, that didn't give her the right to meet with their daughter without his knowledge, even if it only amounted to a ride home. He felt betrayed that Libby would make plans with Amber without consulting him first and worried that if this kept up, Amber would turn to Libby more and more when she got into trouble.

"Amber is well aware that she's supposed to call me when she's been detained, but she didn't do it. She should have known her school would email me. In any case, *you* should have called me and left a message."

"I'm telling you the truth, Cash. I had no idea she'd come from detention! If I'd known she'd asked me for a ride just to conceal it from you, I *would* have called you to let you know."

He glanced at the necklace tangled between her fingers, visually tracing the chain to the hollow of her long, slender neck. Her sleek hair had succumbed to the humidity, springing into tiny golden tendrils that framed her face and covered her shoulders. It reminded him of her as a teenager. Suddenly an old, familiar ache gripped his heart. To get his mind off how much she affected him, he wrenched his gaze upward and looked her square in the eyes. "You were her age once and pulled the same stunts. You should have realized that things didn't add up."

She released the necklace. "Excuse me?"

"I understand that you want her acceptance but chasing across town to pick her up and drive her a couple of blocks without first checking out the facts isn't the way to get it and you know it."

Libby flushed. "Of course, I want her acceptance, but I would never intentionally undermine your authority."

"You just did."

"I apologize." Her cheeks darkened as she placed her hand on his arm. "You have my word that it won't happen again."

The pressure of her fingers against his bicep made his pulse leap. He remembered Todd's troubling words. *Is it really your daughter's heart you don't trust her with? Or yours?*

The warm, humid air in the car suddenly turned suffocating. Sweat clung to the back of his neck. He pulled away and fumbled with the door handle, eager to put some space between them. "So, we have an understanding, right? The next time Amber calls and wants you to do something without my knowledge, you'll check with me first."

"Yes, but—"

"No buts, I insist on this. If I don't give my consent, it doesn't happen."

Libby stiffened at his authoritative interruption. She placed her palm on the top of the steering wheel and clenched her fingers around it as if making a great effort to hold her temper in check. "I understand."

"Thank you." Cash opened the car door and shoved one boot out. A waft of drizzly, fresh air enveloped him.

"Just a minute, Cash." She stared at him, her perfectly-formed brows arched with indignation. "You should be grateful that she called *me* instead of Brian."

The confidence in her statement hinted that she might be holding something back. Worried, Cash paused, halfway out of the car. "What do you mean by that?"

"She's crazy about him."

"Tell me something I don't know."

"She wants to go to his birthday party on Friday night."

"She knows how I feel about that."

"Well, as they say," Libby replied, her voice irritatingly matter-of-fact, "where there's a will, there's a way."

"There's no way she'll get past me. I know my daughter."

"Do you?" Libby sat back, folding her arms into a tight bow, a hint of boldness in her silky voice. "Tell me then—what did she wear to school today?"

"Uh..." He shrugged, wondering what Amber's wardrobe had to do with this conversation. "I don't know, jeans, probably. That's what she usually wears." Nearly every pair she owned lay strewn across her bedroom floor.

"In other words, you don't have a clue, do you?"

He leaned into the car. "I'm getting wet. Make your point!"

"My point is," she said in a serious tone as she leaned toward him with a no-nonsense look, "that you had better wake up."

For a moment, he couldn't pull his gaze away from the fullness of her mouth, mesmerized by the shiny peach tint of her lipstick. Realizing his error, he swallowed hard and pulled back.

"You talk tough," she continued quietly, "but we both know who's really in control at your house."

He snorted, wondering where she got that idea. "That'll be the day."

"Don't delude yourself, Cash! She wore an outfit to school today that would make a truck driver blush."

He'd wondered why Amber had hustled into the house clinging to that silly blanket. The acid in his stomach began to churn. His chest tightened. He got back into the car. "Describe it."

"Skin-tight jeans with a waistband that stopped four inches short of her navel and a tank top about the size of a handkerchief."

Embarrassment and humiliation welled up inside him. "I didn't buy those clothes and you can rest assured she'll never wear them again."

"Oh, I don't doubt that. Tomorrow the clothes will go back to their rightful owner. Problem solved. My question to you is; what's motivating her to make a statement like that in the first place?"

"To show off and act cool."

Libby snapped her fingers. "Bingo. Which brings us right back to—"

"—Brian Hanson. Don't concern yourself with him any longer. I told you, he's history."

Libby tapped her fingers on the steering wheel, exhaling a sigh of frustration. "Listen, Cash, if she wants to be with him, there's nothing you can do to stop her. We both know that much from our past behavior. I'm warning you, if we don't do something to get through to her, our *own* teenage history is going to repeat itself."

"Don't worry about it," Cash replied, unhappy over having his parenting skills questioned. "I've got the situation under control."

Her knowing smile faded. "Are you positive?"

The question made his heart skip a beat. He couldn't afford *not* to. His integrity and Amber's future depended on it.

Chapter 5

"I sure hope you're wrong about this," Medley warned as she pulled her blue Focus into the deserted parking lot at River's Edge High and parked next to a utility building. The digital clock on the dashboard displayed 10 pm. "What makes you so certain Amber is planning to sneak out?"

Libby cut Medley a sideways glance. "I skipped out to meet Cash more than a few times in my day. Why do you think my dad stuck me in a home for unwed mothers out in the middle of nowhere? When I agreed to go to one, I didn't know he had already made the arrangements."

"I remember that." Medley shifted the car into PARK and shut off the engine. "We got lost the time we came to visit you."

Unlike Libby, Medley's conduct mirrored the perfect teenager in her youth. She'd earned top grades, made the Honor Society, sat on the Student Council every year, participated in DECCA, and never caused her parents a moment of distress. Her popularity and reputation never once went to her head, though. Growing up, she'd always exhibited a soft spot for Libby because they shared a common bond of being an only child. As adults, they'd become as close as sisters, but back then they rarely talked except for holiday family get-togethers, passing in the hall at school, and one picture together in the school yearbook.

"She had that look," Libby explained. "It only lasted a second, but when I saw the defiance in her eyes, I knew exactly what Amber had on her mind."

Medley's keys jingled in the dark. "I believe you," she said and stuffed them into her designer jean pocket. "Just the same, I pray you're wrong."

"Honestly, I do, too. Amber's well-being means more to me than telling Cash 'I told you so.' I hope my hunch turns out to be nothing more than a false alarm."

Cash had made his feelings plain on Wednesday afternoon about her interference. She nibbled on her lip, nervous about deliberately going back on her word and becoming involved tonight, but determined, regardless, to go through with her plan.

Then again, if she succeeded, she risked alienating Amber as well. Amber might never trust her again for breaching the girl's confidence. Deep down, Libby knew she had to do what her heart dictated, and not worry about the possibility of unintended consequences with either MacKenzie.

Suddenly, a red Grand Am filled with raucous teenagers zoomed into the lot and parked on the opposite end.

"Well, well, there's the man of the hour," Libby announced wryly as they turned toward the music and loud voices. "It looks like he brought along the entire guest list, too. He's going to be surprised when the star of his show doesn't make her cue. Let's hurry. The performance is about to begin."

The chilly night air enveloped them as they climbed out of the car, partially hidden by the utility building. Libby glanced across the river. Downtown Minneapolis skyscrapers glowed like multi-colored beacons of fluorescent light against the obsidian sky.

Medley shivered and tightened the belt around her charcoal leather jacket. "O-o-o-h. It's cold out here!" A cloud of moisture billowed from her lips, evaporating into the darkness.

Libby wore a black knit turtleneck under a matching velvet workout suit. She zipped up the hooded jacket and stuffed her hands into the front pockets, ready for the short trek to the MacKenzie property. They walked along Eastman until it intersected with West Island Avenue then turned right.

"Cash must be watching Amber like a Doberman," Medley said as they trekked past the darkened athletic field of River's Edge High. "How will she pull it off?"

"She'll stuff pillows under the blankets on her bed to make it look like she's sleeping. If she has one, a fake ponytail or hairpiece will go where her head would be under the covers." Libby curled her fingers into tight balls inside the jacket. "I don't doubt she's skipped out before. Unfortunately, practice truly does make one perfect."

"Yes, but..." Medley shivered again and turned up the collar of her coat. "All Cash has to do is turn on the light to see it's not her."

"She'll probably loosen the bulb in the overhead fixture. That way he'll think it burned out. From the doorway, everything will appear normal."

"That day in my salon..." Medley said with a sigh, "Amber acted so sweet and well-mannered, she stole my heart. She's really a good kid, you know. I just wish you could convince her that this boy is not the answer to all her problems."

Libby pulled her hands from her pockets and zipped her jacket higher. "Life has come full circle, hasn't it? My rebellious attitude drove my dad into an early grave. Amber is doing the same thing to Cash."

"Not exactly," Medley pointed out. "Your dad *worked* himself into an early grave. He spent every free moment he had either campaigning or raising money for his next campaign." She placed her hand on Libby's arm. "Fortunately for Amber, she has you. I don't recall you having anyone to talk to except Grandma Cunningham. I heard my parents discussing it once and my dad claimed that she instigated Amber's adoption."

"It's true. When she found out about my pregnancy, she harbored so much bitterness toward me for disgracing our family that she never spoke to me again. She died a couple of months after I delivered Amber. As far as I know, she never forgave me."

"Lib, I'm so sorry." Medley squeezed Libby's hand. "Growing up, I always wondered why God blessed me with a perfect life while you had so many problems." Her voice faltered. "I-I prayed every night for God to bless you."

"You did?" Libby gave her cousin a heartfelt hug. "That's so sweet of you, Medley. Know what? I prayed every night for God to bless you, too!"

Medley hugged her back and sniffled. "Now I'm praying for Amber. Cash, too. You three make a perfect family."

Libby's chest tightened. "Medley, don't go there..."

Medley held up her palms in a truce. "Okay, but I'm still going to pray for a happy ending! You guys need to be together."

They came upon the railroad tracks and continued on their way.

"I see Cash's house," Libby said as they approached a row of stately, well-maintained homes. "It's the white, two-story with dark green trim and the oval glass in the front door." She waved toward the smaller building to the right of the house. "That's his garage."

She stopped at the cement driveway and looked around. A wicker swing hung in the open front porch. The house looked freshly painted; the grounds reflected meticulous care. For a moment, she wondered what it would be like to live in this house with him, to be cared for as well as he tended to everything he owned. The thought stunned her. Where did that idea come from? Chiding herself, she let it go. She had more important things to concentrate on right now than daydreaming about Cash MacKenzie.

"Where are we going to hide? The streetlight will expose us," Medley whispered as she crept into the narrow front yard. She ducked under a hanging bird feeder. "The bushes are only waist-high."

Libby ignored her question for the moment and walked around the left side of the house. She pointed to a second-floor window near the back. "That's Amber's room."

Medley stared upward. "How do you know?"

"She has beads in place of curtains. I'll bet Amber crawls out there and climbs down the fire escape." Libby leaned against a huge maple tree. "We'll stand here so we've got a clear view."

"You can't be serious." Medley pointed toward the house. "She'll see us. Anyone driving by will see us. We could get hauled off to jail for trespassing!"

Despite Medley's objections, they ended up squatting behind the tree with their backs pushed against the neatly trimmed hedge lining the sidewalk. The minutes slowly dragged by, giving Libby ample time to wonder if Amber had already left the house. She had no way of knowing what Cash's plans were for tonight and whether he'd kept Amber home or sent her to stay with a friend or relative. One thing seemed clear. She needed to cast her doubt and trust God's timing. Worrying didn't guarantee or accomplish a thing.

Every time a car passed, they ducked, crouching on the dew-covered ground. Before long, dampness began to seep into their clothes.

"I'm so c-cold," Medley complained and yanked at a tuft of burgundy hair tangled in a branch. "I need a Starbucks!"

Libby simply rolled her eyes.

"Are you sure she hasn't slipped past us already?" Medley glanced at her watch. "It's a quarter to eleven."

Before Libby could answer, blinding headlights flashed a wide arc across the driveway. A monstrous black Hummer with shiny gold trim pulled up to the garage. The driver threw open the door and hopped out. Tall and as powerfully built as his vehicle of choice, he looked like he'd just stepped off a cruise ship in his snug designer jeans and red Tommy Bahama shirt. Shaggy blond hair brushed a thick gold chain at the nape of his neck. He reached into the vehicle and pulled out a large pizza box, a medium-sized bag, and a twelve-pack of soda.

Medley's eyes widened. She nudged Libby. "Who's *that*?"

"I have no idea," Libby whispered in awe as they watched him stroll toward the front door.

"Look at that swagger. I'll bet 'surfer-boy' thinks he's a real hotshot," Medley murmured with distaste. "Why else would he drive a gas-guzzler the size of a military tank?"

"Maybe he's adventurous." Libby cut her cousin a sideways glance and caught Medley sizing up the man intently.

The front door opened and the bright interior light reflected against the man's handsome, Nordic features as he approached the threshold.

Inside, Amber's voice rang out. "Hi, Uncle Todd!"

*   *   *

Cash sprawled his aching body on the sofa, staring at scarlet flames glowing in the fireplace while nursing a headache and sore feet. He and Amber must have covered every inch of the Mall of America tonight. At least, it seemed that way. A dozen bags and boxes piled high on the dining room table provided more than enough proof.

Todd entered the living room carrying several packages, including a twelve-pack of cola. Amber rushed up to him and relieved him of the soda as soon as she saw the brand. She ripped open the end of the carton and dug into it, pulling out a can.

"Thanks for stopping at the store on your way over, Uncle Todd." The can hissed as she popped the top. "I'm s-o-o-o thirsty and we're out of Coke." She tipped her head back and chugged a couple of ounces.

"Any time, Princess," Todd cooed and slid his arm around her. He winked at Cash across the room. "Did you and Daddy Big-Bucks have an exciting night at the mall?" Todd flashed a toothy grin and gave her a bear hug. "He looks like he's dying over there on the couch."

Amber lifted her head off his chest. "We went to dinner at my favorite restaurant and ordered crab legs. Then we went shopping. Want to see what we bought?"

Todd chuckled. "Sure. Let's see what your old man charged to the company."

From the sofa, Cash snorted at Todd's attempt to be funny then groaned at the shooting pain behind his eyes. He hated shopping. It always gave him a headache and tonight he'd worked up a doozy. He'd taken Amber to the mall to spend quality time with her and keep her mind off *that kid's* party.

Todd threw a small oak log on the fire from a stack piled high in the wood box. A few moments later, he disappeared with Amber into the dining room, giving Cash temporary peace and quiet. Unfortunately, it didn't last long or seem to, anyway. The next thing Cash knew, he awoke as Todd collapsed onto the easy chair across from him. It took all the energy he could muster to pry open one eye. "Why did you buy such a gigantic pizza?"

"I'm hungry." Todd slung one ankle over the opposite knee. "I thought you would be, too."

"Uh-uh," Cash murmured, exhausted. "I had a ton of crab legs for dinner.

My stomach feels like a rock."

Todd's grin stretched from ear to ear. "Matches your head. I got the mega pie with three kinds of meat and extra cheese. I'm such a good customer that the manager threw in some complimentary cheese bread, too."

Cash had all he could do to keep from gagging. "We can't eat all that. You shouldn't have spent so much money on a midnight snack."

"Me?" Todd barked out a laugh. "I'm not the one who bought his daughter a whole new wardrobe. You must have mortgaged this house to pay for all that designer stuff."

"She needed more school clothes, anyway." Cash closed his tired eyes again, relaxing as the heat from the robust fire warmed his aching bones. "She dragged me all over the mall, looking for a pair of jeans with a name I can't pronounce, but they were sold out everywhere we went. I finally talked her into giving up the search by promising to order them on the Internet for her birthday." Easing his head off the arm of the sofa, he warily glanced around. "Where is she?"

"She hauled her loot upstairs."

He massaged his temples for a moment then slowly raised himself to a sitting position. "We made a deal. She agreed to stop skipping class and borrowing clothes from other girls if I bought her some new stuff."

Todd's silly grin morphed into a look of total seriousness. "Bribery doesn't instill good behavior."

"I'm aware of that." Cash exhaled a tense breath, desperately hoping this time he'd truly gotten through to Amber. "However, I don't want Olivia to catch her wearing trashy outfits or to get any more SOS calls from her because she's in detention again. It makes me look like a fool who doesn't know what his own kid is doing and gives Olivia all the more reason to consider me a lousy father."

"How do you know she'd do that?"

Cash thought back to his confrontation with Libby on Wednesday and her blatant suggestion that he 'had better wake up' to Amber's growing obsession with Brian Hanson. "Let's just say I'm not taking any chances."

"It sounds to me like she's gotten the best of you again." Todd leaned back and clasped his wide hands behind his head as he let out a smooth whistle. "You must be carrying an Olympic-sized torch for her. She's still a looker, huh?"

"Give me a break," Cash shot back, trying to appear indifferent. "Her looks have nothing to do with this." The sharp tone of his reply, however, made him sound defensive.

Even so, the scene in her car flashed through his mind, flooding him with the memory of her fragrance, her rain-dampened curls, that soft peach tint on her lips... A small, still voice urged him once again to stop judging her and give her a chance, but the pain of their past clouded his thoughts. He cleared his throat and looked away.

Taking the hint, Todd stood up. "Did you get a movie?"

"Yeah." Cash gestured toward the den where he watched movies and football games on his favorite toy, a high-definition television with a sixty-inch screen. "It's on the coffee table."

"Is Amber gonna join us?"

"Hey, honey bear!" Cash yelled despite the pain, using an endearment from her childhood to get her attention.

Flip-flops pattering on oak flooring echoed from the second-floor hallway. Amber appeared at the top of the stairs. "What?"

"Are you coming down? We're going to watch a movie."

"No thanks," she yelled back.

Todd stopped at the foot of the stairs. "What about the pizza? I've got cheese bread, too."

"I'm still full from dinner. I'm going to bed. Night-night!"

Todd glanced at his watch and chuckled. "My how time flies when you're busy spoiling your teenager. No wonder I'm hungry. It's eleven o'clock."

Ignoring Todd's warped sense of humor, Cash confirmed the time and gave a silent cheer. He let out a loud sigh of relief and glanced toward the stairs. "Yeah, and I thank God that I know where *my* kid is."

*   *   *

"If I sit here any longer, I'm going to freeze in this posture!" With a groan obviously meant to elicit sympathy, Medley clung to the tree trunk and slowly pulled herself up to a standing position. "I *must* have a Starbucks."

"They're probably not open this late." Libby kept her voice even but fought an urge to match Medley's crankiness.

"A venti soy latte..." Medley closed her eyes, shivering, "with extra soy."

The latte sounded great, but the idea of lacing it with soy made Libby grimace. "What's wrong with plain coffee? We can get some at a fast-food drive-thru on the way home."

Medley's face contorted. "I can't believe you said that and actually meant it." She clutched her stomach as though the mere thought had poisoned her. "Ugh! I'd rather drink anti-freeze—"

"Be quiet." Libby grabbed Medley's elbow. "Amber's light just went off."

"Ouch!" Medley jerked away. "You almost pulled my arm off, too."

"S-h-h-h-h." Libby looked upward. "Keep your attention on Amber's bedroom window."

They watched...and waited...and waited.

Libby spotted the silhouette of someone crouching next to the house, slowly and stealthily moving through the dark.

"Don't move," she whispered and grabbed Medley's arm again. "Here she comes."

The figure suddenly rushed toward them, piercing the air with a scream. They jumped away from the tree and grabbed onto each other, muffling screams of their own as a golden Cocker Spaniel shot out of the shadows.

Medley turned to run, but Libby gripped her by the shoulders. "Hold still. Running away will only encourage him to chase you."

Medley stiffened like a pillar of salt but couldn't help looking backward.

Libby knelt and held out her hand, palm down. "Come here, poochie. N-nice doggie." The dog's lip quivered, revealing a healthy set of sharp teeth. A ridge of thick, golden fur surged along his spine.

Oh-oh...

She swallowed hard and slowly rose to her feet. "Go on now," she commanded in a quiet, but firm tone. "Go back to wherever you came from and behave yourself." The dog continued to growl. She took a step backward.

Jaws of steel lunged at her ankle.

"Ah-h-h-h!" In a panic, she swooped down and smacked the dog across the breadth of his long, square nose. To her amazement, the dog yelped and rolled over on its back, raising four furry paws into the air.

"What happened?" Medley inched her way around the tree and stared in shock at the ground, her hand covering her mouth. "Is he dead?"

"Hardly," Libby replied. "He's resting up for round two."

The moment she spoke, the furry hound jumped up and took off, barking as though he had a firecracker tied to his collar. Strangely enough, this time he sounded happy, excited. Libby watched in puzzlement as he raced to the back of the building and began jumping into the air, wagging his fat, stubby tail.

"Medley," Libby whispered, "he's trying to tell us something. I think someone really is lurking behind the house this time."

"That's it!" Medley tossed her slender, manicured hands into the air, and started toward Cash's front door. "I quit! I'm heading for safety and a heat vent. Forget this nonsense."

Libby ignored Medley and ran toward the back of the house; certain she knew who hid in the shadows behind it. Just as she suspected, she found Amber crouched next to the stoop, frantically trying to quiet the dog. Unfortunately, the moment that mutt saw Libby again, his frenzied barking commenced even louder.

"Shut up, Scrappy!" Amber tried to hold him, but he slipped from her grasp and raced a circle around them. "Come here!"

Amber froze when Libby approached her. Their gazes met in the silvery light.

Libby's heart faltered as a flicker of guilt and panic in Amber's eyes told her exactly what she needed to know.

Dear God, don't let me mess this up! Show me how to reach out to my daughter.

Amber glared at her. "What are you doing here?"

"Waiting for you," Libby replied, keeping her voice steady. "You see, I've known since last Wednesday that you intended to sneak out tonight to meet Brian."

"I am not!"

"Then why has he been waiting for you for an hour down in the school parking lot?"

Amber's jaw dropped an inch, but she quickly recovered. "I don't know what you're talking about," she countered abruptly, sounding like Cash. "I just came outside to see why Scrappy started barking."

Libby motioned toward Amber's expensive jeans, suede boots, and matching nut-brown suede blazer. "Dressed like that?"

Amber recoiled with an accusing stare. "You're spying on me!"

"I'm just trying to help you, honey." Libby placed her hand on Amber's shoulder, yearning to make the girl understand. A thought unexpectedly flashed through her mind.

Be courageous and strong. Do everything with love.

"I can't allow you to go through with this," she said softly. "You mean too much to me to stand by and watch you make the same disastrous mistakes that I did."

"What's it to you? Just because you're my mother, that doesn't give you the right to tell me what I can or can't do!" Amber shoved Libby's hand away. "You don't have authority over me!"

The yard light flashed on, blinding them.

"She doesn't, but I do," Cash announced through the screen door, "and I want an explanation." Wearing jeans and a burgundy sweater, he shoved open the door, hustled down the steps in his stocking feet, and stood between the women. "What's going on here?"

Amber refused to speak. She folded her arms instead and stared at the ground, pouting.

Grim disappointment etched Cash's face. He already knew. Libby's heart began to slam. "Amber and I—"

"So much for our understanding," he interrupted softly.

"I know I promised, Cash," Libby replied, jumping to her own defense, "but I'm trying to prevent trouble, not start it."

A blood-curdling scream startled them as it pierced the night air. Libby spun around and saw the tall blond visitor—Uncle Todd—marching around the side of the house, hauling Medley over his shoulder like a bundle of shingles. Scrappy took off on another barking spree, circling Todd and Medley with canine glee.

"Put me down!" Medley kicked her legs and pummeled his broad, muscular back with her fists. "You-you uncivilized brute! Let me go!"

Unfazed, Todd strutted out of the shadows with slow, confident strides. "I caught a burglar," he said, grinning mischievously as he approached them. "I found her peeping through the window in the front door."

"I am not!" Medley shouted. "I did not!"

"I see you've rounded up the other one." Todd leaned over and gently set Medley on her feet. He straightened and pulled his cell phone from a case on his belt. "Did you call 9-1-1?"

"Never mind." Cash gripped his hands on his hips. "I'll handle this myself."

Medley wavered for a moment, as though fighting off dizziness. "Listen, Samson," she snapped and shoved an unsteady fist in Todd's face.

Flashing another handsome grin, he reached out and caught her by the arm.

She easily pulled out of his tender grasp. "I'm the one who should call 9-1-1. How dare you manhandle me!" She gasped in horror and pointed to the back of her hand. "Look at this bruise!"

"That's dirt, Medley," Libby interjected. "Calm down."

Getting a handle on her own attitude, she stepped forward, extending her hand toward Todd. "Hi," she offered humbly, knowing how ridiculous they must look to him, not to mention Cash's neighbors. "I'm Libby Cunningham."

Todd's golden brows shot up to his hairline. "Oh, so you're..." In a nanosecond, he returned her smile. "I'm Todd Trisco." He firmly shook her hand. "Nice to meetcha." Then he shot Cash a questioning look.

The storm door of the neighbor's house swung open and an elderly man's stubbly face peered from behind the screen.

"Say, you people wanna take your party someplace else? I'm tryin' ta get some sleep over here," he hollered in a muffled voice, as though he'd neglected to put in his dentures. He pointed at the dog. "Scrappy! Stop running around and get in this house!"

Oh, great, Libby thought miserably. *Amber won't listen to me, I'm guilty of interfering again and now Cash's neighbors are upset. What else could go wrong?*

The moment the thought crossed her mind, Cash's lawn sprinklers suddenly turned on, showering everyone with a burst of ice-cold water.

Chapter 6

Moisture dripped from Cash's kohl hair, catching on the wide bath towel covering his shoulders as he stood in the living room, attempting to dry himself in front of the crackling fire. The stern look projecting from the profile of his face reflected a barely-held temper in check. Libby didn't know who had infuriated him the most, Amber or her. Both had violated his trust.

He turned and pointedly stared at Libby then Amber. "What were you two doing arguing in my backyard at this time of night?"

Wrapped in blankets, Libby huddled next to Amber on the dark green leather sofa. She gripped the edge of her cushion, ready to explain what happened. She wanted to tell Cash the truth; not to gloat, but to show him that she had acted in Amber's best interest. "We—"

"I went outside to check on Scrappy's barking," Amber blurted, cutting her off. "That's all I know!"

Libby intended to expose Amber's lie, but a small voice in her heart warned her to remain silent and allow Cash to handle the situation.

Cash scrutinized Amber's outfit with a skeptical frown. "Then why are you dressed to go out?"

"I-I'm not." Amber glanced around nervously. "I'm just trying on my new clothes."

"Twenty minutes ago, you told me you were going to bed."

"I-I changed my mind."

"Amber," Cash said in a low, level voice, "were you sneaking out to meet *that kid*?"

Amber glared at him, her jaw stubbornly set. "He's not a kid! Brian turned eighteen today!"

"Where were you supposed to meet him?"

"Nowhere," Amber insisted defiantly.

Cash's face and neck suffused with blood as he slid the towel off his shoulders and tossed it across the back of a chair. He pulled out his cell phone and punched in three numbers. "Yeah," he said into the phone after a moment, "I want to report suspicious activity in my neighborhood involving a red Grand Am."

"No!" Amber sprung off the sofa. The blanket covering her shoulders flew off and dropped to the floor. "He's waiting for me at school. Don't get him in trouble!"

Revealing his bluff, Cash shut off the phone and set it on the Queen Anne coffee table. "He's going to have more trouble than he can handle if he ever comes around here again."

"That's not fair." Tears spilled down her face. "He's my best friend, Dad."

"Not anymore." Cash's cocoa eyes glittered.

"What's wrong with being friends? Brian's fun to be with. We're a lot alike. For one thing..." She glanced at Libby then Cash. "We both know what it's like to grow up with only one parent."

Libby's immediate reaction amounted to first-rate guilt, but Amber's manipulative tone made her mentally pull back. When push came to shove, that girl really knew how to hit the right buttons. She cut a glance at Cash as she retrieved Amber's blanket and piled it on the sofa. The no-nonsense look in his eyes mirrored the same conclusion.

"Best friends don't invite you to make bad choices," he countered with finality. "I don't want you hanging around with him anymore. Understand?"

"Don't preach at me!" Amber smacked her hands over her ears. "You can break us up, but you can't stop me from caring about him!" She charged past them and ran upstairs.

"You're grounded until further notice!" Cash bellowed, still crimson with anger.

Windows rattled as the door to her room slammed.

With a frustrated sigh, he raked his hand through his wet hair. "I wish I could ground her from *all* boys until graduation..."

Todd stood off to one side with his back to the fire. He reached out and clutched Cash's shoulder. "Come on, buddy. You know you don't mean that. Take it easy," he advised in a deep, calm voice. "She's upset because she knows you're right. Give her time. She'll come around."

Libby's heart sunk to her lap. Amber's fight with Cash brought back painful memories of her tenuous relationship with her own father and the disastrous consequences that had resulted. She couldn't let that cycle repeat itself in her daughter's life, too.

She pushed the blanket off her shoulders. "I'm going upstairs to talk to her. I know exactly what's going through her mind right now. Someone needs to talk her out of it."

"That's my responsibility." Cash spun around, meeting her face-to-face. "Please, stay out of this, Olivia. She answers to *me*."

"Cash, she's already answered to you and you got precisely nowhere with her because you lost your temper," Libby replied. "How do you expect to get through to her when you act like that? Forbidding her to stop seeing that boy just because you said so isn't going to fly tomorrow any more than it did tonight. You need to be calm and rational, no matter how she acts."

The color in Cash's face mottled. "I understand your concern, but don't tell me how to discipline *my daughter*."

Libby moved closer. "Then stop yelling at her and start talking to her!"

"Whoa, folks," Todd said and placed his hands on their shoulders, pulling Cash and Libby apart like boxers in a ring. "Time out. Let's cool down."

"He's absolutely right." Wrapped in a blanket like a burrito, Medley sat curled up in one of the wing chairs. "You two sound more immature than Amber. Instead of arguing and finding fault with each other, you should be strategizing the best way to approach her as a team. You're the people closest to her and she needs to see you in agreement. You're not helping her by quarreling. Your daughter needs *both* of you."

A tense silence fell over the room like a heavy cloud.

Libby looked toward the top of the stairs at Amber's closed bedroom door. "I simply wanted to help her."

She turned to Cash. "I'm sorry for losing my temper. Let's start over. I'd like us to go together to our daughter's room and have a heart-to-heart talk with her. What do you say?"

"All right." He gave her a tired nod. "No need to apologize. It was my fault. I'm the one who shouldn't have lost my temper."

Todd pulled out his keys and tossed them into the air. "Hey, beautiful," he directed toward Medley as he caught them and approached her bundled form. Her jade eyes flared at his blatant flirting. "Are you gonna just sit there all night shivering or would you like to warm up with some good brew? I know where there's an all-night coffee bar about five minutes from here that serves up a mean French roast."

Medley instantly perked up. "Real coffee?" She gave him an intrigued smile. "Do they serve latte?"

"Mocha, latte, anything you want." Todd extended his hand to help her out of the chair. "I like a double shot of espresso, myself."

Medley's blanket fell in a heap in the chair as she hopped to her feet. "That sounds like my kind of place. Let's go!"

Todd issued a nod in Cash's direction as he ushered Medley to the door. "Give me a ring when you get things squared away upstairs. In the meantime, we'll be at Sleepy's."

The front door clicked shut behind them.

Libby glanced up the stairs and swallowed hard, knowing she needed God's grace more than ever. She thought she'd already had the most important conversation of her life when she met with Cash at Sandhill Nature Center.

Now it seemed like merely a warm-up for what lay ahead.

* * *

Cash and Libby stood at the closed door to Amber's room. Though he didn't show it, his confidence had suffered a huge hit when her prediction about Amber proved correct. Once again, his stupid pride had made him look like a fool, clouding his judgment and casting doubt on his parenting skills. Once again, Libby seemed to understand Amber better than he did, even though he'd spent nearly sixteen years raising her.

"Let me do the talking," he said, anxious to prove himself. He took a deep breath and rapped on the door. "Amber," he announced with authority, "I'm coming in."

"What do you want?" the voice on the other side snapped.

"She's on the phone with *him*," he whispered and gripped the door handle. He wanted to kick the door down! Instead, he opened it slowly and stepped into the world of a teenager. Empty bags and boxes lay strewn across the oak floor. Amber's new clothes draped her dresser and computer desk like dust covers. In front of the full-length mirror on her closet door, her makeup kit lay open on the floor, its contents spread out on a large pink throw rug.

She lay on her canopied bed with her back to the door, surrounded by pink pillows and stuffed animals, murmuring into her cell phone. Above her, a giant black and white poster of a rock band hung taped to the wall. Their body-hugging, low-rise jeans, and long hair reminded him of Brian Hanson. He wanted to reach over and rip that thing off the plaster, but restrained himself, knowing it would just trigger another meltdown.

As they stepped into the room, Amber angled her head toward them and stopped talking mid-sentence. "The firing squad's here," she grumbled into the phone. "Gotta go." She shut it off and rolled toward them. Her eyes looked red and swollen from crying. "You're both here," she stated warily, as though their combined presence signified an ambush. Her expression, mixed with fear and rebellion, told him she expected another unpleasant incident. "Why? Are you going to gang up on me?"

Her stinging remark wounded his already frazzled nerves. Before he could catch himself, he fired back, "Don't get smart with me, young lady—"

"No," Libby said calmly, cutting him off. "We're here to have an honest and open discussion about what happened tonight."

Sweat collected under the collar of Cash's shirt, but he forced himself to speak with a gentler voice.

"You lied to me, Amber. Why?"

She pursed her lips into a pout. "I wanted to go to Brian's party."

"So, you changed into your new clothes and snuck out." Her disobedience disappointed him, but her lack of remorse hurt him even more. The Bible advised parents to *"Train up a child in the way he should go and he shall not depart from it."* He thought he *had*. Where did he go wrong? He shook his head. "I've tried to teach you to be a better person than that."

Instead of apologizing, she sat up with an air of indignation. "What gives you guys the right to criticize me? You're not perfect, either. You've made mistakes." She glanced from him to Libby and back. "Otherwise I wouldn't be here!"

Her accusation hit him so hard that he didn't know what to say. Yes, he'd made mistakes in his lifetime. His all-time worst error in judgment stood next to him, looking radiant in black velvet. It never occurred to him, however, that Amber understood it, too.

"Our behavior isn't the issue here," he countered. "Yours is—"

Libby's hand squeezed his arm, cutting him short. Surprised, he glanced at her and saw her nodding in agreement.

"You're right," she said to Amber. "We have made mistakes. I can't speak for your father, but in my case, I know that my life would have turned out much different if I'd had even one understanding adult to talk with about my problems. Unfortunately, I didn't have that advantage. You do. You have two people who love you very much—" She looked at him. "Your father and me."

Amber folded her arms into a tight bow. "If you care about me so much, then why did you give me up?"

Cash stood riveted to the floor, gaping as his gaze fixed on Libby. He couldn't believe Amber's boldness or Libby's calm acceptance of her tactless demand.

"At the time I didn't know I had a choice," Libby answered softly. "You see, I grew up without a mother, too. My mom died from an aneurysm just before I started kindergarten. Not long after the funeral, my grandmother moved in with us."

"Where are they now?" Amber asked, firing off the question like an interrogator.

"They've both passed away."

"Why didn't they talk to you?"

"My dad held a public office and didn't have the time, but I know that in his own way he loved me," Libby replied. "He spent most of his life working as a U.S. Senator. My grandmother had neither time nor patience for me. I don't know for sure, but I suspect she never cared for my mother, either."

Amber leaned forward. "Why?"

"I heard once that my dad's demanding job and being gone all of the time put a strain on my parents' relationship. Supposedly, my mother was so depressed about spending so much time apart that she threatened to leave him, and that would have jeopardized Dad's career in politics. Anyway," Libby added and waved her hand as if to dismiss the subject, "I grew up lonely and alone. Your father came along about the time I turned your age. I thought he'd fallen from heaven and I wanted him to be the answer to all my problems." She glanced at Cash, then back again to Amber. Sadness reflected in her eyes. "Instead, I became obsessed with him and got myself into serious trouble."

"Olivia, you don't have to do this," Cash interjected, preferring to keep the private details of their past from becoming a family soap opera. "It's ancient history. Let it go."

"No, don't!" Amber scrambled off the bed, fixated on Libby with a desperate, imploring look. "All my life I've wondered about you and Dad...you know...*together*. Please, don't stop. Tell me—what happened after you met him?"

Cash backed off, feeling like a stray dog at a church picnic. The bond between Libby and Amber seemed to grow before his eyes, pushing him out of the conversation. And their inner circle.

Libby clasped her hands. "I used to sneak out at night, too." She looked squarely at Cash. "To be with him."

They both stared at him. Cash's face burned with embarrassment, as though someone had set it on fire. "I don't know what you're trying to accomplish here," he warned Libby, "but—"

"I made a bad mistake that led to more bad mistakes and permanent heartache," Libby said to Amber, finishing the sentence for him. "When my dad learned about my pregnancy, he felt betrayed and deeply hurt. It caused a rift between us that never completely healed and, to this day, I regret how my actions could have destroyed his political career. Regardless of how sorry I am now, I can't take it back. I can't undo the anguish I caused him and I pray you don't learn that lesson the hard way like I did."

Cash watched Amber's eyes widen as she absorbed Libby's advice. In one short conversation, Libby had made more headway with his daughter than he had in months. He should have been relieved, but instead, it made him feel like a failure. Amber was slowly growing apart from him and, sadly, he didn't know what to do about it.

Amber regarded Libby soberly. "Did your dad make you give me away?"

"Yes," Libby answered simply, "but only after my grandmother coerced us both. I don't know what threat she used against him, but she told me that God would never forgive my sin unless I gave you up. At the time, my youth and inexperience prevented me from realizing she only wanted to protect the family's reputation. Later on, once I realized that God's forgiveness is unconditional, I wanted my baby back."

Cash nearly swallowed his tongue. He knew Libby's grandmother never held any affection for her, but he had no idea that she'd put Libby through so much grief.

Libby selected a picture frame off Amber's dresser. "People assured me that eventually, I'd accept the decision I'd made and get on with my life, but I never did. Instead, I clung to the few memories I had and hoped with all my heart that someday I'd get another chance to get to know you again."

Libby gazed longingly at Amber in her ninth-grade soccer uniform then looked up. "After you were born the nurses wouldn't let me see you. They hid you away in a private room because as soon as I signed the papers, you were going to a foster home to await placement. I understood that once I signed, I had no legal right to know where you went or what happened to you. It hurt me very much, but I couldn't do anything about it."

"Wow," Amber said in a small voice as her eyes glistened. "That's so sad." She looked at Cash. "Why didn't you help her, Dad?"

"Ah...ah..." Cash floundered, suddenly tongue-tied. What could he say without explaining the fact that his parents and the senator had agreed to keep them apart? Amber *absolutely* didn't need to know that about her Grandma and Grandpa MacKenzie.

"It's not his fault," Libby offered, rising to his defense. "My dad broke us up and then sent me away." She set the picture back on the dresser. "The only reason I'm telling you this story, Amber, is to make you understand that there are consequences for your actions. You may think sneaking out is harmless, but it's deceitful and can lead to worse problems. My past is a prime example of what not to do."

Amber bit her lip and stared at the beads hanging in her window, as though preoccupied with something. After a moment, she turned her attention back to Cash. "Um...Dad?" She seemed hesitant to speak her mind, as though his presence made her self-conscious.

"What?"

"Would...you leave us alone for a little while?"

Cash's heart nearly stopped at the prospect of Amber deliberately shutting him out. His stomach churned. "Why? What's wrong?"

"It's..." she stared at her feet, "it's just between us girls."

His heart sunk to the floor. What else could he do but comply? Stricken with helplessness, he shot Libby a worried look and walked out. In the hallway, he debated what to do. Should he go downstairs and wait for them to join him, or stick around and find out what they were discussing? It only took a moment to decide. Without reservation, he stepped close and peered through the space between the door and its frame.

Amber sat on the bed again, cross-legged, facing Libby and hugging a large stuffed rabbit. "When you were with Dad—I mean, back then—did you love him?"

Cash blinked, totally flabbergasted. *Is that what she meant by "between us girls?"* He let out a silent breath of relief, but at the same time, a reckless curiosity overtook him. For some unaccountable reason, he had to hear Libby's answer. He stood in statue-like stillness, afraid to breathe lest he missed it.

"Yes, I did," Libby said after an awkward pause, "once upon a time."

That's odd, he thought. She sounded like she'd been holding her breath, too. He didn't know why, but a surge of elation coursed through him.

Amber hugged the rabbit to her chest. "Do—do you think you could fall in love with him again?"

Though Cash couldn't see Libby's face, his hands automatically clenched.

"I don't think so, honey." Libby shook her head. "What happened between us ended a long time ago."

He cocked his ear toward the door. Had he really heard a note of wistfulness in her voice, or had he imagined it?

"Why not?" Amber's youthful enthusiasm held strong. "There isn't anyone keeping you from being together now."

"Times have changed. Unfortunately, so have we." Libby shrugged, as though the question troubled her. "We're not the same people we once were."

The hopeful light in Amber's eyes dimmed. "Yeah, that's what Dad says, too."

Again, he didn't know why, but his elation sobered. He stepped away from the door and relaxed against the opposite wall with his arms folded, pretending as though he'd been there all along. A minute or so later, feminine laughter erupted from Amber's room. Amber's door opened and Libby stepped out, smiling and clutching the soccer picture to her chest as though it belonged to her now.

"Our daughter wants to have a word with you."

"All right." His arms slowly dropped to his sides, but his heart jumped to his throat. The formality in Libby's words worried him. He walked back into

Amber's room and found her still sitting on the bed.

He stopped directly in front of her. "Amber, what's the matter?"

She nervously fidgeted with the rabbit's soft, floppy ear. "I'm sorry, Dad, for sneaking out of the house tonight. I know it upset you very much. Will you forgive me?"

He nearly fell over. From the time he'd stepped away from the door until Libby came out, he'd missed a crucial moment!

"Of course, honey bear," he replied, purposely using her childhood nickname to show his sincerity. "Can we start over, then, as though this incident never happened?"

Wide-eyed, she nodded.

He held out his arms. "Give me a hug."

She tossed the rabbit aside and flew into his embrace, holding on for dear life.

"I love you, honey," he whispered. "More than you'll ever know."

"I love you, too, Dad." She sniffled loudly.

Despite her positive attitude adjustment, he couldn't allow himself to relax. Part of him believed her, but part of him doubted everything would be okay. He'd dealt with the current crisis, but the fact remained that Amber still wanted to date a kid with a bad attitude, and he still didn't know if he could trust Libby to cease overstepping his authority and taking matters into her own hands.

"Dad?"

"H-m-m-m..."

Amber lifted her head off his shoulder. "I want all three of us to go to church together on Sunday." She sent a pleading look toward Libby, standing in the doorway. "Okay?"

"Well, I..." Libby's eyes widened with apprehension as her gaze darted between father and daughter. "I don't want to intrude..."

"You're not!" Amber pulled away from Cash and went to her mother's side. "Please, come with us? We go to the nine o'clock service at the Four Seasons Church."

Libby fiddled with her cross pendant. "All right," she glanced at Cash, "but only if your father agrees."

He didn't voice any objections to Amber inviting her mother, but somehow it didn't *feel* all right. Sure, Amber's sudden interest in going to church again made him more than happy. Lately, he'd practically had to pry her out of bed with a crowbar on Sunday mornings. Still, he didn't know if inviting Libby, at this point, made sense. Would it encourage Amber to go to church from now on, or would it only serve to give her misguided ideas about the three of them becoming a family?

They stared at him expectantly.

He glanced from female to female—feeling squeezed. The outcome seemed already determined. They'd outnumbered and outvoted him.

Chapter 7

Libby hurried down the stairs, determined to put as much distance between her and Cash as possible. She hadn't expected Amber to invite her to church, and Cash's reluctance to the idea left her unsettled. The more she thought about it, the more she realized she'd made a mistake. Accompanying them to church without Cash's wholehearted approval amounted to intruding upon not only their privacy but her agreement with him not to interfere as well.

At the bottom of the stairs, she pivoted and nearly slammed into him, not realizing he'd followed so close behind.

"I've changed my mind," she declared, bracing her palms against his shoulders to break his momentum. "In retrospect, I don't think it's a good idea, after all, to go to church with you and Amber."

He halted, towering over Libby, his brows lifting with surprise. "If you have concerns, you should've said so in front of her. She's counting on you now to be there." He slid his fingers around her wrists and lifted her hands off his shoulders, as though such close contact made him uncomfortable.

That made two of them.

"It's not Amber I'm concerned about." She slipped out of his grasp and stepped away. "It's you."

He frowned and placed his hand on the newel post. "I didn't object when she asked to include you."

"No, but you didn't look happy about it, either."

He hesitated, as though trying to make up his mind about something. An odd light flickered in his eyes. "I don't care whether you come along or not."

His indecision made her even more convinced she should have discussed it privately with him first. She dug into the pocket of her velour jacket for her cell phone. "You say that now but come Sunday morning you'll be looking for a back seat in the balcony to avoid explaining to your pastor who I am because my presence is undoubtedly going to raise questions," she stated as she speed-dialed Medley's number. She looked up. "I wouldn't want to make you uncomfortable."

"I said I have no problem with it," he blurted. "If you don't want to go, fine, but don't use me as your excuse."

Medley's voicemail greeting played in her ear. Disappointed, she disconnected the call. Her cousin should have been ready to come back by now. Why didn't Medley answer her phone?

"Of course I want to go. Otherwise, I wouldn't have agreed to it in the first place." Libby jammed the phone back into her pocket. "But the one thing I don't want is for unresolved issues between us to make Amber uncomfortable."

He shook his head and lowered his voice. "Whatever happened between us in the past stays there, and the less Amber knows about it, the better off we'll all be."

She glanced past Cash up the open stairway and noticed Amber's door stood slightly ajar. Cash must have sensed her concern for he twisted at the waist and stared at Amber's door as well.

He turned back to her. "I'd prefer that you refrain from bringing up our past around her," he whispered. "Agreed?"

"Someday she needs to learn the truth about what happened," Libby said simply and glanced up, watching Amber's door, "but for now, I'll let it go." Amber had enough issues to deal with already. She didn't need to carry the burden of trying to understand her parents' past failures as well.

Fueled by restlessness and an overwhelming desire to escape his penetrating stare, Libby set the picture of Amber on a small table positioned under the front windows and peered behind the curtains. She'd hoped to find Todd's black Hummer pulling up to the garage, but the driveway sat empty. Frustrated, she yanked out her phone again and started punching in a text message to Medley.

"I'm curious," Cash continued in a low voice, "about how you convinced Amber to drop her tantrum so fast and apologize. What did you say to talk her into agreeing with you?"

He sounded so close; his nearness startled her. She whirled around and found him standing right behind her again. The phone flew out of her hand and skittered across the hardwood floor.

"I didn't talk her into it," Libby replied as she scrambled for her Samsung. "I simply gave her my honest opinion."

Cash reached the phone first. He checked the casing for damage and handed it to her.

She sent the text message, "*Where r u?*" then slipped it back into her pocket, forcing herself to appear calm. "I reminded her that the Bible says not to let the sun go down on your wrath. Since we both had breached your trust, we both needed to make amends with you by asking your forgiveness and put it behind us." She drew in a deep breath. "I guess it's my turn. I apologize for interfering. Please forgive me. It won't happen again."

"Do you honestly mean that this time," he cut another glance toward the stairway, "or are you reserving the right to change your mind again if you decide the situation warrants it?"

"Yes, I mean it." She didn't know why, but he seemed to be testing her. "You still don't trust me, do you?"

He folded his muscular arms. "So far you haven't given me any reason to believe you *can* be trusted. Twice now, you've taken matters into your own hands when you should have consulted me first." A deep frown etched his ruggedly handsome face. "Your actions disappoint me."

She blinked, taken aback. "Excuse me?" The shrill pitch of her whisper cut through the air as his accusation touched a sensitive nerve. "You were the one who supposedly had everything under control," she shot back, lowering her voice. "Only, you didn't, did you? I tried to warn you, but you refused to listen.

If I hadn't stepped in, she'd be partying with Brian Hanson and Jack Daniels right now. She slipped out right under your nose!"

Cash flinched and then sidestepped, blocking her view of the stairs. "You have no idea what it's like for a single parent to raise a teenager. So, until you become an expert in the field, don't criticize me."

"I may not be an expert, but as her mother, I have a right to speak my mind." She backed away and headed for the door, wishing Medley would call or at least answer her text.

"...a mother without experience," he stated abruptly as he followed her.

She glanced back at him. "How would you know?"

"You never married or had a family. You said so yourself."

She stopped at the front door. "That doesn't mean I can't be a good mother to Amber."

"The way I see it," he countered, "you've stayed single all these years because you can't commit to a relationship, and I worry that includes Amber."

How dare he judge me?

"I've never married because my life came to a screeching halt the day they took Amber away. I couldn't move on until I'd found my child." She zipped up her velour jacket and grabbed the door handle. "So, what's your excuse? Surely you've met someone by now who fits your rigid standards."

His dark-eyed gaze pierced her like laser beams. "After what happened with you, I've never been able to trust anyone else."

That did it.

"Take responsibility for your own mistakes, MacKenzie, and stop blaming me," she said between clenched teeth. "I didn't end our relationship. *You did.*" She jerked the door open, intending to storm out when Cash's hand shot out and slammed it shut in her face.

"Do you think it was easy staying away? You have *no* idea what I went through." His voice quavered in her ear. He gripped her by the arm and spun her around. Her breath caught in her throat. "When my parents banned me from ever seeing you again, it made me frantic. I wanted to see you so badly," he persisted, "and find out how you were. Then someone leaked to your father that I intended to ignore the agreement he'd reached with my parents and Frank retaliated with a restraining order. Before I could figure out a way to contact you, you'd disappeared. He'd made it impossible for us to be together again."

"If you'd truly cared for me, you'd have *found* a way. You would have done whatever it took to see me. At the very least you owed me a proper goodbye—" She stopped short, uncomfortably aware that mere inches separated them. He stood so close she could trace a tiny scar on his chin and inhale the scent of his cologne. The spicy fragrance brought back vivid memories and for one crazy moment, she dared wonder what it would feel like to have his strong arms around her again, reassuring her that everything would be all right. She looked into his eyes and the shock on his face suggested he'd read her mind.

The thought unnerved her. She had to leave—to escape this embarrassing moment. *Now.* She pressed her fists against his chest and tried to twist out of his grasp.

As if sensing her desperation, he tightened his grip and drew her toward him. Though she knew what lie ahead she froze, powerless to resist as his mouth claimed hers. In the space of a heartbeat, she became sixteen again. Her pulse quickened, her stomach fluttering with curiosity and fascination as powerful desires resurfaced from deep in the recesses of her heart. Ironically, his arms felt so natural around her, so right, as though God had always meant it to be. Swept into the moment, she dropped her guard and leaned into his kiss...

He pulled her closer, tightening his hold. Her arms flew around his neck, her passion ignited as though the sixteen-year gap in their relationship had never happened. His long arms wrapped possessively around her waist, locking her in his embrace. She let out a deep sigh.

Suddenly, the danger of their foolishness dawned on her. What in the world were they doing? They weren't in love; they could barely get along! Shocked by her impulsiveness, she wrenched free from his arms.

"What do you think you're doing?" Libby stepped an arm's length away, putting the situation in its proper perspective again as she caught her breath and nervously smoothed her mussed hair.

92

"I'm trying to make it up to you for never saying goodbye." He sounded disappointed by her rejection, almost wounded. His dark eyes smoldered, his nostrils flaring as he towered over her. "Isn't that what you wanted?"

She could hardly breathe much less answer him back. Awareness of her vulnerability to him had shaken her to the core. Covering her mouth with the back of her hand, she fell back against the door while her other hand searched wildly for the handle.

As if on cue, headlights flashed through the beveled oval glass in the door. With a silent cry of relief, Libby peered through the sheer curtains and saw Medley's blue Focus pulling up to the garage.

"No," she choked out, her head spinning with confusion and panic, "that's the last thing I expected from you."

"Hey, I didn't mean to upset you—"

"Look, we're not kids anymore. We know what we're doing, so let's not make the same mistakes again. Whatever happened between us in the past stays there...remember?"

She snatched her picture frame off the table and pushed the door wide open. "I'll see you in church."

*   *   *

"Hurry up, Dad," Amber complained for the third time. "Why are you driving like a nerd? We're going to be late!"

Cash glanced at the speedometer and saw the needle resting at 25 mph. He stepped on the gas and sped up to 30 mph, hoping they would be late so he couldn't find a parking space. He'd have justification to drop Amber off but excuse himself from church today. Most of all, he'd be spared an hour of extreme discomfort sitting next to Libby while struggling to act as though nothing had happened between them thirty-six hours ago.

He shook his head. "I don't want to get a speeding ticket, honey. Don't worry; I'll get you there."

Amber pulled out her cell phone and touched the screen a couple of times. After several moments, she said to someone, presumably Libby, "Hi! I'm just calling to make sure you're still waiting for us." She gave Cash an annoyed look. "Dad's driving like a senile old man. I think he's forgotten what time church starts."

Cash picked Amber's water bottle off the seat and pretended to squirt her with it.

"Cut it out, Dad!" She snatched the bottle away from him. "You're not funny." Even so, a smirk curved at the corners of her mouth. She put the phone back to her ear. "We'll be there in a couple of minutes." Her slim brow arched. "At least, I hope we will. Bye."

Cash turned the corner. A massive red brick building and park-like grounds loomed in the distance. His fingers gripped the shifter, squeezing tighter as his tension grew. He only had two blocks to come up with something to say to Libby about his reckless indiscretion on Friday night.

Why did I do it?

Curiosity played a part he had to admit. Once upon a time, he couldn't get enough of her and he wanted to see if she still held the same power over him that she once did. He wanted to experience for himself whether the gentle tone of her voice and the sweetness of her mouth still held the ability to drive him to distraction. Suddenly the memory of kissing her soft, moist lips washed over him like a warm, summer rain...

He sucked in a deep breath of air like a drowning man. *Don't go there*, he thought, exhaling with a tense sigh. *I should never have kissed her like that in the first place.*

But then, she shouldn't have kissed him back like *that* either...

He pulled onto the church grounds and began to search for a parking space. Rows upon rows of cars, SUVs, and pickup trucks stretched across the football-field-sized lot. To his dismay, he didn't have to look far. Just ahead, a dark blue pickup slowly backed out of a parking space. He braked, put his signal on, and waited to pull in.

Amber couldn't hold on that long. She threw open her door and jumped out. "I'll meet you inside!" She hurried toward the entrance, her French braid swinging behind her back like a pendulum. She wore the soft gold skirt, brown leather blazer, and matching knee-high boots that he'd purchased for her last Friday night at the Mall of America. He couldn't help noticing how she looked exactly like Libby from the back. Both stood at the same height. Both had long, slender legs and walked with a graceful, easy stride. His heart swelled with love. Amber meant more to him than his own life.

What does Libby mean to me?

He pulled into the parking space, shifted, and pulled out the keys. *She used to be the love of my life*, he thought sadly. As he shoved the door open and eased out of the truck, a surge of loneliness filled his heart. That one kiss told him everything he needed to know—or wished he didn't know now. He still loved her...more than ever.

Once inside the church, it didn't take long to find the girls. They stood in the Narthex, waiting for him at the wide, open doors to the sanctuary.

Fire began to build under his collar the moment he saw Libby. She stood next to Amber, looking dignified in a navy coatdress with gold buttons down the front. His gaze drew to her blonde hair, swept back into a mass of long, spiraled curls. Mesmerized, he stared at her glossy pink lips for a moment then dragged his gaze to her eyes. Though he knew he should let it go, he had to know if she still regretted that kiss...

Her eyes flared, as though a moment of panic had set in before they silently warned him to keep his distance. Then she quickly looked away. Her hasty retreat disappointed him, but it also made him wonder if his kiss had affected her more than she dared admit to herself.

Without warning, the fire under his collar turned into a nerve-wracking sweat. His tie squeezed his throat like a knotted rope around his neck. He shoved his hands into his pockets to conceal their shaking as he strolled toward them. On Saturday, he'd thought about calling her all day, but couldn't think of the right words to say to apologize for upsetting her. He wished he could speak to her privately right now and set the record straight, but he couldn't say a word about it in front of Amber. His daughter must never know what happened!

"Good morning," he said to Libby. His voice sounded natural, but the words rushed out.

"Good morning." Libby's tight smile appeared to be a front for Amber's sake. Though she made an effort to be polite, tension threaded her voice, making it plain that she'd come only out of respect for Amber's wishes.

Amber waved at someone in the sanctuary and then grabbed Libby by the arm. "Let's go in and get a seat." She turned to Cash. "Come on, Dad. There are hardly any left."

Cash attempted to escort the girls down the center aisle when an elderly, white-haired man just inside the door held up his hand.

"Hold on, please." The greeter smiled and offered him a bulletin. "We're almost full. The usher will be right back to help you find seats."

From the corner of his eye, Cash saw his pastor emerge from the Fellowship Room where confirmation students were serving continental breakfast. The fiery furnace under his collar suddenly became seven times hotter.

Please, God, he silently pleaded, *don't let Pastor Greg notice us.* The strain between him and Libby would be embarrassing, not the actual introduction of her as Amber's mother, as she'd predicted.

The moment the words echoed through his head, Pastor Greg made eye contact and started toward him.

"Good morning, Cash," Pastor Greg called as he crossed the room in his white robe and green vestments. He stood about the same height as Cash, with wavy auburn hair, green eyes, and a dimpled chin. They shook hands.

"Good morning, Pastor," Cash replied then glanced at his watch. "It's almost time for the service to start. We'd better get moving."

However, Pastor Greg didn't seem to be in any hurry. He clasped Amber's hands. "Hello, Amber. How's school?"

"Just great!" She beamed with excitement, much to Cash's surprise. "The varsity football team is six and oh!"

"Awesome!" Pastor Greg held up his hand in a 'gimme five' gesture and smacked palms with her.

He turned to Libby and extended his hand once again. "Welcome! I'm Greg Connor."

Libby's countenance brightened a little. "It's a pleasure to meet you. I'm Libby Cunningham, Amber's mother."

Nonplussed, Pastor Greg returned her smile, but to his credit, he didn't miss a beat. If he found the situation uncomfortable or curious, he chose to overlook it.

"Thank you for coming. I'm glad you could be with us today," he replied warmly. "Enjoy the service." With that, he excused himself and left.

An usher appeared and escorted them into the sanctuary toward the front section. At the pew, Cash stood aside, allowing Libby to enter first. Amber held back, obviously wanting Cash and Libby to sit together, but Cash had no intention of making things any more uncomfortable between him and Libby than they already were. He stepped aside and pressed his hand on the hollow of Amber's back, nudging her forward. Her brows drew together in resistance, but she followed Libby, positioning herself between her parents.

During the sermon, Cash tried to concentrate but couldn't focus as Pastor Greg taught on forgiveness, of all things. Whether sitting or standing, he shifted his feet, fidgeting like a ten-year-old. What little he heard of the message seemed directed to him alone. Unresolved issues with Libby regarding placing Amber for adoption without his knowledge had hindered his faith, and the more he dwelled on it, the heavier it weighed upon him.

He stole a glance at her. She looked preoccupied and withdrawn, as though something deeply troubled her as well. He remembered the surprise on her face after they'd kissed and wondered if his careless blunder still bothered her as much as it bothered him.

Forgive her...

The words echoed deep into his spirit.

Lord, I know what You want, he prayed in agony as he stared at his clenched hands, *but I don't know how to let go of the past.*

Worse yet, he didn't know how he could still be in love with her and not be able to forgive her for that one thing. Why did life have to be so complicated?

God suddenly went silent.

As soon as the last note of the closing hymn faded, Cash bounded to his feet, eager to say goodbye and head for home.

Amber tugged on his sleeve.

"We have to go to the continental breakfast, Dad," she said, raising her voice over lively organ music as she followed him out of the pew and into the throng of people making their way out of the sanctuary. "I told you about it on the way to church. Don't you remember?"

He had no desire to sit across the table from Libby and struggle to make small talk, knowing it would make both of them extremely unhappy.

"Not today, honey. The room is probably packed and we're at the tail end of the crowd. There won't be any place to sit."

"We have to, Dad! Today is the last day that the profits go toward our youth conference. If we don't make enough money, some of the kids in church won't be able to go. Besides, I promised to do my part and help raise the money we need."

Cash dug into his pocket for a twenty and attempted to say he'd be more than happy to give a straight donation instead, but she turned to Libby, cutting him off. "You want to help our youth group, don't you?"

Libby hesitated then took a deep breath. "Sweetie, I have plans after church so I have to get going..."

Amber hooked her arm around Libby's elbow. "Please?"

Libby stood silent for a moment as if wrestling with the situation. "All right," she replied slowly without looking at Cash. "I suppose I could use some coffee."

"Yes!" Amber whirled around, facing Cash. "The vote is two to one, Dad. Let's go!"

Anxiety overtook him as he checked his watch. "Fine, but let's wrap it up in fifteen minutes. I'm due at Todd's place in an hour." Todd held the honor of hosting the football party today for their construction crew. Cash had offered to show up early and concoct a pot of his favored 'atomic' beans while Todd made the barbecue beef.

Amber joined hands with her parents and pressed through the crowd, pulling them along.

They went into the Fellowship Room, a large brick and glass reception area adjacent to a huge kitchen. Cash paid for their breakfast and grabbed a couple of chocolate-frosted doughnuts for himself. Amber pointed out a small table nestled in a corner, away from the crowd, where the couple occupying it stood and gathered their coffee cups, indicating they were ready to leave. With a nod of thanks, Cash escorted the girls to the table and sat down.

At the table, Amber bubbled with happiness, hailing friends across the room and nibbling on a cinnamon streusel muffin. Libby sat next to Amber and gripped her Styrofoam coffee cup with both hands. She had little to say, appearing to focus instead on Amber's non-stop chattering about some choir recital at school next week.

Cash wolfed down his doughnuts and drained his coffee, all the while keeping a close eye on his sports watch, waiting for this unsettling little detour to run out of time.

As if she'd read his mind, Amber pushed her chair back and stood. "I need more juice," she said as she tossed her braid over her shoulder and grabbed her new leather purse. "Can I get you guys some more coffee?"

Almost in unison, they declined, then sat in uncomfortable silence and watched Amber walk away. However, she didn't set out in the direction of the serving window. Instead, she waved at a group of teens across the room and made a beeline to join them. That little schemer had planned all along to desert him! The fire rekindled under his collar.

Across the table, Libby sat as rigid as a post, her expression unreadable as she watched Amber walk away.

"It's obvious what Amber is doing," he said, forging ahead. "I don't know how much she actually knows, but—"

"Whatever she witnessed on Friday night must have been enough to give her false hope." Though Libby spoke softly, the tone of her voice left no doubt in his mind that she held him completely responsible. "We're going to break her heart when she finally realizes that what she wants is impossible. Things will never be the same again."

He winced with guilt then leaned forward, keeping his voice low. "I made an inexcusable mistake on Friday night and I'm sorry. I shouldn't have..." He glanced around, making sure their conversation stayed private, "...*kissed* you without asking you first."

"I'm a big girl, Cash. I can handle it."

Their gazes met and held.

Libby pushed away her cold, untouched coffee. "What I can't handle is giving Amber the wrong impression, especially right after lecturing her on how reckless actions can cause unintended consequences."

Cash expelled a nervous sigh. "I'll talk to her about it on the ride home. The sooner we make Amber understand that nothing happened, the sooner our lives will settle down and get back to normal."

"What exactly will you tell her?"

He swallowed hard, wishing he didn't have to do damage control, but he needed to set Amber straight. He'd vowed not to allow Libby to hurt her. Ironically, his impulsive indiscretion may have already caused irreparable damage.

"I'll simply point out the truth; that she lives with me and she visits you. We share a common bond in her, but there is no *us.*"

She stared at him, unblinking, though white-knuckled hands clutched her purse. "I totally agree."

She shoved her chair back and rose to her feet. "As a matter of fact," she added quietly, "I think it would make things easier on everyone if you and I avoided each other from now on."

Looking straight ahead, she walked out.

He stared after her, wondering if she really didn't want to see him again, or if being together made her as nervous as it made him. He should have been relieved to know that she didn't want anything to do with him. It made life simpler for everyone involved. Instead, his sadness deepened as that lonely spot in his heart suddenly expanded into a crater-sized cavity. He tried to deny it to himself, but Libby's words undeniably rang true. After what happened between them two days ago, none of their lives would ever be the same again.

*   *   *

"What did you do to make her leave without saying goodbye?" Amber matched Cash's pace stride for stride as they hiked across the church parking lot to the truck. She swung her arms; her boots stomped on the blacktop, each step sounding like a small explosion.

The accusation in her voice put him on the defensive. "I didn't do anything. She chose to leave of her own accord, that's all."

"I don't believe you." Amber scorched him with an accusing glare. "You said something to upset her, didn't you?"

He knew better than to refute it, but couldn't give Amber a detailed explanation, either. She already knew more than she should. He stopped at the driver's side of his truck and fished into his pocket for the keys. When he looked up, Amber stood at the passenger side door, still glaring, still waiting for an explanation.

"We reached an agreement on a couple of things," he mumbled as he unlocked the doors with his remote-control keypad and opened his side.

Amber climbed in and slammed the door. "What things?"

"We discussed priorities."

She looked confused. "What priorities?"

"You live with me, you visit her," he said, looking straight at her, "and going forward we're committed to ensuring you have quality time with each of us."

Her mouth gaped. "You mean, like, separately?"

He nodded.

She hooked her seatbelt into place and then looked up, her eyes searching his. "Why?"

She sounded like a five-year-old again, asking questions he found difficult, if not impossible to answer. *How many stars live in the sky? Where do they come from? Why do my friends have a mommy and I don't?*

"It's better that way."

"This really isn't about me, is it? This is about your stupid break-up back in the ice age that nobody even cares about anymore. At least, I don't! Why can't you just forget about it?"

An old, familiar pain laced with guilt pierced his heart. He took a deep breath and gripped the steering wheel. "Someday," he replied in a softer, fatherly tone, "when things settle down, I'll explain everything. I promise, honey. Okay?"

"That's a lame explanation, Dad." She folded her arms and sat like a statue. "All I want to know is why you guys can't be friends *now* for my sake. I mean, what happened between you two in the old days is sad, but you're grownups now. Why can't you get over it?"

When he didn't answer, Amber turned away and stared out the window. She understood more than he'd given her credit for and it worried him. The distance that had steadily grown between them since she became a teenager stretched wider than ever and he didn't know how to breach the gap. Everything he said and everything he did seemed to drive her closer to Libby, and farther away from him.

Chapter 8

The incident on Sunday played havoc with Cash's morale for several days. He couldn't stop thinking about Amber's resentment toward him or her criticism of his discussion with Libby, even though she didn't know why they'd parted ways. A small voice in his head kept urging him to tell her everything, including his past with Libby.

Deep down, he wanted to set her straight on what really happened. It sounded like the right thing to do, but he feared that Amber would judge him for the mistakes of his youth, even though he'd had no control over Libby's fate once her father found out about her condition. Most of all, he didn't want Amber to find out about the role his parents played in keeping him and Libby apart. Amber loved her grandparents and didn't need to know they'd disapproved of his relationship with her mother as much as the senator did.

The thought of Amber searching for answers on her own and possibly getting misinformation made him uneasy as he drove his pickup home from work on Wednesday afternoon. He pulled into the driveway and turned off the ignition.

Maybe I should talk to Amber, he thought, waffling, *and get it off my chest.* He stared out the windshield for a while, mulling over what to say.

"Forget it," he grumbled to himself a couple of minutes later and jumped out of the truck. "Trying to explain the past is a complete waste of time. You can't go back and fix it, so why bother digging it up? It's only going to result in hurting people again. *Today* is all that matters."

He walked into the house expecting to find Amber on the phone instead of doing her homework, but to his dismay, the place sat eerily quiet.

"Amber?" Cash's voice echoed off the walls as he wandered through the house looking for signs of her presence—her jacket tossed over a chair, her backpack piled on the table, or a loaf of bread drying out on the counter next to an open jar of peanut butter with a knife stuck in it but he found none of those things. He bolted up the stairs to the second floor, taking two at a time, his work boots pounding like kettledrums on the oak treads. "Amber!"

Her bedroom door stood slightly ajar. He nudged it open with the toe of his boot and peered inside. The room looked normal. A fluffy, pink comforter lay in a crumpled heap on the end of the bed. Her open cosmetic case covered the matching throw rug in front of the mirrored closet door and discarded clothing dotted the floor. However, he found no sign of his daughter.

He snatched his phone from the clip on his belt and speed-dialed her cell number. After several rings, she answered, whispering. "Hello?"

"Amber, it's Dad. Why aren't you at home working on your school assignments?"

"I'm at choir practice," she whispered. "Our concert is tonight. I told you about it last Sunday when we were eating breakfast in the Fellowship Room. Don't you remember?"

"Oh." He hesitated, trying to recall that particular point in time. Unfortunately, he didn't have a clue. "Ah, yeah..." He jammed his fingers through his thick hair. "What time is the concert again?"

"Seven."

"What about dinner? Are they feeding you?"

"We're having pizza in a half-hour. I have to go, Dad. If Mrs. Riker catches me on the phone she'll send me to the principal's office."

"All right, honey. See you then."

He disconnected the call and jammed the phone back into the clip. Although he loved watching Amber sing, swelling with pride over his daughter's beautiful voice, choir concerts didn't rate high on his list of Wednesday night entertainment. A hot shower and a good movie on his big-screen television sounded more exciting than sitting in a stuffy auditorium listening to *"Oh, Susannah! Oh, don't you cry for me..."*

At least she found merit in something else besides that Hanson kid, he thought gratefully.

The clock downstairs on the fireplace mantel chimed, alerting him that he had two hours to clean up, find something to eat, and grab a quick nap before driving to school. On his way out of her room, he almost tripped when his foot tangled in some clothing. He picked up Amber's new designer jeans and a shiny plastic package dropped out of the back pocket. It bounced off the toe of his boot and skittered across the floor.

He dropped the jeans and stared, stunned. Even from where he stood, he couldn't mistake what he saw. Slowly, he walked over to the square plastic package containing a bright purple condom and picked it up. Where did Amber get this? Why did she have it?

As if he didn't know...

Panic and shock washed over him with the force of a tsunami. No way, not Amber, not his little girl...

His panic turned to dread and the worst state of helplessness he'd ever experienced in his entire life. His heart pounded as he stared at the package and wondered how he could have been so blind to the situation. Amber's obsession over *that kid* had always bothered him, but it should have set off warning bells louder than a civil defense system when she snuck out of the house to meet the boy. Guilt and a deep sense of failure seeped into his heart.

Lord, what did I do wrong? I've always done the best I could to raise her according to your Word.

He stared at the package for several moments then pulled out his phone and speed-dialed Todd's number. The phrase 'misery loves company' never seemed so appropriate before. Instantly, Todd's voicemail boomed in his ear. "Call me," he said once the message ended. "It's important!"

He ended the call, thought better of it, and redialed. "Forget the phone call. Just get over here!"

Feeling numb, he left Amber's room to take a shower. Five minutes ago, he'd faced the prospect of a boring night. Now, the bottom had literally dropped out of his world.

*   *   *

Twenty-five minutes later, Todd burst through the front door carrying a large bottle of water, dressed in jeans and a black Ralph Lauren polo shirt. His damp, blond locks looked freshly showered.

"What's the problem, Cash?"

Cash stood in the living room holding a roast beef sandwich in one hand, a can of cola in the other. His hand shook as he set the cola on the coffee table.

"I want to show you something," he said and reached into his pocket. He tossed Amber's purple package onto the coffee table. "Do you know what this means?"

Todd's golden eyebrows nearly disappeared under his blond bangs as he stared at the object. "Sure," he replied and stuffed his hands into his pockets, "but if you're getting that serious about Amber's mother again, I suggest you get married first."

What?

Cash nearly choked on a mouthful of roast beef. He grimaced and swallowed hard as the food went down his throat like a fist-sized rock. "It's not mine," he managed to say and dropped the sandwich on a plate sitting on the coffee table. "I found it in Amber's room."

"You did? Oh-oh..." Todd's deep blue eyes mirrored shock and disbelief as he stared at the package. "What are you going to do about it? Ground her until she's thirty?"

"She's already grounded for that little stunt she pulled last week. I don't know what to do about Amber, but I've got a pretty good idea of what I'd like to do to Brian Hanson..." He made a fist with one hand and slammed it into his open palm.

"Take it easy, buddy." Todd pressed his long fingers against Cash's shoulder, pushing him toward the sofa. "That's not a smart move and you know it."

Overwrought, Cash collapsed onto the sofa and buried his face in his hands. Life had a way of coming full circle when a person least expected it. He realized now what Frank Cunningham must have gone through after learning about him and Libby. Most of all, he understood why Frank had threatened him.

"I'm getting what I deserve, aren't I?" He groaned into his hands. "I'm finally reaping what I've sowed."

"I think you're jumping to conclusions." Todd gently squeezed his shoulder. "You don't even know if it belongs to her. Maybe she found it at school."

Cash jerked his hands away from his face. "Yeah—right in *that kid's* back pocket! I should never have sent her to River's Edge High School. She's facing too many temptations there."

Todd dropped his long, muscular frame into an easy chair across from the sofa. "I doubt if that makes any difference. She's gonna be tempted no matter where she goes to school. You can't protect her from the world."

"I've tried to talk to her about drugs and explain the facts of life," Cash said as his frustration mounted, "but obviously I didn't get my message across very well."

"Don't be so hard on yourself." Settling into the chair, Todd slung his size twelve sneaker over the opposite knee. "She's a woman. You're a man. You don't talk the same language. This is a conversation she should have with her mother."

Cash started to object when he suddenly realized the truth lay right under his nose. He sprang from the sofa. "That's what happened!" He tossed his hands toward the ceiling as he paced the room. "Ah, man, I should have seen it coming!"

Todd's brows knit together as he unscrewed the cap off his water bottle. "What are you talking about?"

"Don't you see?" Cash spun around. "That's where Amber got the...ah...that *thing*..." He stammered, unable to say the word as he pointed to the purple package on the coffee table. "She told Olivia how much she liked *that kid*, and Olivia gave it to her for protection. Instead of telling me about it," he jammed his thumb toward his chest," Olivia took it upon herself to handle the situation and leave me out altogether."

Sweat beaded on his upper lip. The words, though true, wounded him to the core of his being, making that crater in his heart turn into a chasm as wide as the Grand Canyon and just as empty.

Todd took a hefty swig of water and replaced the cap. "It sounds plausible, but you don't know for sure. I mean, why would Amber's mother deliberately give such a thing to her own daughter? That's like throwing gas on a fire."

"Because," Cash countered, "Olivia knows firsthand what it's like to be a pregnant teen!"

Neither spoke as his emotional outburst sunk in. Cash snatched his cola and guzzled it to cool down. The sweet, fizzy liquid brought temporary relief to his parched throat but did nothing to quench his nerves.

"I have to talk to Amber about this," he announced desperately. "I have to find out if Olivia is the person who supplied it to her. If that's true, I..." He looked at Todd, feeling helpless. The fact that Libby had Amber's complete trust put him at a total loss as to what to do next. "I don't know what I'm going to do."

Todd leaned his arm across the back of the chair and relaxed as he watched Cash continue to wear a path on the floor. "*I* think you should marry the woman," he said matter-of-factly. "That would solve all your problems."

Cash jolted to a stop. His jaw dropped, nearly bouncing off his chest. At first, he didn't know whether to laugh or to tell his best friend to shut up. "You can't be serious."

"Completely," Todd replied with a know-it-all grin. "From what I've seen, you two are perfect together. Besides, it's obvious you're in love with her."

Cash almost swallowed his tongue. Did his feelings really show? "Are you crazy?" he said, attempting to sound aloof. "We're so opposite, it's ridiculous."

"See what I mean? You complement each other."

Cash shook his head. "I don't know where you're coming from, Trisco. It would *never* work." He pointed to the purple package on the table. "Not after *this* development, anyway."

"Life is what you make of it, buddy." Todd casually rose from the chair and looked toward the open stairway ascending to the second floor. "Where's Amber now?"

"She's at school practicing for a choir concert tonight," Cash replied. "I think I'll walk down there instead of driving. That way I'll have more time to talk to her about it on the way home."

Todd stared hungrily at Cash's sandwich going stale on the coffee table. "I jumped into the Hummer and raced over here as soon as I listened to your message. I didn't even take the time to grab a burger or something for dinner." Licking his lips, he pointed to the chunky slab of roast beef and sliced tomatoes stacked between two pieces of whole wheat bread. "Are you gonna eat that?"

"Help yourself." Distracted, Cash shoved the plate across the coffee table and turned away as Todd attacked his leftovers with disgusting gusto. He had greater issues on his mind right now than food.

He didn't have any idea what to say to Amber or even how to approach such a delicate subject. However, one thing proved certain; he needed God's grace more than ever to get through to his daughter.

*   *   *

By the time Cash arrived at River's Edge High School, the small auditorium overflowed with people. At the entrance, a student greeter welcomed him to the concert and offered him a program. Murmuring thanks, he grabbed the handbill from the freckled, sandy-haired kid and charged through the door. Once inside, he couldn't locate a single empty seat except for an area in the front reserved for faculty. Other latecomers also streamed into the noisy room, lining the walls to watch the concert.

He stood in the main aisle, contemplating which side of the room would provide the best view when Libby walked in, her black satin trench coat draped casually over her arm. The moment he saw her, his heart began to thump uncontrollably.

She didn't see him at first. Realizing his advantage, he entertained the urge to slip out before she noticed him. He considered it wise not to speak to her until he'd first talked to Amber. Besides, after what happened during their last conversation, he didn't know *what* to say to her this time.

His hesitation cost him the option to escape when she suddenly pivoted in his direction. She wore a soft pink dress and short, matching jacket, trimmed with satin ribbon and pearl buttons. The simple style accentuated her slender frame. The color complemented her ivory complexion and sleek, blonde hair.

Before he realized his mistake, his gaze drew to her glossy pink lips. Instantly, the memory of their tender warmth washed over him like an ocean wave on a balmy Maui beach. He stood dazed for a moment, caught between an innate impulse to enjoy the experience and common sense warning him to guard his heart.

Their gazes collided. At first, she appeared surprised. Then, as if struggling to compose herself, her cheeks darkened and she spun away. Only then did he realize he'd deliberated too long. She'd caught him staring like a smitten teenager.

He shoved his hands into his jacket pockets. "What are you doing here?" he heard himself say in an effort to cover up his mistake.

She whirled around. "My daughter invited me."

"I figured that," he countered, unintentionally sounding defensive. "What I mean is...do you have any idea what you're in for tonight? These things can get long, drawn-out, and plain boring." Right away, he knew he'd said the wrong thing again.

She acknowledged his comment with a smile. "Maybe it's just you."

A middle-aged man with a thinning, brown ponytail and goatee pushed through the crowd. Wearing designer jeans and a dark blazer over a black T-shirt, he looked like an upper-class hippie from the 60s. "Folks, let's take our seats. The show is about to begin." He stared pointedly at Cash. "Have we met before?"

Unfortunately, yes. Cash recalled seeing the man in the hall several weeks ago when he'd stopped by to pick up Amber after her first date with detention. He gingerly extended his hand. "I'm Cash MacKenzie, Amber's father."

"Ah, yes," the man replied enthusiastically with a vigorous handshake. "Russ Reynolds here, Amber's drama teacher."

Cash swallowed hard, hoping the teacher wouldn't seize this moment as an opportunity to lecture him on Amber's attendance issues. Amber skipped his seventh-hour class the most. Ironically, the man had barely pumped Cash's hand before turning his attention upon Libby. "...and this beautiful lady in pink is Mrs. MacKenzie, I presume?"

Libby flushed three shades of red before she found her voice. "No, we're not together. I-I'm Libby Cunningham," she replied and shook his hand, "Amber's mother."

Reynolds' gaze dove to her bare ring finger.

"This is my first visit to the school," Libby continued. "I'd like to find a seat, but it looks like the room is filled." She tried to pull her hand away. Instead of releasing her, the teacher clasped her hand in both of his, holding her captive as he gazed into her eyes.

"That won't be a problem." He grinned then cupped his right hand over her left elbow. "Come with me. I've got the best seat in the house—for you."

Libby flashed a radiant smile. "Why, thank you very much."

The gallant tone in Russ Reynolds' voice raised a red flag in the recesses of Cash's mind. He didn't care for the man's boldness or the predatory glint in Reynolds' eye. Before he could stop himself, he shook his head in disapproval. Libby caught his reaction and arched one brow, silently questioning him.

"Excuse us," Russ Reynolds announced in a business-like manner and turned his back on Cash, leading Libby through the noisy, shoulder-to-shoulder crowd.

Out of concern for Libby and the prospect of gaining a good seat, Cash trailed them to the reserved row in front, all the while focusing on the teacher's hand possessively guiding Libby by her elbow. He tried to remain cool, but with each step, his jaw clenched tighter. The more his irritation grew, the more it fueled the temptation to peel the man's hand away.

Let it go, MacKenzie, his internal critic harped. *Mind your own business. She's not your girlfriend anymore and she's made it plain she doesn't welcome your interference.*

The thought jolted him back to reality as he maneuvered his way through the crowd to the front of the room, but his heart wouldn't give up the fight.

Reynolds offered Libby a seat and deposited himself at her left. Uninvited, Cash scrambled for the only seat available, situated on Libby's right. He dropped into the cushioned chair and attempted to ask Libby a question to pull her attention away from the teacher, but he never got the opportunity. Libby abruptly turned toward Reynolds and leaned close, engrossed in a private conversation about Amber. Cash tapped her on the shoulder several times, but she ignored him.

Their chance to talk passed the point of no return when the red velvet drapes on the stage silently swept open. Thunderous applause shook the room as the gold-robed choir marched onto the stage in single file and took their positions on the risers.

After that, Cash couldn't make out much of Libby's conversation with the teacher, but he did manage to overhear that Reynolds wanted to give her a backstage tour after the concert. He opened his mouth to object then stopped himself when he realized he had no right to tell Libby what to do. Nevertheless, he didn't trust Reynolds. The man came on too strong.

Scanning the choir, he found Amber standing in the back row. His stomach churned at the thought of the critical discussion he needed to have with her on the way home. Deep in his heart, he held out hope that she had a plausible excuse for having the purple package in her pocket. He wanted to believe she'd found it or that it belonged to someone else, but he also knew better than to delude himself into accepting anything less than the truth. He knew firsthand the consequences of making moral mistakes. If Amber had traded her innocence for acceptance from *that kid*, he needed to acknowledge it and forgive her. At the same time, however, he'd make sure it never happened again.

Shaking off his worrisome thoughts, he caught Amber's attention, greeting her with his customary wink and smile. Her eyes widened with amazement as she glanced back and forth between him and Libby sitting together in the front row among her teachers. She responded with an ecstatic smile of her own and a vigorous wave.

The choir director, a red-haired woman in a black, tuxedo-style pantsuit, took her place in front of the singers. She cued the student musicians in the small orchestra pit to begin the opening song.

Cash rested his elbows on the armrests and tried to give Amber his total concentration as she sang a folk-sounding tune, but the scene unfolding next to him made it difficult to focus. Reynolds plied Libby with a low, steady stream of chatter about a parent's role in helping his or her child develop a greater appreciation for the arts. Cash couldn't hear Libby's answer, but when Reynolds suggested she visit the class one day next week as Amber's guest, he couldn't keep quiet any longer.

"Amber has an amazing voice," he whispered and nudged her with his elbow, "doesn't she? Did you hear her hit that high note just now?"

Libby raised her gaze and smiled at Amber but didn't acknowledge his comment.

He nudged her again. "Hey, did you notice in the program that she's listed with Dylan Sikes to sing a duet?"

Once again, Libby gazed at Amber but kept up her conversation with the drama teacher.

Throughout the next few songs, Cash sat in silence, listening as Libby discussed options with Reynolds for improving Amber's dismal grade in his class. He should have been taking mental notes, but Reynolds' obvious attraction to Libby began to make him so jealous he couldn't get it out of his mind. He fixed his gaze on Amber, but his thoughts smoldered over the attention given to Libby by a 21st-century clone of The Bard. Instinct warned him that Russ Reynolds had only one thing on his mind, and it had nothing to do with Amber's education!

Cash's eyelids began to grow heavy, causing him to involuntarily slump in his seat. His weekdays commenced early and usually ended about this time. Yawning fiercely, he sat up to keep from falling asleep when his shoulder bumped against someone's hand. He looked to his left and nearly jumped out of his seat. Reynolds had draped his arm across the back of Libby's chair.

Every muscle in Cash's body tensed, every nerve sharpened as his attention zeroed in on Russ Reynolds' blatant attempt to pair himself with Libby. He didn't know why it triggered such a strong response in him, but the guy's slick maneuvering made him mad.

In one swift move, he leaned sharply toward Libby and with a jerk of his shoulder, shoved the hand away. Caught off guard, Reynolds' outstretched tentacle slipped off the back of the seat and disappeared. Cash pretended to yawn and extended his arms, bringing his elbow to rest behind Libby.

The movement behind her prompted Libby to lean forward. Twisting at the waist, she gazed down at his elbow camping on the back of her seat then focused on him with a puzzled look. Mere inches separated them. "What's the matter?"

Mesmerized by the clear blue of her eyes, he froze for a moment then pulled back to put some space between them. "Oh, I'm just stretching," he answered innocently and eased his arm across the seat. "This arrangement is too close for comfort." He leaned back and shot Reynolds a pointed look. "If you ask me."

Libby suddenly straightened and turned her attention back to the concert. "Move over," she said staring straight ahead. "You're giving someone the *wrong* idea." With a curt nod, she gestured toward the stage where the choir clapped to a fast-paced tune. In the back row, Amber stood motionless, her brows knit together, her eyes blinking furiously as she took in their every move.

Realizing his blunder, Cash sat forward and folded his hands, determined to keep them out of trouble for the rest of the concert. He'd succumbed to the wrong impulse twice in less than a week, and each time his actions may have given Amber an unrealistic impression of his intentions toward Libby. He peered at his watch in desperation. A mere twenty minutes had passed. Would this night ever end?

*   *   *

The concert lasted a little over an hour. When it finally wrapped up, Cash followed Libby and Reynolds out of the crowded auditorium, anxious to round up Amber and head for home. Surprisingly, Amber stood outside the entrance with her best friend, Jenny, waiting for them. Her eyes sparkled when she saw her parents walking side by side with her teacher.

"Oh, I'm so glad you came together!"

Cash opened his mouth to say that they had run into each other at the concert, but the words evaporated on his lips when she brushed past him and went straight to Libby.

"Thank you for inviting me." Libby tactfully reacted to the 'together' comment by sidestepping the subject and instead gave her a quick hug. "I enjoyed every minute. Aren't you going to introduce me to your friend?"

"Oh! This is Jenny," Amber said as she hung on the diminutive, pink-cheeked brunette with green eyes and straight, chin-length hair. "We've been best friends since third grade. We've got three classes together this semester."

She turned to Cash. "Hey, Dad, can we go for ice cream? Jenny's mom said she could go if we drove her home afterward."

Cash folded his program and shoved it into his shirt pocket. "I didn't drive, honey. The weather has been so warm this week that I decided to walk. We'll go next time, okay?"

Undaunted, Amber turned to Libby. "Can we ride with you? There's enough room in your BMW for all four of us."

Libby cleared her throat and glanced at Reynolds, standing off to one side in conversation with another parent. "I'd love to go for ice cream, but I've already committed to taking a backstage tour with your teacher."

Amber gasped with surprise and excitement. "Can we come, too? When we're finished, we'll show you and Dad our other classrooms!"

"Like the science lab," Jenny chimed in, "where we always get Jeremy Waddell into trouble for talking!" Their laughter rose above the din of the crowd milling around, drinking coffee, and munching on cookies from the hospitality table.

"Girls, girls, quiet down," Russ Reynolds said, his voice resonating with disenchantment as he stepped back into the group. "It's up to Libby." He cut Cash a questioning glance. "If she wants all of you to join us on the tour, you're welcome to come along."

The girls crowded around Libby. Cash stood silently to one side as he observed Amber toying with one of the buttons on Libby's jacket. "Please?"

Libby smiled at their enthusiasm. "Of course, you can come."

"May we go for ice cream after that?"

"I might let you talk me into it."

"Yeah!" Amber hugged Libby with renewed excitement as Cash watched his plans for a heart-to-heart talk with her dissolve in the merriment of a turtle sundae.

"C'mon, Dad." She grabbed him by the hand and tried to pull him along. "Let's get a cookie before we go on the tour."

"Sure, honey," he replied, making an effort to keep his frustration under control.

He leaned toward Libby. "We have to be home no later than ten."

Libby turned to him. "Of course. I'm aware she has school tomorrow."

He nodded curtly and allowed Amber to lead him toward the refreshment table. On the way, they passed a young couple, not much older than Amber. The teens gazed adoringly into each other's eyes, holding hands as they walked along the main corridor.

Amber glanced away, but not before Cash noticed a yearning in her expression that gave him the chills.

"Dad," she said after a few moments of thought, "you said that when I turned sixteen we'd talk about dating and stuff."

Alarm bells went off in his head, clanging so loudly he could barely think. "You're not sixteen yet."

"I will be next week."

From the corner of his eye, he saw the couple share a kiss. The chill in his soul sent a shiver down his spine as a vision of Amber flashed through his mind, sitting in a dark car and locking lips with *that kid...*

"What's the hurry? There's plenty of time for that," he answered hastily.

She looked straight ahead, her jaw stubbornly set. "As soon as I get my license I'm going to ask a...a friend to go with me to a home game."

The clanging in his head ramped up louder than a ten-alarm fire. It didn't take a genius to figure out whom she'd set her sights on. "One thing at a time," he said with finality. "First we'll work on your grades then tackle the driver's license. After that, we'll discuss the dating issue."

Her face darkened. "But, the quarter is almost over. It'll take another whole quarter to raise my grades!"

He struggled to keep his voice calm. "I can't help that, honey. When you start maintaining an acceptable level of responsibility, you'll be granted more privileges."

Her dark eyes flared in defiance. "You're just trying to keep me from being with Brian."

You bet I am...

"No," Cash replied evenly, all the while fighting to keep his sanity. "We've already been through this several times. I don't approve of your dating older boys, no matter who they are."

She stopped at the refreshment table and confronted him. "I have *two* parents and the other one doesn't think Brian's age matters. She even wants to meet him." Amber lifted her chin. "She told me so."

The ugly truth began to unfold. Unknown to Amber, her own words confirmed what he'd suspected all along; her mother not only condoned Amber's relationship with the boy, but Libby had also supplied Amber with the purple package to keep her safe.

He understood why Libby tried to help Amber, but he could not excuse it. The mere thought of her counseling Amber behind his back made his heart sink in disappointment. How could she do this to him?

"It doesn't matter what Olivia thinks." He picked up a napkin and used it to grab a couple of cookies off a large silver tray. "I'm your father and I make the final decisions in our house." He held out a palm-sized peanut butter cookie. "Let's not argue about this anymore. All right?"

She pushed the treat away as angry, defiant tears filled her eyes. "I don't want one now. Somebody just made me lose my appetite."

He bit into a sugar cookie and watched her stomp back to the group. Little by little, Amber continued to slip away from him and he couldn't seem to stop it. He needed a plan, a sure-fire strategy to keep his family together because if he didn't come up with something soon, he wouldn't have one much longer.

Chapter 9

Late again.

Libby sat alone in the center of a wide, leather, and mahogany banquette at Stefano's Restaurant, waiting on Medley to join her for lunch. She reclined against the padded upholstery and folded her arms, willing herself to stay calm despite Medley's habitual tardiness. Unfortunately, the longer she spent cooling her heels, the more she'd have to rush at the end of the day to get things done so she could leave at a decent hour. Not only that, but it also meant she had more time on her hands to replay in her mind the scene between her and Cash the night Amber tried to sneak out of the house.

Since that disastrous event, the mere thought of his kiss made her heart shift into overdrive. She tried to push it out of her mind, but when she least expected it, their foolish encounter would flash through her head like an annoying commercial on late-night TV, launching shivers down her spine. No matter how much she tried, she couldn't stop thinking about it. She couldn't stop thinking about *him*.

Why couldn't she let his memory go and get on with her life? The truth was hidden deep in her soul...

She'd never stopped loving him.

The moment she saw him at the game, a small flame had ignited in her heart—a flame that grew brighter every time she met up with him again. Then the unthinkable had happened, causing that flame to flare into a major forest fire and it had been scorching a hole in her soul ever since.

Stop this, she thought miserably. *Be thankful for what you do have. You've found your baby!*

Her assistant, Brianna, approached her, looking apologetic.

"Libby, I'm sorry to interrupt you, but..." The slender redhead paused, hesitant to finish. "You have a phone call."

"Is it Cash MacKenzie again?"

Since the night of the concert, Cash had repeatedly called both her cell phone and her work phone and left messages, pressing her to call him on an 'urgent' matter. He'd even stopped in at the restaurant one day, but luckily, she'd gone to a hospitality conference downtown at the Minneapolis Convention Center. He wouldn't elaborate to Brianna on his reason for stopping by but went so far as to imply that Libby's avoidance of him convinced him of her guilt. Guilty of what? Getting involved in Amber's sporadic school attendance and dropping grades? Interviewing her drama teacher to get a handle on her performance in his class? Guilty as charged!

"Not him," Brianna said and pursed her lips. "Ardelle Johnson is holding on line two and she demands to speak with you *right now.*"

Libby groaned inwardly. *Now what?* "Did you inform her that, as my assistant, you could answer her questions?"

"Of course." Brianna's fair cheeks flushed. "She won't work with me."

Ardelle Johnson's phone calls had progressively grown more erratic and imperious as the day of her daughter's wedding reception approached. The temptation to refuse the call nagged at Libby's heart, but she knew from experience that Ardelle would simply call back, more upset, and more obnoxious at being inconvenienced. She forced a reassuring smile as she slid out of the horseshoe-shaped booth. "That's okay, Bree. I'll find out what she wants."

Her position at Stefano's afforded special privileges, such as an executive credit card for complimentary food and beverages. Nevertheless, she seldom dined in peace at the restaurant. The likelihood of making it through an entire meal without interruptions by either an urgent phone call or a client who dropped in without an appointment proved the norm rather than the exception.

Resolved to handle Ardelle's latest issue as quickly as possible, she walked back to her office and picked up the phone. "Good afternoon. This is Libby."

"*This* is Ardelle Johnson. I've been waiting all morning for your call. Why are you ignoring me? You *said* you'd get back to me today to go over the menu." Her shrill voice bordered on hysteria. "I had to cancel my medical appointment because I couldn't leave the house until I knew—"

"I'm not ignoring you, Ardelle," Libby replied in a soft, but firm tone. "I've spoken with our executive chef and he's assured me that he'll personally contact you this afternoon to review every one of your menu choices. That way, if you decide to make changes, he can work directly with you to be sure he fully understands what you want."

"I'm counting on you both. If anything goes wrong..." Ardelle's bitter voice cracked.

"Nothing will go wrong, I guarantee it. My team is one of the best in the business. They'll have the Florentine Room ready hours before your guests arrive. I've already spoken to the banquet captains and they've agreed to come in early to supervise the setup. Every item listed on your contract will be checked and double-checked."

"Are you sure that you've accounted for—"

"—two hundred and fifty guests," Libby interjected quickly.

"The room must be open—"

"—by 6 pm. The harpist will be in place and performing when the first guest walks through the door. Appetizers and punch will be on the buffet."

"Well..."

"Relax, Ardelle. You're going to have a wonderful evening."

Libby ended the call and went back into the dining room, wishing she could manage her own life with the confidence and success that she handled other people's affairs.

Her banquette still sat empty. Armed with Ardelle's file, she slid in and set her mind to go over the details again. Sadly, she knew the document so well she could recite it in her sleep and suddenly couldn't bring herself to suffer through it one more time. Shoving it aside, she sat back and folded her arms again, absently observing the activity around her as she waited for Medley.

Reminiscent of pre-World War II Italy, Stefano's Restaurant replicated a large family dining room with starched white tablecloths, fresh flowers, family portraits, and oil paintings, softly illuminated by amber-colored chandeliers.

The pungent aroma of sausage, prosciutto, and southern Italian red sauces permeated the air as servers scurried through the swinging doors of the noisy kitchen, their arms laden with hot platters of steaming food. Amidst the din of conversation and tinkling of silverware, the soft crooning of Dean Martin's 'Amore' filled the large, but comfortable room.

The romantic nostalgia of Stefano's should have lightened her spirits. Instead, the atmosphere provided a sharp contrast to the loneliness and boredom that currently defined her life. The highlight of her week centered on her Tuesday lunch with Medley. Her cousin, however, didn't rank their date high enough to show up on time. *Ever...*

A stanza of "Here Comes the Bride" cut into her thoughts. She dug into her blazer pocket for her cell phone. M. Grant appeared on the Caller ID.

"Medley, where are you? I've been expecting you for fifteen minutes!" Today, of all days, she'd hoped Medley would be prompt. She desperately needed the support of a friend.

"I'm in the mall parking lot," Medley chattered nonchalantly, as though she'd bopped in fifteen minutes early. "I'll be there as soon as I find a parking spot."

Another fifteen minutes dragged by before Medley breezed into the dining room, waving cheerily as she approached the banquette.

"Hi!" She slid out of her pumpkin-colored Cashmere sweater coat and tossed it on the empty side of the banquette. "I parked in Nordstrom's ramp." She placed her gold clutch purse on the table and slid in. "That way I can do some shopping on my way out."

Stefano's sat on the west side of Wooddale Mall, sandwiched between a busy seafood supper club and a French Bistro—a long way from Nordstrom.

No wonder it took her so long to arrive.

A server wearing immaculate white slacks, a white oxford shirt, and a red, floor-length apron appeared at the banquette like a well-trained retriever. Her nametag read 'Andrea.'

"Welcome to Stefano's," she said to Medley. "Would you care for a beverage?"

Medley motioned toward Libby's glass of iced tea, garnished with a wedge of lemon. "I'll have one of those, please. Oh, and bring a side of honey, would you? Thanks, Andrea."

Andrea acknowledged her request and departed.

"How is the situation going with Amber?" Medley asked as soon as they were alone. "Is she behaving herself?"

Libby lifted her glass of iced tea and sipped the cool, tart liquid before answering. "I haven't received any phone calls from her in detention hall, so I assume she's showing up for class. At least, I hope she is."

"What about Cash?" Medley unrolled her napkin and placed it on her lap. "Are you two on cozy terms yet?"

"It's impossible to be on cozy terms with someone who can't forgive me," Libby said, referring to her emotional confrontation with Cash that day at Sandhill. She pushed her menu aside. "Honestly, I don't blame him. It took me years to come to terms with giving up Amber myself, even though I had no choice in the matter." She sighed. "If only things had been different..."

She thought about their chat on Sunday and their agreement to avoid each other for Amber's sake. The decision made sense, but even so, she couldn't help noticing an unintentional thread of disappointment in her voice. Had Medley detected it, too?

Medley didn't have a clue that Cash had kissed her and she'd vowed to herself never to share that awkward little detail with anyone, especially her matchmaking cousin.

Andrea's serving assistant appeared at the table carrying two tall bottles and a woven basket filled with warm loaves of fresh bread. He placed the basket in the center of the table.

"The white bread is sourdough and this..." he pointed to a darker piece, "is our new sesame loaf made with soy and honey."

He took a liner plate off a small stack sitting next to the salt and peppershakers, set it in the center of the table, and poured a golden puddle of olive oil into it.

Medley smiled at him. "Pour one for each of us, please."

"Would you like Balsamic vinegar added?" the assistant asked politely.

Medley's face brightened. "Yes, please."

Libby placed her hand over her dish. "No thank you, Brandon."

After he left, they bowed their heads and blessed their food.

Medley selected a pair of liner plates from the stack on the table and placed one at each setting. "Libby, you can't continue to avoid Cash. It's affecting you more than you realize. You seem so sad all of the time," Medley declared as she chose the sesame bread from the basket. She broke it in half and set the pieces on her liner plate. "You must agree to put your differences aside for Amber's sake. It's going to take a unified front—and that means both of you— to deal with her about lying, skipping school, and that boy-crazy attitude of hers."

"Actually, we are unified now when it comes to Amber." Libby removed the lid of a tin of grated Parmesan and Asiago cheese. She picked up a spoon and some scooped out. "But it would take a miracle to bring Cash and I to the point where we could be good friends again. At least before Friday," she said as she sprinkled a generous serving of cheese over her dish of olive oil.

"Why?" Medley asked curiously. "What's coming down on Friday?"

Libby extracted a small, square envelope from her blazer pocket. "Look at this." She set it on the table. "It arrived in my mail this morning."

Medley's fingers, clutching a chunk of sesame bread, stilled over her oil and Balsamic mixture as she stared at the writing on the envelope. "What is it?"

"It's an invitation to Amber's birthday party. She's turning sixteen."

"That's wonderful! She's invited you to her party!"

Libby's silence pulled her up short.

Medley's smile faded, her forehead furrowing with concern. "You look absolutely miserable. What's wrong?"

"What's wrong?" Libby repeated with incredulity. "According to this invitation, there are only going to be three people present and one, namely the birthday girl herself, isn't eating because she's doing all the cooking and serving."

"Really?" Medley's jade eyes grew larger than her liner plate as she snatched the envelope and pulled out a pink card. Her pumpkin-colored smile widened. "O-h-h-h... This is so sweet!"

"Sweet, my eye! It's a parent trap."

Medley ignored the comment. Instead, she stared at the card with misty eyes and read aloud, "Chef Amber requests the presence of her parents at a candlelight dinner—"

"S-h-h-h-h!" Libby snatched the card away. "Don't announce it to the entire restaurant!"

Medley grabbed the card back. "—given in her honor on Friday, October nineteenth to celebrate her birthday. Appetizers and chilled cider cocktails will be served promptly at six pm." She wiped a small tear from her eye and laughed. "It's perfect."

Libby snorted. "It's an exercise in futility."

"She forgot the RSVP."

"No, she didn't." Libby slid the invitation back into the envelope. "Read between the lines. Declining is not an option. She's trying to create the perfect romantic environment to make her parents fall in love again."

"You wouldn't decline, anyway," Medley stated matter-of-factly. "It would hurt her feelings."

Libby smoothed out the creases in the white linen napkin on her lap. "No, I don't want to hurt her feelings, but at the same time, the last thing I want to do is build up her hopes of getting her parents back together. If she's doing it for our sakes, she'll end up being hurt and disillusioned."

Andrea arrived with Medley's beverage and a small ceramic pitcher of honey. "Have you decided what you'd like for lunch?"

"I'm s-o-o-o hungry." Medley opened her menu and quickly scanned its contents. "I'll have the spinach salad with walnut vinaigrette dressing on the side. No cheese, thank you."

Libby handed her unopened menu to the server. "I'll have my usual chopped salad with chicken, Andrea. The half-order. Oh, and leave off the green onions, okay? Thanks." After Andrea left them, she let out a tense sigh.

"Lib, Lib, relax," Medley lectured as she lifted the little pitcher of honey and poured some into her tea. "It's only dinner. What could possibly go wrong?"

Libby broke off a chunk of sourdough bread and swirled it in her cheesy oil. "I'm not objecting to Amber having a party, it's just the way she's going about it that makes me uncomfortable. She only turns sixteen once; her birthday should be a special event where she is surrounded by family *and* friends."

Medley picked up a teaspoon and stirred her tea. "It appears to me that she *is* planning a special event, all on her own."

"I can't do it her way." Libby dropped the cheese and oil-soaked bread on her liner plate. "Innocent though it may be, it'll end up badly."

"Of course, you can. Don't be ridiculous. You'll disappoint her!"

Libby wiped her fingers on her napkin. "I'm not trying to be ridiculous. Rather, I'm trying to save Amber the heartbreak of disappointment when things don't turn out as she'd planned. I'm going to take her out to dinner instead— just the two of us." She glanced at the time on her cell phone. "Amber's on her lunch break at school right now." She picked up her phone and touched the screen to access her contact list. "I'll make early reservations at her favorite restaurant and then we'll go on a shopping spree. We'll have a wonderful time."

Medley stiffened. "But, that's not what Amber wants."

"You know I want only the best for her," Libby said as she pulled up her daughter's number. "That's why I can't allow this to go any farther. I don't want to spoil her birthday and neither does Cash. When he receives his invitation, I know he'll agree with me."

"So far, he's not spoiling anything. You are!" Medley snatched the phone from Libby's hand and disconnected the call.

"Medley, what part of this conversation don't you understand? Cash and I are not getting back together. It would be deceitful to allow Amber to go through with this because it would only give her false hope. That's not fair to her."

Medley pursed her pumpkin-colored lips into a pout. "What I don't understand is why you two can't simply put your differences on hold for a couple of hours for your daughter's sake."

Self-conscious, Libby glanced around, hoping no one overheard. "We've tried," she whispered, "and it's impossible."

"It's selfish." Medley pointed a professionally manicured finger at her. "You're going to Amber's dinner party, even if I have to drive you myself."

"Wrong."

"Why not?"

"You weren't invited."

"Well, then, I can easily fix that, can't I?" Medley hit the green icon on Libby's phone to find Amber's number. After a couple of punches, she pressed the phone to her ear. "I have it all figured out. I'll be the chaperone."

Medley's unexpected show of temper surprised Libby, but she didn't try to stop her cousin from making the call. Instead, she rested her forehead on the heel of her hand, trying to be patient. "What are you doing?" She didn't have a headache, however, given the circumstances, she expected one would be coming on shortly.

Medley put the phone to her ear and sat back with a mischievous smirk. "I'm calling my second cousin to request an invitation to her birthday party." She put her hand over the phone and smiled. "I really wanted to go, anyway."

Libby squeezed her eyes shut in disbelief. Some day she just might learn to keep her mouth shut around Medley. Too bad today couldn't have been that day.

Thanks to her, Amber's birthday dinner for two just turned into a three-ring circus.

*   *   *

"I should never have let you talk me into this!" Todd paced the floor of Cash's den as they waited for the other half of Amber's birthday dinner guests to arrive. "I don't know why I agreed." He stopped and rubbed the back of his neck. "I must be nuts."

"You had to agree." Cash folded his arms and leaned against the doorframe. He angled his head. "You owe me."

Todd raked his hands through his blond hair. Wearing snug-fitting jeans, duck boat-sized hiking boots, and a red plaid shirt, he looked like Ole the Lumberjack. Not exactly GQ material tonight, but he'd do.

"Yeah, well, I'm not asking you to do me a favor ever again." Todd pointed an accusing finger at Cash. "The next time I get into a jam with a girl, you're the last person I'll turn to."

"I should be so lucky," Cash answered with a wry smile, "but we both know you will." Since college, they'd been through this little drill more times than he cared to remember. "You've got me programmed on speed dial as your private 9-1-1."

Cash didn't possess half the confidence he projected, but he couldn't allow Todd to see that. If Todd even suspected he had doubts, Plan A would go up in flames. For now, he and Libby stood evenly matched. He had Todd in his corner tonight for reinforcement and Libby claimed to be bringing Medley, that eccentric cousin of hers—the one who talked like Tinker Bell and dressed like a fashion queen. She'd make a good diversion. He hoped.

As things stood, Plan A had better work out because he didn't have a Plan B.

Todd paced to the door, passing between an overstocked bookcase and a pillow-back, velour sofa. A pile of books stacked haphazardly on the top shelf suddenly shifted and crashed to the floor with the force of a small explosion. Covering his head with his hands, Todd pivoted to see what happened. He stared at the mess for a moment then bent to pick it up. From a half-crouching position, he pointed an accusing finger at Cash. "I mean it this time,

127

MacKenzie. From now on, you're on your own. Todd Trisco ain't gonna be your fall guy no more."

Cash collapsed onto the sofa. "You sound like a gangster masquerading as Paul Bunyan. Relax. It's only for a couple of hours. Hey, she's half your size. You can handle her."

Todd straightened and dumped the books in a loose pile on Cash's oak desk. "That woman is too opinionated!"

Sounds like a match made in heaven, Cash mused and wondered if Todd had purposely worn that grubby-looking outfit to discourage any attraction on Medley's part. "Come on. You don't know her that well. You've only met her once."

"Met her? I had to suffer through a whole cup of coffee with her. Remember? Thirty minutes of non-stop rant on social issues. I've never been so thoroughly sermonized in my life." He clapped his hands over his ears. "Save the whales, boycott furs, stop global warming," he mimicked in a high-pitched, squeaky tone. "Lord," he added in his normally deep voice, raising his palms heavenward, "make me deaf for just one night."

"You should be glad you're not in my shoes. I've got two opinionated women on my case."

Cash hadn't spoken to Libby since the choir concert. She'd purposely avoided him and he knew why. She didn't want to confess that she'd had *the talk* with Amber and had supplied her with protection. He planned to confront Libby about it tonight but had to find a way to discuss it with her in private. He wished with all his heart that she would prove him wrong, but the facts didn't lie. She had motive and opportunity.

That and the prospect of sitting through a 'romantic' dinner with Libby had caused him nothing but sleepless nights ever since Amber shoved the invitation in his face. Why couldn't he just take the birthday girl out for dinner to a fine restaurant in...say...the Caribbean instead? Somewhere far, far away from Libby Cunningham and the haunting memory of her kiss...

But Amber wouldn't agree and he couldn't figure out why. How many times had she bugged him to take her on an exotic vacation? How many magazines had she left on the kitchen table, flipped open to an advertisement for a cruise or a luxurious, all-inclusive resort in the Bahamas? Now that he'd decided to give her idea a shot, she'd suddenly developed a case of selective amnesia. Women!

The doorbell chimed to the tune of Big Ben, startling them. They froze, exchanging looks that suggested going down with the Titanic would have been a better gig than this. At least they'd have had a chance to escape.

"I'll get it!" Amber's boots click-clacked on the hardwood floor as she hustled past the den.

Todd tiptoed to the door and pried it open a quarter of an inch. He jammed his hands into the pockets of his jeans and peered into the living room. "They're here."

No kidding.

Soft strains of classical music and the chatter of female voices filtered through the crack. Two of them were almost identical. The third one sounded giggly and a tad excited.

"Hmmm..." Todd mused aloud as he spied on the newcomers. "Your 'ex' is lookin' good. Real good."

Cash's attention sharpened. "What's she wearing?" he mumbled, not realizing until too late that he'd spoken aloud.

Todd stood riveted to the floor, his eyes wide as he spied on the women. "Huh?"

"I said *whatever*." Cash cleared his throat. "She's not my *ex*."

Todd stood silent for a minute, apparently absorbing the scenery. "She looks beautiful." He turned and stared at Cash, looking like a raccoon caught in a spotlight. "Take a look." When Cash made no move to get up, he turned back to spy on them again. "She's wearing a silver top that shimmers and black slacks. They're loose-fitting and when she walks, they kinda sway...like poetry in motion."

What?

Cash sprang from the sofa. "Lemme see..."

He craned his neck to look over Todd's shoulder. Libby and Medley stood in front of the fireplace, drinking cider from crystal flutes. Bright flames reflected off Libby's face, giving her skin a soft, ivory glow. Her sleek hair, tied back with a white ribbon, fell past her shoulders like liquid gold.

His mouth gaped. *Wait a minute—*

The silky slacks and the shimmering top did look sharp, but not on Libby. Todd had described Medley's outfit! Libby wore an ivory dress made from textured material. A string of pearls adorned her long, graceful neck like crown jewels.

Funny, but she looked just like a bride...

A bolt of nerves shot down his spine as the thought sunk in. He let out a tense breath and wiped at the sheen of sweat collecting on his upper lip. Where in the world had that idea come from?

Suddenly Todd stepped backward, tripping over his own feet and nearly falling on top of Cash. They galloped like a couple of buffalo to get away from the door just before it flew open and Amber charged into the room. She wore a black turtleneck top and slacks, overlaid with a black, full-length chef's apron. The words "Birthday Girl" sprawled across the bib in sparkly gold letters. She'd fixed her hair in a French braid with a twig of tiny red flowers fastened behind her right ear.

"C'mon you guys. It's almost six o'clock and our guests are here." Her high cheekbones flushed as she beamed with anticipation. A smudge of chocolate decorated her chin like a beauty mark. "It's party time!"

Chapter 10

Libby clutched her flute of sparkling cider with a death grip as the door to Cash's den swung open. Amber marched out first with Todd then Cash following single file. Todd's ornery, pained expression reminded her of a ten-year-old who'd just returned from an unpleasant visit to the woodshed. Cash, on the other hand, looked grim, like the punishment-administering parent. The picture they created gave her a sudden urge to laugh, though she didn't understand why. Funny didn't begin to describe this evening.

She met Cash's cool gaze. The memory of his kiss suddenly seared her lips. The warmth of his strong arms holding her close enveloped her once more and sent a surge of longing through her.

And dread...

Act natural, she thought as she forced a smile in return. She couldn't allow anyone, least of all him to suspect her discomfort. After their...agreement...at church, she never expected to see him again; at least until she'd buried the memory of his kiss so deep in her mind that his presence wouldn't resurrect it. The night of Amber's choir concert, she'd planned to arrive at the last minute, sit in the last row, and be the first one out the door after the final song ended. She hadn't counted on Cash being late, too. More than that, she hadn't expected an encounter that ended up causing them to be in each other's way all evening.

"Hello, Cash," she said lightly and approached him, putting forth her best effort to appear relaxed.

He stood tall and handsome as ever as his dark, unreadable gaze seared hers. "Hello, Olivia. Why didn't you return my calls?"

The abruptness of his question startled her. Behind her, a trio of voices burst into laughter over the chocolate smear on Amber's face.

I didn't want to be interrogated about getting involved in our daughter's education without your permission, she thought to herself.

"If my memory serves me correctly, we agreed not to associate with one another for Amber's sake," she said in a low voice, wondering why it hadn't actually worked out that way. She edged closer to him. "Please, stop calling me Olivia."

He raised one ebony brow. "Why not? That's who you are."

"I don't identify myself with that name and never have."

"I didn't know you were so sensitive about it. I'll be more careful about it from now on." Bearing an innocent smile, he turned his back to her and joined in the other conversation.

His reply made her pause. She took a mental step backward and reined herself in.

This is Amber's first birthday with both of her parents and it should be memorable for her. No matter how uncomfortable this situation is, I need to focus on my daughter and enjoy the party she has painstakingly planned.

She gazed at Amber as the girl hurried back to the kitchen. A diamond-hard lump grew in her throat. She loved Amber so much! She vowed never to allow anyone or anything to separate her from her child ever again. Silently she thanked God for blessing her with the opportunity to spend this night with Amber and the people who cared about her. A girl turned sixteen only once in her life. She deserved to have a wonderful time.

"Hello, Todd," she said, doing her best to sound light and carefree as she extended her hand.

His strong fingers engulfed her palm and squeezed it gently. "Hello, there, little lady." His deep blue eyes twinkled. "You look beautiful tonight."

"Why thank you," she replied, warmed by the compliment. "How sweet of you to notice."

He didn't look too shabby, himself. Even though he wore what amounted to hiking clothes, she couldn't find a thing to dislike about his appearance. His plaid shirt and heavy-duty jeans gave him a rugged quality that actually enhanced his attractiveness. He struck her as the kind of guy who loved to ski, fish, hunt and view his favorite sports from a front-row seat. In other words, he loved being alive.

Todd stepped forward and angled his head close to her ear. "I'd sure like to know what Amber's doing in the kitchen," he murmured. "She's got something sitting in the sink..." His golden brows knit together. "I don't know exactly what it is, but from here it looks like the world's biggest ball of twine."

Libby whirled toward the arched doorway to the kitchen and cast her gaze upon a tangled mound of something white in the stainless-steel sink. My goodness! She smiled back at Todd with an understanding nod. "Maybe I'd better see if I can lend a hand."

He roared with laughter. "Yah, sure. You do that."

She immediately headed for the arched doorway. "I'm checking out your kitchen, birthday girl," Libby said, greeting Amber in a cheery voice as she hurried into the room. "How is dinner coming along? Need any help?"

From the looks of things, Amber needed disaster relief from the National Guard. Dirty dishes, open jars, empty boxes, and bottles littered the gray and white granite countertops. A large dribble of chocolate slid down one of the lower cabinet doors. In the sink, that ball of twine Todd mentioned looked suspiciously like a mountain of cold, cooked spaghetti. That must be dinner. She winced.

Suddenly her foot slipped on something. In a panic, she grabbed onto the refrigerator door to steady herself and looked down. What in the world had happened to the floor? A narrow stream of water covered the tiles from the stove to the sink.

And speaking of the stove...

A medium-sized, stainless steel pan of spaghetti sauce bubbled like a cauldron, splattering red blobs across the stovetop and just about everything within striking distance.

Amber stood at the opposite counter with her back to the stove, arranging golden crackers on a frosted glass serving plate. A can of snack cheese sat by her right hand, next to the plate.

"No, thanks," she replied happily and picked up the can, positioning the nozzle over a cracker. "I've got everything under control."

"I—I see that." Libby clasped her hands, itching to jump in and help.

Suddenly a blob of sauce exploded out of the pan and rocketed toward her. She jumped backward as it flew past her and landed on the floor with a loud splat.

"Oops." Amber put down the aerosol can and grabbed a roll of paper towels. "I'll get that." She ripped off a sheet and dropped it on the tile floor, rubbing the towel over the sauce with the toe of her boot.

"I'll cover the pan for you, sweetie," Libby said, unable to resist one little suggestion. She bent down and opened a large cabinet door next to the stove to look for a lid. In one swift move, she reached into the cupboard for a cover with one hand and turned the flame down to simmer with the other.

Amber came up behind her. "Thanks for offering to help," she said and put her hands on the back of Libby's shoulders as Libby stood up and placed a cover on the saucepan, "but you're not supposed to be in here." She giggled and pushed Libby toward the door. "You're my guest, so go back into the living room. I need you to keep Dad busy so he doesn't come into the kitchen and flip out over the dirty dishes! I'm serving the appetizer in two minutes."

Libby left the kitchen wondering if Cash had plans for tomorrow. If he did, they were short-lived. Judging by the mess, she estimated it would take all day to scour dried sauce off the walls and appliances.

She went back into the living room and found her dinner partners sipping cider and staring silently at the fire. She took a seat next to Medley on the leather sofa. Cash and Todd sat in matching Windsor-backed chairs, facing them. The coffee table, piled high with presents for Amber, served as a buffer of sorts.

"How is she coming along?" Medley asked in a stage whisper.

A loud groan echoed from the kitchen. Everyone turned toward the noise.

"Hmmm..." Libby snatched her flute off the coffee table. "How's the cider?"

No one answered. She tipped her head and tossed it back.

Moments later, Amber spared everyone the pain of idle conversation when she emerged from the kitchen carrying a plate of assorted crackers and toppings.

Todd helped himself to a golden cracker garnished with a glob of cheese, a stuffed green olive, and a toothpick decorated with an American flag. He raised both his glass and his flag-bearing cracker in a toast to Amber. "Happy birthday, Princess, and God bless America."

Amber responded with a wide, beautiful smile. "Thanks, Uncle Todd."

After everyone took their fill of the crackers and had their cider replenished, Amber motioned toward the dining area. "Dinner is ready."

They trudged into the dining room to take their assigned places. On the way, Libby and Medley hung back.

"Did you catch that look on Cash's face when you and Todd were laughing?" Medley whispered, cupping her hand over one side of her mouth. "He looked green with jealousy to me."

Libby rolled her eyes. "You're imagining things," she whispered back then wondered why Cash would care that she enjoyed Todd's company. "What do you think of that blond hunk, Todd Trisco?"

Medley flushed but pursed her lips into a pout. "He's a highly-opinionated know-it-all."

Libby smiled inwardly. Like two peas in a pod, as the saying went. "He's been a perfect gentleman around me."

"He owns a Hummer!" Medley whispered primly, as though driving a glorified tank somehow amounted to a major flaw in the man's character.

Libby entered the dining room and looked around, taking in the rich look of the wainscoting and built-in, mirrored buffet of dark-stained oak. Amber's birthday cake, a quarter-sheet covered with ivory frosting, pumpkins, a scarecrow, and the number "16" surrounded by fall-colored leaves, took center stage on the buffet.

Please, Lord, she prayed as she approached the table, *let this be a night we'll always remember.*

*   *   *

Cash held Libby's chair, anxious for the evening to pass. He'd suffered through barely fifteen minutes of this fiasco called a dinner party and his nerves had already strained to the breaking point. He'd already managed to upset Libby, had to be reminded of their agreement, and didn't have the slightest idea how to get her to talk to him in private now.

"What a beautiful table cloth," Medley remarked as Todd pulled out her chair. "I just love Battenberg lace." She sat down and spread a matching ivory napkin across her lap. "It goes nicely with your rose-patterned china."

"Thank you," Amber replied shyly. "My friend, Jenny, helped me decorate." She pointed to the centerpiece, a small bouquet of red roses flanked by crystal candleholders. "Jenny's mom gave me these. They're the last ones from her garden this year."

Medley picked up her crystal goblet filled with ice water. "Did she furnish you with everything else, too?"

"Uh-uh." Amber blew a strand of hair from her face. "Dad got it all at a garage sale."

Cash's face and neck grew hot at the burst of laughter around the table. "That's not the whole story," he blurted, rushing to his own defense. He pushed in Libby's chair and took the seat across from her. "I acquired everything from my mother's estate sale before my parents retired to Florida. She wanted to give it to me, but I insisted on paying for it."

"Hey, that's not where you're supposed to sit," Amber complained as she picked up his hand-written name card and glanced around the table. "These things got mixed up." She shot Cash an accusing glare as if to suggest he'd tampered with them. The present arrangement placed Libby and Medley on one side of the table, him and Todd on the other. Her disappointed tone made it plain that she had planned to seat her parents next to each other.

Libby cut Medley a knowing glance. Medley returned the favor with a mischievous, 'I-told-you-so' smirk.

Okay, so they'd guessed he'd played musical place cards before everyone arrived. Why not? Things were awkward enough without having to rub elbows with Libby all night, too.

Amber extracted a small box of stick matches from the pocket of her apron and lit the slender white tapers. She took a step backward, reached into the pocket of her apron again, and pulled out her phone. "Smile everybody. Say cheese, Mom." She snapped a picture. "I can't wait to post this on Myspace. I want all my friends to see you!"

Cash stared at Amber in surprise as she and Libby exchanged smiles. When did she start addressing Libby as Mom? Had he missed something? Until now, Amber had always referred to her mother as either Libby or *she*, as though she hadn't made up her mind. Obviously, something had recently changed and he had a good idea of what had made the difference. Libby could be trusted with Amber's deepest secrets. A tight knot formed in the pit of his stomach.

A small, still voice in his heart urged him to calm down and let go of his fear. Amber had plenty of love to go around.

Given the stakes, he didn't know if he could.

"Now it's your turn." Libby reached under the table and produced her phone as well. "Happy birthday!"

Amber's smile radiated a level of happiness Cash hadn't seen in a long time. Beholding her in such good spirits should have warmed his heart. Instead, it only reinforced his feelings of isolation and loneliness. Since the day he brought his baby home, it had always been just the two of them and they'd always been close, but the night Libby came into their lives, things began to change. He didn't blame Amber for wanting to know her mother. Libby filled a void in Amber's life that only a mother could satisfy. Unfortunately, the more Amber grew into a woman, the more she needed her mother, and the less, it seemed, she needed *him*.

Chapter 11

"The first course is coming up," Amber announced and dimmed the crystal chandelier. Her long, black braid swung over her shoulder as she scurried into the kitchen.

Music echoed softly from the living room. Todd stretched out in his chair and attempted to build a simple structure with the place cards. Cash made a major project out of synchronizing the time on his watch with the grandfather clock in the corner. He couldn't think of anything else to keep himself busy until Amber returned with the food.

He glanced up to double-check the time and caught Libby watching him. Suddenly, he realized he'd made a colossal mistake. It never occurred to him at the time he rearranged the place cards that he would end up face to face with her!

She looked startled that he'd caught her staring. Before she looked away, he noticed the intense blue of her eyes. They reminded him of the sky at twilight. Funny, but he'd forgotten how beautiful they were. Candlelight reflected off her face, giving her skin a soft glow. His gaze slid to her glossy, pink lips...

Todd's elbow nudged him in the ribs. "Hey," he whispered, "after dinner, do you want to go somewhere for a pizza?"

At first, he thought Todd had lost his mind. Eat again? Then he mentally summarized Amber's culinary talents and figured a late-night, fully-loaded, sixteen-inch pie would be a lot more satisfying. He'd probably have antacids for dessert but decided to risk it. He cut Todd a slight nod to concur.

Amber marched into the dining room humming to the music. Her feminine voice sounded contented, rising above the soft strains of Mozart's "Moonlight Sonata" as she carried a silver tray holding small bowls, plates, and soupspoons. "You first, Mom," she said as she hovered over Libby. Cash watched her proceed around the table to serve Medley, Todd, and lastly, him. She spoke to everyone, but him. What had he done to deserve the silent treatment? Did she still hold a grudge over their conversation after the choir concert at school?

She placed the tray on the buffet and wiped her palms on her apron. "Please give the blessing, Uncle Todd."

"Me?" Todd sat up straight and looked around as though he didn't have a clue what to do.

"Yes, it's your turn. Dad gave it the last time you had dinner with us," Amber replied then looked pointedly at Cash. "Everyone has to hold hands." She joined hands with Medley and Todd, forcing Cash to join both hands with Libby. Once more, he regretted messing with the place cards. He reluctantly clasped her hands. Her soft, slender palms fit perfectly inside his.

Todd bowed his head. "Thank you, Lord, for the food we are about to receive..."

Cash tried to concentrate on the prayer, but the awareness of Libby's fingers intertwining with his distracted him so much he could hardly keep his hands steady. Todd's baritone voice melted into a blur of syllables as Cash's thoughts traveled at hyper-speed back to a certain Friday night two weeks ago. In his mind's eye, he saw Libby's face stain rose red with shock, heard the finality in her voice as she spun around and jerked open the door. An unaccountable rush of desperation surged through him as he relived the moment his hand reached up and slammed the door in her face. The scene fast-forwarded and he pulled her into his arms. His mouth covered hers. He suddenly couldn't breathe...

Todd cleared his throat.

Zooming back to the present, Cash's head bobbed up and he discovered everyone staring at him.

"What?"

Todd regarded him with a curious look. "Do you want to add something to the blessing?"

He blinked in confusion, trying to get up to speed with the group. "Ah...no. Good job."

Libby attempted to pull away, making him realize he'd been clutching her hand. Had she guessed his thoughts? Self-conscious, he let go.

The house phone rang.

"I'll get it!" Amber snatched her tray off the buffet and dashed into the kitchen.

Cash decided he'd better get started on his tomato soup. Looking down, he saw cheesy, fish-shaped crackers floating on the surface. Gingerly, he dipped his spoon into the mix, took a sip, and almost spit it out. He hated lukewarm soup!

He spent the next ten minutes trying to convince himself to eat it. If either Libby or Medley realized the first course had been spooned from a can and hastily cooked in a microwave, neither let on. He found it mind-boggling to watch them steadily sip it away, acting as though they thoroughly enjoyed it.

He lowered his spoon, wondering what to do. If he didn't eat his soup, Amber's feelings would get hurt. If he did eat it, his stomach's feelings would get hurt. He glanced around for a place to stash the slimy stuff. Unfortunately, the main floor bathroom was currently under construction so the only available bathroom was tucked away upstairs. Unfortunately, he didn't own a dog to slip it to under the table or a decent plant to use for an emergency compost, so that left him no alternative but to eat it. He gritted his teeth, put the spoon to his lips, and forced it down.

Yuck.

"What's wrong?" Medley gestured with her spoon toward Todd's untouched soup. "Aren't you going to eat that?"

"No!" Todd's lower lip thrust out.

"Why not?"

"I hate tomato soup."

Medley's jade eyes widened. "I beg your pardon?"

"You heard me."

"How can you not like tomato soup? Don't you realize it's loaded with Lycopene, antioxidants, and vitamin C?"

Todd shoved his bowl away and crossed his arms. "I don't care if it's loaded with Red Bull. I'm not gonna eat something I don't like."

Medley waggled her finger at him. "You're going to hurt Amber's feelings." She darted a glance toward the kitchen. "At least give it a try."

Todd shook his head, apparently unconvinced.

"Then give it to me." She reached over and exchanged bowls. "I'll eat it for you."

Fighting back the urge to gag, Cash dug his elbows into the table and slapped his hands over his eyes. Why couldn't she have offered to take it five minutes ago? He would have gladly given his away!

Amber hung up the wall phone in the kitchen and reentered the dining room armed with her tray. She approached the table and stared at Medley's full bowl with dismay. "You didn't finish. Don't you like it?"

Todd went rigid, watching Medley's reaction.

"It's wonderful." Medley dipped her spoon into the soup and smiled sweetly. "I'm a slow eater."

Amber picked up Todd's empty bowl. "That's okay. I didn't mean to rush you."

"Don't worry about it." Medley giggled. "I'm having a wonderful time!"

Amber gathered up the rest of the dishes and left the room, promising to return in due time with the next course.

Cash refused to watch as Medley slowly devoured Todd's leftovers. Still, he couldn't help swallowing every time he heard her take another sip. He gulped some ice water to clear the sticky, slithery feeling from his throat. It didn't work.

He cut a glance at Todd and caught him staring at Medley with a dreamy, faraway look, as though Todd had just noticed something attractive about her that he hadn't been aware of before. A half-hour ago, he didn't want anything to do with the ditzy redhead. Now he couldn't take his eyes off her. Brother!

The next course turned out to be a mixed-greens dinner salad with Italian dressing, black olives, and croutons.

Cash picked up his fork and breathed a sigh of relief. "This looks...safe," he said to no one in particular. "I can do this." After all, how could anyone screw up a salad?

Nevertheless, something didn't seem quite right. He couldn't put his finger on the problem until his third bite when the back of his throat burned hotter than if he'd eaten gunpowder. He grabbed his water goblet and put out the fire.

Suddenly everyone at the table began coughing into their napkins and reaching for their water goblets. Cash peered at Libby through bleary eyes and saw a tear running down her cheek. She clutched her throat and tried to swallow.

He leaned forward. "Are you okay?"

She nodded and gulped her water.

Curious, he turned over a couple of torn pieces of lettuce with his fork and found the cause. Amber had garnished the salad with a hidden layer of red pepper flakes.

He pushed his barely-eaten salad out of the way and leaned back in his chair, feeling like a contestant on *Survivor*. Unfortunately, no one at the table possessed either the inclination or the guts to vote him off the island. In this case, misery insisted on company!

Todd stared at his salad, absently pushing lettuce around the plate with his fork. All of a sudden, a black olive pitched through the air, landing on the table between his plate and Medley's. Both reached for it, but Medley got there first. Todd's hand smacked on top of hers, pinning it to the table.

They stared at each other in amazement, as though they couldn't quite comprehend what had happened. With gazes locked, they slowly pulled their hands apart.

"Excuse me?"

Everyone turned toward the kitchen. Amber stood in the arched doorway holding a large pair of tongs. "Are you ready for the entrée?"

Cash held out his plate. He could barely talk. His throat burned as though someone had torched it. "I am."

Amber approached the table, frowning at his half-eaten salad. "But, Dad, you—"

"I'm saving my appetite for the main course." He displayed a wide grin as he handed her the plate.

Amber shoved the tongs into her apron pocket. As she went around the table and gathered the salad plates, a buzzer went off in the kitchen.

"Oh-oh, I'd better hurry. That's the garlic bread."

Then the cell phone in her pocket began to scream out music. She piled the last of the dishes in her arms and scurried into the kitchen. Cash winced at the clatter of china crashing in the sink.

"Who does your hair?" Medley asked Todd.

"Why?" He ran his hand self-consciously through his long, shaggy locks. "What's wrong with it?"

Medley scrutinized his mane with concern, reminding Cash of a landscaper inspecting a diseased tree. "You need a good trim."

Todd folded his arms again and leaned back, rocking on the rear legs of his chair. "There's nothing wrong with my hair."

"You need layers." She tapped her finger on her chin as she studied him like a pro. "Layers would give your hair fullness, more body." Her fine brows arched. "And camouflage that thinning spot on your crown."

Todd bolted upright, nearly losing his balance. The chair's front legs slammed on the wood floor. "What thin spot?" His eyes widened with panic as one hand flew to the top of his head; the other grabbed the table edge for support. "Can you see it?"

"Not from here, but I'm sure you have the beginning of one. Thinning is normal," she replied casually, "for a man *your* age. Don't worry; I can style your hair so no one will notice." She reached down and snatched her black purse from under the table. "I do it for clients every day."

Todd rubbed the back of his neck. "Yeah...sure." He sounded anything but confident. "I-I'll call you on Monday morning and make an appointment."

"I'm fully booked next week," she stated and offered him a business card, "but I'll make time...for you."

They stared into each other's eyes again, mesmerized.

Amber interrupted their epiphany as she wheeled a shiny brass and glass serving cart through the door. The top shelf held a metal colander of spaghetti and a stainless-steel pan of red sauce. The lower shelf held a woven basket filled with garlic bread.

She stopped at Libby first and piled a mountain of cold spaghetti on Libby's plate. "Say when, Mom," she said in a sugary voice as she spooned the sauce over it.

Libby smiled and raised her palms right away. "That's plenty."

Amber bustled around the table like a honeybee flitting among the flowers as she doled out a portion of the cold, wiry spaghetti and a ladle of sauce to each of her guests. No one spoke as she went about her business, but Cash couldn't help noticing the stoic looks on the faces of his dinner companions as they surveyed the next installment of *Survivor*, MacKenzie-style.

Amber placed the basket of toast on the table. "I'll check back to see if you want seconds. I...um...accidentally made too much."

Cash gazed down at the stringy mess on his plate. Boy, that pizza sure sounded good right now. He picked up his fork and glanced around the table. The others stared at their plates in dismay and bewilderment, obviously not knowing what to do with their portions, either.

"Bon appetite," Amber announced cheerily as she wheeled the cart back into the kitchen.

He picked up his fork and murmured, "I'll never complain about having to cook again..."

Using her large spoon, Libby proceeded to twirl the spaghetti around the fork, but the stiff, wiry strands stuck together and wouldn't cooperate. Something lumpy rolled to the edge of her plate. Upon closer inspection, Cash concluded that she had a mini-meatball, the ready-made kind that came with the sauce.

Medley erupted into an explosion of giggles. She let go of her fork and it stuck in her pasta like a fence post in cement.

Todd reached across the table with his fork in hand and attempted to help her untangle the pasta but ended up getting the tines of his utensil stuck in hers. Then their gazes tangled and he exploded with laughter, too.

A glob of spaghetti dropped into Medley's water goblet. Their merriment intensified into a unified roar.

Cash met Libby's questioning gaze and shrugged innocently to show he had no idea what had gotten into either Medley or Todd.

Amber popped into the doorway with a pitcher of ice water. "Is everything okay?" She approached the table, wide-eyed with curiosity as she refilled their water. She held up Medley's goblet. "Hey, you guys act worse than the kids at school." Shaking her head, she took the goblet and disappeared into the kitchen.

Cash picked up his knife and fork. *Might as well get this over with,* he thought and began to crosscut the spaghetti. He'd made it past one hurdle but still had to swallow it.

He spied the garlic toast, baked to a golden brown. Now that looked edible—almost tasty. With high hopes, he picked up a piece and took a large bite. It tasted odd.

He turned it over. The underside looked like a briquette. He downed his cold food with the help of a large gulp of water and showed the toast to Libby, flipping it from one side to the other. "How did she manage that?"

Libby picked up her piece and turned it over. "I'm not sure," she replied, examining it. "Maybe she cranked the heat too high, or maybe she should have set the pan on a lower rack."

"Maybe she should have ordered out," he whispered and covered everything on his plate with a thick layer of grated cheese, hoping it would salvage the meal. "I would have gladly picked up the tab. The only food she's ever showed an interest in cooking is macaroni and cheese, and half the time she scorches that."

Scooping up a forkful, he shoved the cheese-covered spaghetti into his mouth, followed by a large bite of charred toast. He chewed and swallowed, washing it down with a hefty gulp of ice water. Even so, it went down like a chunk of brick.

"It's not so bad," Libby remarked over Todd's obnoxious belly laughing.

Cash paused, his fork suspended in mid-air. "Not if you like rubber spaghetti mixed with scorched sauce and cinders for toast."

"You should have seen the first meal *I* tried to cook," she said, suppressing a chuckle. "I put pieces of a frozen chicken into a deep-frying pan filled with hot oil and it caught on fire. Well, the truth is that it practically blew up the kitchen. The alarm went off and not more than five minutes later, three squads and two hook and ladders showed up at the house."

He stuffed a forkful of cold spaghetti in his mouth while she talked, but the comical expression on her face made him burst out laughing. Unfortunately, the food stuck in his throat, nearly choking him. Laughing and coughing at the same time, he gulped a mouthful of water.

Libby picked up her napkin and blotted her lips, trying to conceal her amusement.

He caught himself watching her closely again. *Forget it, MacKenzie,* he told himself and went back to work on his meal. *Get your mind off her and concentrate on your food or you'll never get through this.*

"What's the matter with you two?"

Surprised, he looked up from his pasta and paused as Libby glared at Medley and Todd.

"Have you lost your minds?" she asked.

"No, I lost my meatball," Medley said and roared again.

"No, you didn't." Todd pointed to the edge of her spaghetti with his fork. "It's hiding."

"Good," Medley countered, giggling uncontrollably. "That's where it belongs—out of my sight."

"Why? Aren't you going to eat it?"

"Of course not." Medley pursed her lips in a lousy attempt to feign offense. "I'm a vegan."

Todd shot her a puzzled look. "A what?"

"A vee-gan."

"Oh, yeah?" Todd displayed a toothy grin as if suddenly getting the point. "I'm part Nor-vee-gan myself."

Cash forced himself to keep a straight face and in doing so, almost chomped down on his tongue. "She said vegan, Todd. Not Norwegian. In other words, she's a strict vegetarian."

"Say, what?" Todd gaped at Medley as though she'd come from a distant planet. "You mean—you don't eat meat?"

"No," she answered sternly, pointing the tines of her fork at him, "and you shouldn't either. All that cholesterol is bad for your health."

Todd seemed to absorb that information for a moment then pointed his fork at her meatball. "Can I have it?"

Cash shook his head to convey an "I give up" gesture as Libby covered her flushed cheeks with her hands to conceal her laughter.

For the remainder of the meal, Cash sat quietly, taking in the show. Even though Todd's antics annoyed him to no end, at the same time, it gave him an excuse to keep quiet and focus on something other than Libby. Between the four of them, they somehow managed to consume not only all of their spaghetti but the entire basket of toast as well.

Amber cleared away their empty plates and returned with a stainless teapot of hot water and a jar of instant coffee.

"I don't know how to make coffee," she said to Libby in an apologetic tone. "I made hot water instead so you could mix your own." She set the coffee jar on the table. "Is that okay, Mom?"

Libby held out her cup for some hot water. "That's fine." She placed her hand on Amber's arm and smiled approvingly. "We'll all have some."

They were still stirring their coffee when Amber returned with dessert plates, each bearing two strawberries, frozen and dipped in chocolate.

"Even though we're having cake for dessert, I wanted to start it off with a little treat first. I hope you like it." Amber set a dish in front of Libby. "I made this just for you."

"How thoughtful! Thank you, Amber," Libby said with a twinkle in her eye. "How did you know chocolate-dipped strawberries were my favorite?"

Amber's cheeks turned crimson. "I guessed." Her quick reply, however, suggested just the opposite. With cell phone in hand, she backed toward the doorway, as though she found the moment uncomfortable. "Don't worry, Aunt Medley, they're organic. I have to get back to the kitchen. Enjoy!"

Cash watched Amber make a hasty retreat. "I hate to think of what that room must look like."

Libby stirred her coffee but looked straight at him with a knowing smile. "I wouldn't go in there if I were you."

His strawberry-laden fingers stopped in mid-air. "Why?"

"You wouldn't want to spoil your dinner."

Cash almost laughed at the irony in her statement. At that very moment, his dinner lay in his stomach like a lump of setting concrete. From the corner of his eye, Cash saw Todd feed a strawberry to Medley. "What are you doing over there, Trisco?"

Todd beamed. "What does it look like? I'm sharing my dessert."

Medley giggled and leaned forward for another bite of a ruby-red, palm-sized berry.

Todd gazed at Medley, all starry-eyed like a kid with a crush on his favorite movie star. In this case—Elle Woods. "She's sweeter than chocolate."

Cash couldn't stand to watch Romeo and Elle play *The Dating Game* any longer. In actuality, it seemed more like *America's Funniest Videos*, but he didn't think they deserved a ten-thousand-dollar grand prize for performing

America's most adolescent behavior by an adult. Cash shoved his chair back and patted the pockets of his blazer.

"What's up?" Todd gave him a curious look. "Did you lose something?"

"Yeah, my antacids," Cash exclaimed as he cut Todd a disgusted frown.

Todd glanced toward the kitchen and laid a silencing finger across his lips.

Hah! Are you kidding me?

Taking his cue, Libby tossed her napkin on the table and began to gather the soiled plates. "Let's call Amber in here to cut the cake."

"Sounds good to me." Cash stood with renewed enthusiasm. "Hey, honey bear," he yelled toward the kitchen. "Get off the phone and come in here. We're going to light the candles."

Libby cleared the center of the table as Cash went to the buffet and retrieved the cake. He placed it on the table just as Amber came into the room carrying her tray laden with a bucket of ice cream and a scoop, a small stack of clean plates, forks, and a large knife. He grabbed his butane lighter from the buffet drawer and lit all sixteen candles.

"Make a wish, sweetheart." He stood back. "Then take your best shot."

Amber gazed wistfully at her parents standing together.

Cash's heart crashed to the floor. The way she looked at the two of them told him what she had on her mind, but he couldn't do a thing about it.

Or...could he? An idea became finalized in his mind. Something he'd been tossing around in his thoughts for about a week.

Amber closed her eyes and went still for a moment then drew in a deep breath. She blew out the candles with air to spare.

Though she kept it a secret, he knew exactly what she'd wished for, but he had a sinking feeling it might be the one present he could never give her.

Chapter 12

"Let's take our coffee in the living room," Cash announced after everyone, except Medley, who'd declined dessert, had finished eating cake and ice cream. Smiling, he tugged on Amber's thick braid. "My little girl is eager to open her presents." Amber giggled as he shoved back his chair and stood, motioning everyone to follow suit.

Libby rose from the table, dreading this part of the evening most of all. She could handle Amber's lack of cooking skills and Cash's reference to her as Olivia, a name she hated. She could even tolerate Medley's incessant flirting and Todd's annoying belly laughs. However, she couldn't bear Amber's disappointment if two of the first gifts she'd selected for her daughter turned out to be a mistake.

She'd chosen the items with the intent of giving Amber something meaningful, rather than just the usual material things people gave a girl her age. Now she agonized over her choice. Clutching her china coffee mug with trembling fingers, she followed the others into the living room, wishing she had played it safe.

A small mountain of gifts covered the coffee table, wrapped in a jewel assortment of paper, ribbon, and bows. Only one package, hidden under the pile, came from her. Though small, it held several things near and dear to her heart. In giving them away, she'd sacrificed a piece of her past and the only link she'd possessed to the faceless, nameless daughter she'd cherished for sixteen years. She hoped with all her heart that the items would mean as much to Amber as they had meant to her.

Cash went straight to the fireplace and stoked the fire before tossing several small logs into the crackling flames. Medley and Todd claimed the sofa, deep in whispered conversation, leaving Libby and Cash to occupy the twin easy chairs facing them. Amber had the floor, so to speak.

Libby gripped her flowered mug with nervous anticipation as Amber sorted through the boxes and bags. First, she selected a large box wrapped in gold foil, trimmed with a red velvet ribbon and matching bow.

After skimming the card, she gleefully ripped open the paper and tore off the cover. She pulled back several layers of tissue and then gasped with excitement. The box tumbled to the floor as she held up a pair of designer jeans and a sparkling gold belt.

"They're just what I've been waiting for!" She went to Cash and hugged him. "Thanks, Dad, for remembering how much I wanted these!"

Cash relaxed in his chair with a big smile, looking more than pleased with his choice of gifts. His ease, however, in knowing Amber's wish list peeled away yet another layer of Libby's confidence.

Next, Amber opened a box from Todd. Inside she found a fuzzy brown bear. The bear held another box the size of a large ice cube, adorned with a tiny bow and matching ribbon looped around its paw. The little package contained a glittering pair of diamond earrings, baguette-style in a buttercup setting.

"Oh..." Amber's eyes widened as she ogled the pair in their black velvet case. When she looked up, her eyes twinkled brighter than the stones. "Are— are they real, Uncle Todd?"

Todd placed his hand over his heart, pretending to be hurt. "You know me better than that. Of course, they're real." He held out his arms. "Come here, Princess, and give me a hug."

Amber threw her arms around him. "I love you, Uncle Todd. You always give me the coolest stuff!"

"Only the finest is good enough for my God-daughter." He released her and sat back, grinning. "Every girl should get diamonds on her sixteenth birthday."

His reply struck a chord with Libby. By her sixteenth birthday, she'd spent most of her time waiting for her dad to come home from Washington and wishing she had the loving, caring family life Medley enjoyed. Little did she know, back then, that in a few weeks she'd meet a boy at a basketball game who would fill that void in her heart. Unfortunately, that fateful encounter with the young and cocky Cash MacKenzie resulted in altering her attitude and ultimately the course of her life.

Amber opened her gifts, one by one. She received more jewelry, makeup, perfume, and a gift certificate from Medley's salon.

"Here ya go, the last one," Todd announced as he picked up the last package. He handed Libby's gift to Amber.

Amber carelessly ripped open the card and read aloud in a bored tone, "You're invited to a 'girl's only' luncheon at the restaurant of your choice, a matinee, and a shopping trip for a complete outfit at the Mall of America." She jammed the card back into the envelope and dropped it on the table, unaware that her cool reception succeeded in crushing more than the paper.

If she didn't like that, Libby thought nervously, *she's going to hate the rest.* She held her breath as Amber pried open a flat, white box. Inside she found two separately wrapped packages in soft pink tissue paper. She tore the paper off the first one and froze, frowning in puzzlement.

Libby's heart caught in her throat.

Amber held a small, but thick book in her hands—a homemade baby book. The yellowed photo album contained a collection of mementos that Libby had cataloged from the hospital when she gave birth to Amber.

For years, Libby had kept it a secret, though she'd never meant to hoard it for herself. She had always trusted that one day her life would come full circle so she could present it to her own daughter, the person for whom she'd lovingly created it. Now she wished she'd waited to give it to Amber when they were alone.

Everyone watched as Amber sat on the floor and stoically leafed through the pages of stiff black paper. She held up a page displaying a tiny plastic identification bracelet. "Where did you get this?"

Libby expected questions. Rather, she'd hoped Amber would want to know more about her past. "It's from your ankle." She pointed to the torn clasp. "I snuck into your room in the middle of the night after you were born and took it from your foot. I'm sure the nurses knew what happened to it even though they didn't question me. The next day they put another one on you," she confessed and pointed to a larger strip on the next page. "I wore this one."

Amber continued to pour through the little keepsake in silence, studying items such as the pink identification card from her bassinette and a tiny pair of plain white bootie socks. There were smaller, everyday items as well, such as swabs and cotton balls, now stretched and flattened into thin, ivory spots. After she paged through the mementos, she found a yellowed collection of birthday cards—fifteen in all, written to her from Libby.

Libby didn't know how to gauge Amber's silence, but as the seconds ticked away, doubt overshadowed her. Did Amber find this gift boring, too?

Amber suddenly looked up, blinking away tears. "This is...awesome," she said in a thick voice. "Growing up, I always wondered who you were...and whether you cared." She jumped up and threw her arms around Libby. "Thank you, Mom. You've given me the best gift of all."

Relieved, Libby wrapped her arms around Amber and hugged her tight. "Finding you is the best gift I've ever received."

Medley began to sniffle. Libby looked up and saw Todd snatch a napkin off the coffee table. He crushed it into a ball and gently patted away Medley's tears as he wrapped his long, muscular arm around her narrow shoulders.

Behind her, Cash stirred.

Self-conscious, she pulled away from Amber and picked up the remaining piece of her daughter's gift. She hadn't intended to turn Amber's party into a family melodrama. "Don't forget this."

Amber wiped her eyes with the backs of her hands and accepted the small, flat box. With a loud sniff, she ripped off the paper then pried open the cover and gaped at the photograph inside. Her questioning gaze met Libby's straight on. "Is this you?"

Libby smiled, warmed by Amber's interest. "And you."

Fascinated, Amber pulled out the antique gold frame containing an old

153

Polaroid 'instant' color photo. "Wow," she said with amazement, "you look so young...like *my* age."

Everyone gathered around them, peering over their shoulders to get a better look.

The picture showed Libby at seventeen with straight, elbow-length hair standing in a stark white hospital room wearing a flowered nightgown. In her arms, she cradled a tiny bundle wrapped in a pink receiving blanket. Her eyes sparkled as she posed for the camera, beaming with a joyful, radiant smile.

Amber marveled over her newborn picture. "It's so hard to imagine that's me. I mean, I'm so small. I look more like a doll than a real baby." She looked up. "Who took this?" She stared pointedly at her dad. "Did you?"

Cash's face turned scarlet. His mouth flapped open and shut like a fish out of water, but no words emerged.

"The craziest thing happened that day," Libby remarked, abruptly changing the subject. "Remember when I told you how the nurses hid you in a small room behind the nursery? I saw a chance to sneak in there the next afternoon to peek at you while the nurse on duty held a discussion with one of the doctors. I planned to pull the covers back a little and just feast my eyes on you, but when I saw you were awake, I couldn't resist the urge to take you out of the crib. Wouldn't you know it," Libby chuckled to herself at the irony, "the moment I picked you up, a housekeeper came into the room to clean it. I expected her to run straight to the head nurse and bust me, but she didn't. She said she understood how I felt. When she left me alone again, I thought she'd gone back to work, but she returned a couple of minutes later with a Polaroid Instant Camera to take my picture."

Amber scrunched her brows together in confusion. "What's a Polaroid Instant Camera? Didn't you have digital cameras back then?"

Everyone burst out laughing.

"It's a camera with a special film that we used back in those days to take 'instant' pictures. You took the picture, pulled out the raw photograph, and waited a minute or so until it developed before your eyes." Libby smoothed a stray hair away from Amber's face, tucking it into her braid. "I don't know where she got it, but I've always assumed she borrowed it from one of the other mothers on the floor."

"This totally rocks. Thank you, Mom!" Amber crushed the frame to her heart. "I can't wait to show it to my friends!"

As if on cue, her cell phone blasted out an old Jonas Brothers song. She pulled it from her pocket, checked the number, and swiped the screen with her finger. "Hey," she chattered excitedly as she scurried into the den, "you wouldn't believe what I got for my birthday!" The door slammed behind her.

Amber's departure created a gaping hole in the conversation but established one thing; the birthday party had officially ended.

Medley arose from the sofa. "I'll take care of these dishes." She collected the empty coffee mugs and took them to the kitchen while Todd tended to the fire.

Taking the hint, Libby began gathering the discarded wrapping paper. An odd feeling made her pause. She glanced past her shoulder and saw Cash standing behind her with his hands jammed into his pockets.

"Olivia..."

There he went again, calling her by the name on her birth certificate, not the one she used every day. His deep, commanding voice sounded serious. She shot him a warning look but didn't turn around. Instead, she kept on straightening up the living room, pretending to be uninterested.

A strong, work-roughened hand gripped her elbow and pivoted her toward him. "Listen...ah...we need to talk."

Her pulse thundered. "I'm sorry, Cash. I didn't mean to embarrass you in front of everyone by giving Amber the memory books of my hospital stay. I should have presented her that gift in private."

She glanced around, hoping to use Medley as an excuse to get away. Medley and Todd, however, had disappeared, leaving her and Cash alone in the center of his living room.

She tried to pull her arm away.

"Don't worry about it," he insisted. "Frankly, I've given up on our agreement." His grip tightened. "There is something else I need to talk to you about."

She straightened to her full height and said softly, "But it's Amber's birthday. Why can't we postpone the discussion until tomorrow?"

He shook his head as his dark-eyed gaze burned into hers. "This can't wait."

Medley emerged from the kitchen just as Todd came through the front door with an armload of wood. The door to the den remained closed.

Libby sensed Cash's discomfort and used the distraction to pull her arm free. "Is this about Amber's grades? Look, if you're considering hiring a tutor," she whispered, "I totally support your decision, but this is neither the time nor the place to get into it."

"I don't intend to discuss anything here. It's a clear night. We'll take a walk."

"Why?" Libby suddenly became alarmed. "What happened?"

His jaw tensed. "I'll get your coat."

"Cash—"

The door to the den opened and Amber appeared with a cell phone in her hand.

Medley approached them. "Amber's going to need some assistance in there," she said, blinking in disbelief as she gestured toward the kitchen. "I think we'd better stay a while and help her get the damage under control."

"It's no big deal!" Amber shoved her phone into her pocket as she rushed toward the group. "I can clean up the mess by myself. I've done it lots of times."

"Medley's right," Libby said, jumping on the idea as she stuffed the last of the loose paper into the box that had held the toy bear. "We should all pitch in and help her."

"Oliv—I mean, Libby and I are going to take a walk first," Cash announced abruptly. He came up behind them with Libby's coat draped over his arm. "I need some fresh air and a decent cup of coffee."

Amber turned to Medley. "Why don't you and Uncle Todd go, too?" She anxiously twisted a couple of loose strands of ebony hair around one finger. "I'll load the dishwasher while you're gone."

Todd gave one last stoke to rejuvenate the fire then placed the poker back into its holder. "You guys go and get your coffee," he said to Cash. "I'll stay and help these two beautiful women get the kitchen cleaned up."

He grinned at Medley, gazing into her eyes like a smitten teenager.

Libby watched Medley's gushing reaction, concluding that if she'd been made of wax, Todd's smile would have melted her on the spot.

Amber smacked her lips in disgust.

"Thanks, Medley, for offering to help. Just load the dishwasher and stack the pots in the sink." Cash turned to Amber. "You and I will get up early tomorrow to take care of the rest."

He took the box stuffed with crumpled wrapping paper from Libby and handed it to Medley then held Libby's black satin trench coat, assisting her as she slid her arms into it and then pulled it over her shoulders. Taking her by the elbow, he firmly guided her to the door.

The clock on the fireplace mantle chimed eight times.

Libby paused at the doorway, giving Medley one last chance to complain about being stuck with all of the work. One word from her cousin would give her the excuse she needed to put off being alone with Cash. Medley's dreamy smile, however, indicated that her mind couldn't have been further away from cleaning.

Todd moved to her side, cradling his hand at the nape of her neck. They made a perfect pair—like the little china bride and groom on top of a wedding cake.

"We'll be back in a little while," Cash said to Todd and escorted Libby onto the front porch. The door shut behind her with a heavy thud.

Libby squared her shoulders and stepped off the porch into the peaceful, starry October evening, wondering what Cash MacKenzie had on his mind.

*   *   *

Now that Cash had Libby alone, he didn't know what to say. He did know,

157

however, that he only had one chance. He had to get it right the first time and win her cooperation or risk losing the only thing that mattered in his life.

She looked surprised when he took her hand but didn't pull away. As they walked along West Island Avenue, the deep roar of water rushing over St. Anthony Falls and the rumble of traffic crossing the Hennepin Avenue Bridge enveloped their silence. A whisper of a breeze, unseasonably warm, made the weather seem more like an August night than the third week of October.

They were nearing River's Edge High School when Libby tugged on his hand. "Aren't you going to tell me what's bothering you?"

He shoved both of his hands into his trouser pockets and looked away. He'd been asking himself the same question since they left his front yard. Every approach he came up with sounded desperate, almost like begging. Somehow, he had to muster the guts to swallow his doubt and go through with it.

"I'm thinking," he said. His voice shook slightly as he spoke, and he wondered if Libby suspected his apprehension. Little, it seemed, got past her. That quality in her had a lot to do with his coming to this decision in the first place.

Her growing influence over Amber simply blew him away. All through dinner, he'd studied the interaction between them, noting every time Amber referred to her as Mom. Inwardly, he hurt every time Amber showered her with special attention while ignoring him. Little by little, he saw himself eased out of the picture as Libby mothered her way into Amber's heart and the center of her life. His thoughts ran in so many directions he couldn't remember who said, "If you can't beat 'em, join 'em," but the more he considered it, the more it made sense.

He took a deep breath. "Something has been on my mind all night. I-I..." The words stuck to his tongue.

"Are you upset with me because I went along with Amber's plans to put on a dinner party for her birthday?" she asked, finishing the sentence for him. "I couldn't bow out without hurting her feelings and neither could you."

Do it.

Cash opened his mouth again to speak, but this time his throat closed up. He clamped his jaw shut.

He looked up, struggling for courage. Lights outlining the Hennepin Avenue suspension bridge shone through the night like topaz-colored beacons.

Lord, give me the guts to go through with this, he prayed as they approached the Nicollet Island Inn.

A worried voice ricocheted through his head. *What if she says no?* He shoved his fists deeper into his pockets. *What if she says yes?* His heart pounded so vehemently at the prospect that it hammered in his ears.

"Libby, I..." That horrible food he'd forced down at dinner threatened to erupt in his throat. He swallowed back the burning bile, vowing to himself to never again eat so much as a piece of Amber's toast until she went to cooking school!

"Amber got detention for skipping class again," Libby stated bluntly. "Is that it?" Her brows shot upward. "And you think I've been covering for her. I told you the day I brought her home from detention I would never do that and I meant it!"

He shook his head. *Lord, if only the problem was that simple...*

Suddenly, Libby gasped with shock as a fresh revelation rocked her. "You're planning to send her away to a private school to separate her from Brian Hanson, aren't you? That's why you're having a tough time breaking the news to me." She stomped her high-heeled foot on the sidewalk. "Well, that's not going to happen, do you hear me? I forbid you to treat my daughter as though she's nothing but a burden." Her voice quaked with anger. "Like my father treated me!"

"No, no..." He shook his head. "I'm trying to ask you—"

"I won't let you, Cash! Do you understand? You're not taking her away from me—"

Something in his heart tripped, pushing him over the edge. He grabbed her by the arms and pulled her face close to his. "Shut up, Libby, and just listen, would you? I'm not sending Amber away. Are you crazy? I couldn't live one day without her. I'm trying to work up the nerve to ask you to marry me!"

The lights of the Nicollet Island Inn reflected off her beautiful, but stunned face. He watched her crimson cheeks instantly pale. Her wide blue eyes went into a trance-like stare; her jaw dropped in slow motion as she absorbed his incredulous announcement.

"I mean it," he argued in his own defense. "I know this isn't what you expected, but it will make sense once I explain." He held up one hand. "Please, don't make a decision until you hear me out. Amber needs *us*," he contended stubbornly, "both of us, together."

She didn't agree or disagree. She didn't speak at all, and he wondered why.

"Oliv—Libby!" He shook her gently to bring her to her senses. "I realize we've got a long way to go to reestablish our relationship, but I'm willing to make a fresh start with you."

"You...have...got...to...be...kidding," she said incredulously, leaving no doubt in his mind how much he'd shocked her.

"I've never been more serious in my life," he replied, knowing that he'd figuratively just opened his mouth wide enough to shove both feet and his pickup into it. "I don't play games and you know it."

"You don't? Then what do you call this outrageous proposal, a business deal?" Her voice trembled as she pulled her arms out of his grip. "You're the one who's crazy if you think I'll marry you just to be your housekeeper and round-the-clock chaperone."

Huh? Cash stared at her, baffled. *Wha-what did I do wrong?*

"Marriage is sacred, Cash. It's a lifetime commitment of love and devotion between two people and the Almighty. I've never heard of anything so absurd in my life. You've not only insulted me, but you've also mocked God!" She spun around to go back the way they came.

"You're taking this all wrong," he replied helplessly as her rejection sunk in. Not knowing what else to do, he stepped in front of her, blocking her way. "I-I didn't mean to upset you. I thought you'd understand. You said once that you wanted to be involved in your daughter's life because she needed you more than ever. I'm offering you that chance."

She didn't answer. Instead, she surprised him with a one-eighty turn and began speed-walking past the Nicollet Island Inn, toward the wooden walking bridge that connected the island with the east bank of the river and the cobblestone streets of the historic St. Anthony Main retail complex.

Frustrated, he threw his hands into the air and trailed her like a hunting dog on a fresh scent, determined to finish what he'd started. Never in his life had he made such a fool of himself, but never had the stakes risen so high, either.

"Stop, please! Don't walk away from this discussion without hearing the rest of my plan. You can't make an informed decision without all of the facts."

"I've heard all the *facts* I need." She increased her speed, her four-inch pumps clicking a staccato beat on the sidewalk. "Your ego needs a lesson in humility!"

He caught up with her and hooked his fingers around her elbow. "Slow down. You're going to trip in those high heels and end up in the river if you don't watch out."

She jerked away from him and started across the bridge.

"Libby," he demanded gruffly, trying a different approach. "I'm talking to you!" That line always worked with Amber, but it apparently didn't faze her. She kept walking.

"You may be talking, but you're not making any sense," she yelled over her shoulder.

He followed her to the street and slid her arm in his as she stepped onto the cobblestones.

She tried to pull away, but he held on.

"I can't marry you if you fall and kill yourself." He kept a firm grip on her as they crossed the bumpy, uneven surface of the street and walked another half-block along the brick storefronts of several small shops. Once they reached Sleepy's Coffeehouse, he charged ahead and threw open the door for her.

In a far corner of the room, a half-circle of easy chairs faced the scarlet-tipped flames of the gas fireplace, occupied by coffee drinkers either reading or doing homework. In the adjacent corner, a lone guitarist sang the last bars of a melancholy song. A few patrons responded with applause.

Cash ignored the reverie and stayed close behind Libby as he squeezed between rows of people crammed around small round tables, maneuvering his way toward the serving counter.

"Tell me, once and for all," he shouted above the noise, refusing to give up. "Will you marry me?"

"*No.*"

Wrong answer. "Why not?"

She turned her head just enough to view him from the corner of her eye. "You're not asking me to be your wife. You're offering me a job." She pushed her way through the crowd to the coffee bar.

Behind the counter, a young woman with dark brown hair sporting a boyish cut adjusted her black horn-rimmed glasses. "May I help you?"

"I'll take a mocha," Libby shouted above the crowd. "Make that a large one."

The girl squinted at Cash. "And you, sir?"

"Nothing, thanks, but I'll pay for hers." He couldn't fathom eating or drinking anything right now. He reached into his pocket and pulled out his money clip.

Libby pushed his hand away and shoved a handful of dollar bills at the cashier. "Keep the change."

A brawny young man wearing a maroon workout suit boldly wedged himself between Cash and Libby. "Are you okay, lady?"

Libby turned away to wait for her mocha. "I'm fine."

The young buck's protectiveness toward Libby generated a fresh dose of jealousy in Cash that he hadn't experienced in a long time—at least, not since the night of Amber's choir concert at school.

"Hey," the young man persisted, giving Cash a thorough once-over, "if this guy's bothering you, just say the word and I'll get him out of your way."

"Men!" She whirled around.

Libby grabbed her mocha, heavily garnished with whipped cream, and walked out. Shaking his head, Cash shoved his hands into his pockets and followed her, feeling like a lost puppy.

Taking her advice, however, he took a humbler approach once they'd crossed the cobblestone street and started back across the walking bridge to the island.

"I'm sorry I upset you. I blew it. Let's start over. All right?"

Libby stared straight ahead as they passed a stand of large cottonwood trees lining the riverbank. "I don't see why. I won't change my mind."

"Give me one good reason why not."

She sipped her fancy coffee and grimaced. He couldn't tell whether the hot liquid caused her reaction or his refusal to give up.

"Cash, the day we met at Sandhill, you told me you didn't trust me. Two weeks ago, on the Friday night that Amber tried to sneak out, you accused me of not being able to commit to a relationship."

"I never said being married would be easy," he argued, "but I promise you this—I'll give our relationship everything I've got."

They reached the end of the bridge and continued to Merriam, starting the final leg of their journey back to the house.

Libby took another sip of coffee. "What's happened in the last fourteen days to change your mind?"

"You," he stated plainly. "You seem to be one step ahead of Amber all the time. She listens to you, even if she doesn't agree with what you're saying. When she invited you to church, I realized how much she'd begun to care about you. She wanted everyone to see us as a family."

Libby winced. "That day at the choir concert, I caught the look on her face when she saw us together. There's no doubt in my mind that she wants us to become a family in the truest sense of the word." She pursed her pink-tinted lips. "Obviously, when she saw you kiss me that night at your place she became convinced of the idea."

He agreed, hoping his compliance would put him another step closer to persuading her to accept his proposal. "That's also why she insisted on making dinner for her parents on her birthday instead of having a party with her friends."

"So, you've decided that making us into an instant family will solve all her problems. And yours."

"*Our* problems," he said. "No, but it's a start. I'm willing to do whatever it takes to bring us together."

"Even marrying a woman you don't love? Or trust?"

He cupped her elbow, halting her. Then he gently turned her around, ready to bare his soul. "The truth is, I've never stopped loving you," he confessed, softening his tone. "It's obvious by the wariness in your eyes that you don't believe me, but I do. I figured you wouldn't buy into that because of what I said at Sandhill, so I thought that appealing to you on Amber's behalf would make more sense. I'm not denying that we have issues. I'm asking for a chance to resolve them." He looked deeply into her eyes. "This may sound corny or clichéd, but life *is* what you make of it."

Funny, but that line sounded strangely familiar, like something Todd said once...

Libby stared at the ground for a few moments. When he lifted her chin, her eyes glistened with tears.

"As much as I love my daughter, I won't give her false hopes. That's why I can't marry you and gamble that things will miraculously work out between us. I'm sorry, Cash. My final answer is no."

They returned to the house in silence. Libby's rejection had deeply disappointed Cash and placed his future with her in doubt. Deep in his heart, he knew he couldn't give up on her, but for now, he accepted her decision.

As they approached the front yard, something seemed out of place.

"I don't see any lights on in the living room," Cash said, craning his neck to see the usual stream of light filtering through the oval glass in the front door. "Do you?"

"No." Libby shot him a concerned look. "Todd's Hummer is gone. Medley's car is gone, too. I wonder if Amber went somewhere with one of them."

He pulled out his phone and dialed Amber's number. "She's not answering. Let's hurry." He grabbed her free hand and they swiftly walked to the front porch. Cash reached out to open the front door and found it locked. Where had everyone gone? He didn't recall either Todd or Medley mentioning taking Amber anywhere with them after they'd cleaned up the dishes. Todd must have taken Amber out for pizza instead of him. In any case, Todd should have called his cell to let him know. He shoved his key in the lock and stepped into the living room. Libby followed close behind.

A healthy fire still burned in the fireplace, but darkness permeated the rest of the house. At first, he didn't understand why. Then his gaze rested upon the sofa. He jammed his keys into his pocket and flipped on the light. It took him a moment to adjust his sight. He froze.

Amber and Brian Hanson lay on the cushions in a tangled web of arms and legs.

One of his worst fears had suddenly become a reality.

Chapter 13

The nightmare unfolded before her eyes.

Libby dropped her empty cup and bolted after Cash as he charged into the living room. She caught up with him just before he reached the sofa, making a frantic, but futile effort to stop him.

"What's going on here?" He glared at Brian. His hands balled into fists at his sides.

"Calm down, Cash," she urged and gripped his arm. "Nothing good can be accomplished by losing your temper."

As soon as Amber saw them burst into the room, she scrambled to her feet, hastily attempting to straighten her appearance at the same time. "Dad! Um...wh-what are you doing home so soon? I-I thought you and Mom were going for coffee—"

Before she could finish, Cash brushed past her and seized Brian by the front of his black T-shirt. With one hand, he hauled the kid to his feet. "I asked you a question. What are you doing with my daughter?"

"Dad! Stop!" Amber cried as she tried to wedge herself between them. The coffee table turned over during the scuffle. "Don't hurt him. It's not his fault!"

Cash ignored her plea and nudged her out of harm's way. He confronted Brian's defiant glare as they stood nose to nose.

"Take your hands off me, Mr. MacKenzie!" Brian backed away, straining his shirt as far as the black fabric would stretch.

"I warned you to stay away from her."

"I didn't touch your precious daughter!"

Amber began to sob as the confrontation between Cash and Brian escalated to heated threats and shouting. "Stop it! Stop it!"

With a tear-streaked face, the girl threw her arms around her mother. "Do something, Mom. Make them stop before someone gets hurt!"

Libby gave her daughter a reassuring hug then broke away and gripped Cash by the arm again with both hands. "Settle down, Cash, or you're liable to do something you'll regret."

"I've already done something I regret—not taking action the first time I caught him hanging all over my daughter," he bit off each word without taking his gaze off Brian. "This is between him and me."

"No, it isn't. This is a family matter and right now, you're not behaving like a responsible head of this household. Stop acting like the hothead you were at eighteen and exercise control!"

Cash froze, his gaze switching from Brian to the death grip she held on his arm. He looked her in the eyes. "I should have known that if it came down to a choice, you'd take *his* side."

He released his hold on Brian and turned to her. "Ever since you met Amber, you've been trying to gain her confidence and draw her away from me by condoning her obsession," he pointed at Brian, "over him. Don't deny it, Libby." He shoved his hand into his pocket, pulled out a purple square, and held it up between his fingers. "I've got the proof right here."

Amber gasped. "Dad, where did you—"

"What proof? What are you talking about?" Libby looked down to see what he held in his hand.

"I don't know where you got that," she said, suddenly realizing what he'd flashed in front of her face, "but I've never seen it before and I'm disappointed in your accusation. After all, that's happened between us in the last three weeks, you should know by now that I'd never influence Amber to compromise her values! Why don't you trust me?"

"Time and time again, I've tried to trust you, but you say one thing and do another." Cash swept back the panels of his black blazer, gripping his hands on his hips. Disillusionment and regret threaded his voice. "I knew it would take a lot of adjustment, but I wanted to believe the three of us could make it as a family. Why do you think I asked you tonight to marry me? I offered you the chance to start over, to take my name and become my wife for better or for worse, but you're not interested in what you consider a mere *job*."

Libby winced at hearing their private conversation made public. She saw the astonishment on her daughter's face and knew how difficult it would be now to make Amber understand her reasons for declining his proposal. "Cash, don't—"

"The only thing you want from me is Amber," he continued bitterly, "but I won't let her go." The rugged lines on his handsome face were etched with anger and pain. "She's been the center of my life ever since you wrote her out of yours, and I'm not letting you turn her away from me by pitting me against *him,* not now...or ever."

In a surprising show of support, Brian moved to Libby's side, as if to defend and protect her.

"That's enough, Cash," Libby said. "You've made it plain that you're upset—"

"Yes, I'm upset—because I should have known better. Everything you've said or done since we met at Sandhill has been for one purpose only; you're determined to get your daughter back, no matter what it takes. You said so yourself."

For a moment, Libby could only stare at him, stunned. "That's not true," she replied in astonishment. "I'd never do anything to turn Amber against you!"

"Your actions speak for themselves. I knew that you condoned Amber's friendship with him over my objections, but I still chose to give you the benefit of the doubt. I should have followed my instincts instead of putting up with your interference." He pointed toward the door. "Go home, Olivia. We both need some time to think about what this means and how we're going to proceed from now on."

"No, Cash. I can't imagine where you got such a ridiculous idea, but you're wrong, and I'm not leaving until we straighten out this misunderstanding."

"I have nothing more to say about it tonight. I'm tired and I just can't take any more family strife. I need some time to decide on my next move."

He motioned to Brian with his thumb. "I never want to see your face on my property again. Do you hear me? Get out of here before I change my mind and call the police."

Amber ran to Libby and threw her arms around her mother. "Please, don't go! Don't give up, Mom. You have to make Dad see that he's wrong about you—" She raised her hand toward Brian, "And about you, too."

Cash came up behind her and gripped his daughter's arms, pulling her out of Libby's embrace. "Please, go," he said to Libby. "I'd like to talk to my daughter *alone*."

"Mom, don't leave!" Amber pleaded and started to cry.

Libby struggled to hold back the tears stinging the backs of her eyes. "I'm sorry, honey. Don't cry. This is all a misunderstanding, but we'll get it straightened out. I won't give up on you like my family—" She cut a pointed look at Cash then turned back to Amber, "—and others gave up on me." Her throat thickened. "I promise."

"Brian, don't believe him! It's not your fault. It's mine!" Amber cried.

Through blurred eyes, Libby made eye contact with Brian and started for the door, knowing that Cash meant what he'd said about calling the police on the boy. Brian reached the door first. He opened it and stood waiting for her.

"I hate you! I hate you!"

Libby spun around in time to see Amber break away from Cash and race upstairs to her bedroom. At the top of the stairs, she shouted, "I love Brian, and I'm going to be with him, no matter what you say!" She ran into her room and slammed the door.

Libby stumbled out of the house and stopped on the porch, staring up at the sky. The cloudy night seemed bright compared to the darkness plaguing her heart.

Behind her, Brian paused on the threshold. "I know you won't believe this, Mr. MacKenzie," he announced to Cash in a bold voice, "but I didn't show up here to take advantage of Amber."

"You're right," Cash thundered, "I don't."

Brian shut the door and silently moved past her, stepping off the porch. At the bottom porch step, he turned around and offered his hand to assist her.

"I'm sorry about what happened, Ms. Cunningham. I never meant to cause you any trouble and neither did Amber. She loves you. I know because ever since she met you, she hasn't stopped talking about what a cool person you are. She's so happy she found you."

Libby opened her mouth to speak, but only a tiny sob escaped as a tight knot formed in her stomach. Brian's words should have been a soothing balm to her soul. Instead, she couldn't stop remembering the crushed look on Amber's face when Cash accused her of rejecting his marriage proposal. Amber's happiness meant more to her than anything else in the world. Would she ever stop failing to be there for her daughter?

Brian gave her a brief hug as if to console her. "Amber's old man shouldn't have characterized you the way he did. It's not true."

"What isn't, Brian?" she managed to say.

"Everything he said about you." Brian walked across the small patch of the front lawn, heading in the direction of the high school. "Goodbye, Ms. Cunningham."

Libby held up her hand and waved him off, even though he didn't look back. She couldn't speak and cry at the same time.

*   *   *

Cash awoke in the darkness with a start. He thought he'd heard a car pull up to the house, but didn't know if he'd imagined it, or if one had truly awakened him. Raising his shoulders off the bed, he turned his head just enough to squint at his alarm clock. The LCD showed 1 am.

Expelling a weary sigh, he lowered his head back down to the pillow and placed one arm over his eyes. Something still didn't seem quite right, but it took a while before he realized that his body lay spread-eagled across the bed, fully clothed. He didn't even remember lying down, much less falling asleep.

Suddenly that annoying Cocker Spaniel next door screamed as though something had scared the wits out of the silly mutt.

"Wouldn't take much..." he muttered. Fully awake now, he rubbed his hands over his face and sat up. Now he remembered...

Even before Libby and Brian Hanson left the house, his head had started to throb. The stress of dealing with everything had given him a nasty headache and a queasy sensation in the pit of his stomach. He'd taken something for the pain and stretched out on his bed, hoping to ride it out when he'd fallen asleep.

Fighting back nausea, he went into the hallway and descended the stairs in his stocking feet to get a bottle of lemon-lime flavored water. The house seemed eerily quiet as he padded across the wood floor of the dining room.

In the kitchen, he stood at the open refrigerator, trying to focus his eyes clear enough to read the labels on the bottles when a familiar sound caught his attention. He stopped and listened for a moment. There it went again—a mewing sound. Curious, he stepped toward the back door and peered through the rectangular window. Muffin, Amber's gray and white cat, sat perched on the wooden porch railing, waiting for someone to let him in the house.

"That's odd," he muttered as he turned the knob. "This door isn't locked." Muffin dived off the railing and landed on the shoe mat with a solid thud. Then he ambled into the kitchen and arched against Cash's pant leg, purring like a finely-tuned engine. Cash reached down to ruffle the cat's thick, soft fur. "What are you doing outside in the middle of the night, mister?" Thinking back, he remembered nearly tripping over the fuzzy critter at the top of the stairs when he'd come up to his bedroom to lie down.

Muffin ducked under Cash's hand and made a beeline to his dish. Cash looked down at the animal feasting hungrily and scratched his head. The food looked untouched. Muffin always helped himself to a bedtime snack and frequent snacks thereafter. That's how he managed to stay 'round as a muffin.' How long had the fur ball been outdoors?

A passing thought whizzed through his head—and boomeranged right back.

Muffin ended up on the porch with the help of only one person. Amber must have accidentally let him outside...*on her way out.*

He slammed the bottle on the granite countertop so hard the carbonated water shot through the opening like a geyser, scaring Muffin and causing him to scuttle under the dining room table. Ignoring the splatter on his shirt, Cash charged out of the kitchen, dashed through the house, and took the stairs three at a time to reach Amber's room. He threw open her door and flipped on the light.

Nothing happened.

He groped around in the dark until he found the reading lamp on her desk and touched the brass base, flooding the room with soft light.

Her bed looked rumpled as usual but empty. The door to her bathroom, however, gaped open. He poked his head inside and turned on the light. Cosmetics, clothes, and long strands of dark hair covered the closet-sized space, but he didn't find Amber.

She's with him, Cash thought, and recalled the last words Amber had shouted before locking herself in her room.

"I'm going to be with him, no matter what you say!"

Panicking, he ran back downstairs and lit out the kitchen door, combing the area for any sign of her or Brian Hanson's red Grand Am. His search turned up nothing.

"Stay calm," he told himself, gasping for breath as he trudged through the backyard, tramping through the dew-covered grass in his stocking feet. "She's okay. She's okay." He went back into the house, peeled off his muddy, wet socks, and went straight into the den. In the darkness of the small room, he groped for the pull chain on his banker's lamp and turned on the light. He punched in Amber's cell number on his desk phone and collapsed into his office chair as he waited, gripping the edge of the desk mat with white-knuckled fingers.

The call went straight to voicemail. "It's Dad," he said after the beep. "Where have you gone? Call me, honey bear. *NOW.* I'm worried about you." He hung up and redialed the number, got the voicemail greeting again, and left another urgent message.

He repeated the process two more times before giving up. Why wouldn't she answer her phone? Did something...happen to her? The thought of Amber being out all night with *that kid* sent his imagination into a frenzy.

The slamming of a car door brought him back to his feet, hopeful his phone messages had yielded results. He raced to the living room and peered through the sheer curtains veiling the oval glass in the front door. The driveway and street in front of his house sat empty. The sound must have been generated from a neighboring house. Discouraged, he turned away from the window and slumped against the wall, rubbing his eyes with the heels of his hands.

"Dear God, I can't stand not knowing where Amber is or if she's all right. Tell me what to do!"

Call Libby.

The words filled his head as distinctly as though someone had spoken directly to him. He pushed himself away from the wall and looked around.

"Hello? Todd, is that you?" No one answered. He wheeled around and jerked open the front door. "Who's there?" Again, no one answered. Confused, he shut the door and marched back into the den.

He used the desk phone to call Todd's cell, but after four rings, the call went to voicemail. Cash disconnected the line, not in any mood to leave an SOS message. Didn't people answer their phones anymore?

Call Libby.

The words ricocheted through his head again, giving him momentary hope. Perhaps Amber had gone to her mother's house, or at least called to let Libby know of her whereabouts!

Desperate, he picked up the receiver again and punched in Libby's number.

She answered on the second ring. "Hello?" The word came out in a muffled whisper, as though she'd been crying.

"Is Amber with you?"

"What?" Libby sounded confused. "Amber? I don't understand. What do you—"

"She's gone." He tried to suppress the worry in his voice, but he couldn't conceal it. "I don't know what time she snuck out of the house, but if she's not with you then it's my guess she's gone somewhere with Brian Hanson."

"Are you sure?" Libby sounded completely coherent now and beginning to panic. "How do you know she's with him? Did you talk to her?"

"She's not answering her phone and if she's not with you, then where else would she go?"

"I have no idea. Cash, I haven't talked to her since I left your house."

The subtle reference to their last conversation created an awkward silence. He swallowed hard, finding it difficult to ask her for support after the things he'd said to her last night. He shouldn't have taken out his frustration on her—

"What can I do to help?" she asked, obviously choosing to let it go.

"Try to get a hold of her and talk her into coming home." He let out a tired sigh. "She's not taking my calls. If she doesn't answer her phone or call you back, stay home and wait. Perhaps she'll eventually show up at your house."

"Okay, I'll try to find out where she is, and if I do, I'll go and get her myself."

"Thanks, Libby. I appreciate it."

"And Cash..." The resolve in her voice put him on notice. "When Amber comes home, the three of us are going to sit down together—I don't care what time it is—and have an honest, open discussion about all of our issues. We're putting everything on the table and if it turns out that we can't resolve some concerns, we're going to pursue family counseling. No more arguing over who's in charge or which parent knows best. The focus is going to be on our daughter and how much we love her. Amber's disappearance is more than a wake-up call; it's a cry for help and her message is coming through, loud, and clear. She needs us more than ever."

Her voice, threaded with quiet determination, told him that things were about to change again, but this time he didn't object—because he knew she was right. She'd been right all along...

"Yes, Amber is all that matters," Cash said solemnly. "I agree with everything you're saying, but all I can think about right now is bringing her home."

"Fair enough," she replied, sounding relieved. "We'll talk about this again after we find Amber."

"All right…and, ah, Libby…"

"What?"

"I'm sorry for losing my temper earlier. I should have listened to you instead of letting anger get the best of me. If I had, we wouldn't be dealing with this crisis."

"We all need improvement in that area and I think it should be the first item on our family agenda," she said firmly.

"I agree. Talk to you soon. Bye." He hung up the phone, relieved to get that off his chest.

Almost immediately, the desk phone jingled. Without looking at the number, he snatched up the receiver again.

"Amber?"

"It's me, Todd. You rang?"

"Yeah." His voice sounded hoarse, strained as he rubbed the back of his neck. "Amber's gone."

"Gone?" Todd paused tentatively, as though distracted. "What do you mean, she's gone?"

"She snuck out again. I've left message after message, but she's not answering her phone. I'm worried about her."

"What did you two argue about this time?"

"It doesn't matter now. Are you busy?" He had no idea why he'd asked that absurd question, given the fact that the clock on his desk read 1:40 am.

"Yeah, sort of…"

Cash hesitated. Todd never mentioned having late-night plans tonight—except to eat again. "Are you having pizza right now?"

"Nope," Todd answered with a contented note in his voice. "I'm at the

Cake and Steak with Medley. We've just finished breakfast."

Cash didn't know what to make of that. A few hours ago, Todd had vigorously claimed 'that woman' drove him crazy, but since dinner, they'd been inseparable. "I just wanted to find out if, by chance, Amber had contacted you."

"Sorry, Cash, but I haven't talked to her since we left your house. We straightened up the kitchen and left at about eight-thirty. Medley and I have been here ever since, drinking coffee and reading the Bible together."

Reading the Bible together? Cash couldn't believe his ears. *What's next,* he thought, *an engagement party?*

"Have you called your *ex?*" Todd asked, breaking into his thoughts. "Amber might be with her. If not, Libby should be told about it."

"She's not my—" Cash started to say 'not my ex' then decided to let it go. Todd couldn't seem to get his facts straight, anyway. "I've already called Libby and she hasn't seen or heard from Amber, either."

Todd's words sounded muffled as he held his hand over the phone. After a few moments, he came back on the line. "If you're sure Amber has taken off then we've got to start looking for her. Sit tight. We're coming over. And hey, stop worrying, okay? We'll find her."

Todd hung up, leaving Cash with nothing to do but pace the house and stress out until they arrived.

Restless and plagued with 'what if' thoughts, he paced from room to room, trying to shake off an increasing feeling of foreboding. The clock in the living room chimed the half-hour, echoing a hollow tune through the house as he waited nervously for Amber to call back. After a couple of minutes of wearing a path on the floor, he wandered back into the den and parked himself on the sofa. Dropping his head into his hands, he began massaging his throbbing temples.

With nothing else to do but think, his mind replayed tense situations with Amber over the last couple of weeks.

"I shouldn't have vented my frustration upon her after the concert," he murmured, feeling like a total failure, "or that night Libby caught her sneaking out of the house." He exhaled a long sigh as a wave of remorse swept over him. "We used to be a rock-solid family. What's happened to us?" Nothing mattered anymore except regaining closeness with Amber, and the mutual trust and respect for each other they once held.

His gaze fell upon Amber's picture sitting on his desk. He gripped the phone, ready to call the police and report Brian Hanson for violating city curfew with a sixteen-year-old girl when he heard someone pounding on the front door.

Dear God, he thought as his heart slammed against his ribcage, *don't let it be the police bringing bad news...*

He rushed to the door, flipped on the porch light, and peered through the sheer curtains.

Brian Hanson stood there. Alone.

Cash couldn't believe his eyes. Given the scene in his living room a couple of hours ago, Brian Hanson ranked as the last person he expected to find banging on his door in the middle of the night. Instead of his low-riders and T-shirt, the kid now wore khaki pants and a tan polo shirt. Despite his long hair, his solemn air and stylish clothes made him look older and surprisingly, more mature.

Cash swung the door open wide. "Where is she?" He moved his bulky frame into the doorway and visually searched the surrounding area. "Where's my daughter?"

The tall, brown-haired youth didn't even flinch at the demand in Cash's voice. "That's what I've come to talk to you about."

"I don't negotiate with you or anyone else where she's concerned," Cash said in a low, level voice. "I want her back home—now!"

"I hear you loud and clear," Brian replied, boldly staring at Cash, "but I can't make her do anything she doesn't want to do. She's a control freak. Just like you."

Cash's heart nearly slammed out of his chest. "Get in here and explain what you're talking about. I want a straight answer." His voice shook. "What have you done with her?"

"Nothing, sir. I don't know where Amber is right now," Brian said in a steady voice, "but I know what she's doing. That's why I'm here. I want to help her."

"What do you mean you don't know where she is?" Cash studied him suspiciously. "What is she doing?"

"She's looking for me."

Fantastic... Cash thought anxiously. "If you don't know where she is, how do you know she's looking for you?"

"She's sending me a text message every ten minutes. She keeps begging me to run away with her." A loud beep-beep interrupted them. Brian dug into his pants pocket and pulled out his iPhone. "She just left another one."

Cash's heart crashed to his knees at the thought of Amber running away. He held out his hand. "Let me see that." Brian hesitated at first then handed over his expensive toy.

Cash started pressing buttons, trying to call her back.

"Don't do that," Brian said and thrust out his palm to recover his iPhone. "She's really upset with you. If she finds out I'm here, she'll think I've double-crossed her."

The gizmo suddenly rang. Ignoring Brian's warning, Cash pressed a button and shoved the phone to his ear. "Amber? Amber, this is Dad. Don't hang up, honey, please. Let's talk—"

The buzz of a disconnected line roared in his ear. "Amber? Amber!" He held the phone at an arm's length and stared at it in confusion. "She cut me off." He hit the redial. It rang until her voicemail message played. He repeated his earlier message to call him on his personal cell phone then reluctantly returned the device to Brian.

The kid refrained from commenting, but the look in his eyes made it clear he wanted to say, "I told you so."

"You did the right thing by letting me know," Cash said, forcing himself to calm down, "but I'm curious. Why aren't you calling her back?"

"I don't want to come between you and her. I simply want to be her friend."

The kid's reply floored him, but before Cash could get a word in, Brian answered his unspoken question. "My girlfriend gets jealous when Amber hangs on me."

"If you have a girlfriend, what were you doing in my house lying on my sofa with my daughter?"

Brian shoved the iPhone deep into his trouser pocket and boldly stared back. "I made a mistake and let her pull me down on the couch, thinking we were going to sit and talk, but that's not what she had in mind. I didn't want to get her into trouble when you walked in, so I kept my mouth shut and took the blame."

Cash's brows shot up in disbelief.

"It's not the first time I've covered for her."

"I see," Cash said with fresh skepticism. "Tell me why you've 'covered' for her."

"I really like her. She's a beautiful girl." Brian's jaw tensed. "No offense intended, sir, but...she's also pretty spoiled."

Taken aback, Cash refrained from commenting. He wanted to hear the kid's version of the story first.

"One of my friends introduced us during the first week of school. After that, every time I went to my locker I'd find her hanging around, waiting for me." Brian glanced down at the class ring on his right hand. "I never gave her this ring. She asked to look at it and then wouldn't give it back until the night you saw us together at the football game. You blamed me for being a bad influence on her, but I never encouraged her to skip school or stop doing her homework." He glared at Cash. "I didn't bother to argue with you because I knew you wouldn't believe me, anyway.

"After you told me to stay away from her," Brian continued, "I didn't want any trouble so I decided to cool it with her and instead got interested in someone else. When I told Amber that I just wanted to be friends, she became upset— wouldn't accept that I liked another girl. She started texting me all the time and following me around."

Cash took a deep breath, afraid of what else he might hear, but knowing he had to find out. "Did you, by any chance, have detention on Wednesday a couple of weeks ago?"

"Yeah," Brian said and rolled his eyes. "I worked the night before and didn't have time to get my homework done so I had to do it before school. I didn't notice the time and ended up getting detention for being late. Amber purposely got caught skipping class so she could sit next to me. She got a charge out of doing it." He shook his head, as though the episode irritated him. "I just wanted to do my time and get out of there."

Headlights flashed through the glass in the front door. Expecting to see Todd pulling into the driveway, Cash walked over to it and pulled back the sheer curtain. The car passed by. He let go of the curtain and turned around. "I'm still waiting to hear why you were covering for her tonight."

Brian looked indignant, as though he found the whole episode ridiculous. "She started bugging me at school today to pick her up after some dinner she had to cook for her birthday," he said, keeping his manner civil. "She planned to sneak out after you went to bed. When she called tonight, I said I had a date, but she started to cry and begged me to come over right away or I'd spoil her birthday." He gripped his hands on his hips. "I didn't know she would be alone. As soon as I walked in the door, I told her about my new girlfriend. She started to cry again and it made me feel like a real jerk. When I put my arm around her to console her, she pulled me down on the sofa and started kissing me. That's when you walked in."

Something didn't quite add up here. Either this kid had a gift for lying or he knew of a side to Amber that Cash had never seen. Suddenly Amber's words echoed through his head. *"Brian, don't believe him! It's not your fault. It's mine!"*

Maybe he had never wanted to see it...

Emotionally drained, Cash closed his eyes and rubbed the back of his neck. "Why didn't you tell me this right away?"

"I told you," Brian replied, his voice rising a notch. "I didn't want to get Amber into trouble."

The words 'get Amber into trouble' made Cash shiver inside. Nevertheless, he pulled the purple package from his pocket and shoved it in

Brian's face. "How did she get her hands on this little goodie? Did you give it to her?"

"Don't blame that on me!" Brian's grayish-green eyes narrowed as he shoved Cash's hand away from his face.

"Then where did she get it?"

"It's a status symbol in school. Some girls flash 'em around to make the guys think they're cool, but I'm not impressed by that. Amber traded lunch money to one of *those* girls for it. When she showed it to me, I told her she didn't need to play that game to attract a guy. She just needed to be herself."

The kid didn't know it, but his levelheaded answer had elevated him several notches in Cash's eyes. It also made Cash realize that he'd wrongly accused Libby. A spark of regret pierced his heart, but he didn't have time to dwell on it.

He meant to question Brian further about Amber's situation at school when Todd's Hummer roared into the driveway. Within seconds, Todd strode into the house with Medley in tow. Todd appeared different somehow.

"Did you hear from Amber? Did she come home yet?"

When Todd saw Brian standing off to one side he raised his brows in surprise but didn't ask about the kid's presence.

Cash couldn't quite pinpoint what had changed in his best friend, but it made him wonder how Todd could be concerned about Amber yet stay so calm. He started speaking when the door burst open again and Libby rushed in. Her dark blue pea coat flapped open as she marched toward him.

"I got here as soon as I could," she cried. She glanced around at the people in his living room and when she saw Brian Hanson, she let out a loud gasp. "Where's Amber? Did she come home?"

Chapter 14

The defeated look on Cash's face confirmed Libby's worst fear. Their daughter's MIA status had not changed.

"What are you doing here?" Cash placed his hands on his hips as Libby rushed toward him. "Why aren't you at your place, waiting in case Amber comes to you? She could be knocking on your door right now."

She stopped, breathless. "I've called her a dozen times and her phone keeps defaulting to voicemail. I can't sit around, waiting for something that may not happen. I have to stay busy or I'll go crazy, so I've decided to join you in the search for her."

Cash blinked in surprise. "Who told you we were meeting here to organize a search party?"

Brian and Todd stared blankly at each other.

Medley raised her hand. "I did."

Cash turned back to Libby. "I know you're worried about her, we all are, but what if Amber shows up at your house and you're not there to let her in? Look, why don't you go home and wait for her, maybe try to get some sleep? I'll call you if she comes home or if I get any information on her whereabouts."

Sleep? How could anyone sleep at a time like this?

"If she wanted to contact me, she'd have done it by now, especially after receiving all the messages I've left her." Libby gestured toward the window and the darkness beyond. They didn't have much to go on, but she refused to give up. "Amber is out there, wandering the streets, Cash, distraught about what happened tonight. Every minute is precious. We *all* need to get moving and find her!"

He didn't answer at first, but the anguish that flashed in his eyes spoke volumes.

She pulled her cell phone from her pocket to check for any missed calls. To her disappointment, Amber had not tried to call. She looked up, focusing on Cash. "Did you call 9-1-1?"

Medley raised her hand again. "I did! The operator told me to call the non-emergency number. So, I called that number and an officer took down the information, but he told me that they don't file a report until the person has been gone for twenty-four hours." She looked apologetically at Cash. "The police aren't actively looking for Amber, but if they happen to cross paths with her, she'll be taken straight to the juvenile detention center for being out after curfew."

"She's all I have, Cash," Libby said as her heart quaked with despair. Her greatest fear had come upon her. "If anything happens to Amber, I'll never forgive myself for not doing all I could to find her. I'm going out to search for her—and I don't care how long it takes."

"I'll help, too," Brian piped up. Until now, he'd been standing off to the side, silently watching their exchange. He briefly filled her in on the events leading him back to Cash's house. "I know of a few places where she might go to hang out."

"Thank you!" Libby smiled with relief as she approached the young man. "You probably know better than any of us where to look for her."

"I'll do everything I can to help track her down, Ms. Cunningham." He glanced away, his expression stern. "I know what it's like to search for someone in your past. You and Amber need each other."

She wondered whom he had lost, but since he hadn't willingly offered the information, she decided it would be inappropriate to ask.

That little detail didn't interfere with Medley's curiosity, though. She perked up. "Did someone in your family run away?"

"Not exactly," Brian answered with a hard glint in his eyes. "My old man just up and took off before I was born. He didn't even bother to marry my mother. A month ago, I finally tracked him down. I wanted to get to know the guy but he...ah...didn't agree. He told me he wanted to leave things just as they were."

Cash stared at the young man for a moment then looked away as though Brian's answer had struck a nerve.

"Well, I'm grateful to you for coming forward." Libby patted Brian's shoulder, not sure of what else to say. Cash's reaction puzzled her, but she let it go. "Call me Libby, please."

"Sure...Libby," Brian replied as his face brightened. Though he sported shoulder-length hair and spoke with a man's voice, Brian's smile reminded her of a sad little boy.

"Hold on." Cash wedged himself between her and Brian. "Nobody's leaving here until we strategize a plan."

A loud sniffle interrupted the discussion. Libby pivoted toward the noise and found Todd and Medley huddled together on the sofa, holding hands. Medley's eyes brimmed with tears.

"This is awful," she said and released a hiccupping sob. "Where could Amber be? I can't bear to think that my cousin's sweet little daughter might be roaming the streets all alone. If she runs into the wrong people, she might—" Her voice choked off as a round of sobs overtook her.

Todd slid his arm around her and tenderly pulled her close. "Don't cry, darling," he whispered into her hair as she buried her face in the center of his chest. "We'll find Amber and bring her back. God is watching over her. It's gonna be okay. I promise."

Libby stared with amazement, realizing that somehow in the last few hours, Todd and Medley had not only become friends but had fallen in love, too. She looked away as a wave of discomfort washed over her. Though she tried to deny it, witnessing their budding romance caused the emptiness in her own heart to grow.

She turned around to find Cash standing closely behind her. The loneliness in his eyes sent shock waves down her spine. Deep down, she wanted to reach out to him, but given the discomfort that existed between them, common sense propelled her in another direction.

"I'm going up to Amber's room," she informed everyone as she dropped her keys and purse on the coffee table and then shoved her cell phone into the front pocket of her jeans. "I want to look around to see if she left any clues as to where she might have gone." She slipped her coat off and tossed it over a nearby chair. "I want to know what's going through her mind right now." She turned toward the stairs, relieved to put some distance between her and Cash.

Her opportunity for privacy didn't last long. Like a shadow, Cash followed on her heels.

* * *

At the bottom of the stairs, Cash halted and turned toward Brian. "Get on that fancy gadget you're carrying around and call Amber, okay? Send her a text message," he waved his hand, "or whatever it is that you do with that thing to get her attention. Even if she doesn't respond, keep trying! I'll be back in a couple of minutes."

Brian held up his iPhone as he dropped into a sofa chair. "Will do, Mr. MacKenzie."

Cash took the stairs three at a time to catch up to Libby. He'd already walked through Amber's room and failed to find anything useful but admitted to himself that he could have overlooked something. If he did, Libby would find such a thing. Nothing slipped past her.

Besides, he needed to get away from the lovebirds downstairs. What had gotten into them, anyway? How two opposite strangers could literally fall in love overnight proved beyond his comprehension. He didn't know why it bothered him. After all, Todd possessed the right to find his true love and live happily ever after.

Putting the thought out of his mind, he crossed the hallway and entered Amber's bedroom. Libby stood in the center of the square room on a chair, tightening the light bulb in the ceiling. The bulb flashed on. Without a word, she dismounted and put the chair back where it belonged then went to Amber's ivory-toned chest of drawers and began emptying items from the girl's backpack.

He stood in the doorway for a moment and stared at the ceiling, wondering how she knew the bulb merely needed tightening. Curious...

He watched Libby pull out a couple of wire-bound notebooks and slowly page through the top one. She stopped and stared at it for a few moments, as though trying to keep herself together.

"Libby, what's—"

"Look at this," she said in astonishment, cutting him off. She thrust the open notebook toward him. Amber's artistic handwriting, penned across the cover in red metallic gel ink, revealed a secret that saddened him.

"Mr. and Mrs. MacKenzie," he said, reading Amber's doodling aloud, "Libby MacKenzie, Libby Cunningham-MacKenzie." Stars and a happy face made the second name stand out as the one that obviously garnered her approval. He looked up. "Did you ever do silly things like this in high school?" Once the question came out, he regretted his impulsiveness, but for some reason, he still wanted to know.

If she found his boldness inappropriate, she didn't say so. Instead, she stared at the notebook. "I used to sit in study hall and tattoo your name all over everything I owned, including my tennis shoes." She gave him an odd look. "I even painted it on my wrist with gold eyeliner..." After setting aside the notebook, she looked into the backpack again, pulled out a calculator stuck to a half-eaten candy bar, and gingerly set it on a used piece of notebook paper on the dresser.

Absorbing that piece of information, Cash grabbed the notebook and flipped it open. Inside he found more doodling gems, namely a rough sketch of Amber's birthday dinner invitation and a mock wedding invitation. From this, he concluded that Amber must have assumed her brilliant plan of a one-on-one dinner party for her parents would be the deciding factor to bring them together. He winced with guilt over the things he'd said about Libby in front of Amber, knowing his words must have destroyed her fragile hope for the future.

He held out the page with the wedding invitation. "Did you see this?"

"Of course, I did." Libby dumped the remainder of the backpack onto the top of the dresser. "It didn't surprise me, either. I read between the lines last week when I opened my invitation to dinner. I should have turned her down flat instead of putting up with Medley's interference!"

"I got the same pressure from Todd." He handed the notebook back to her. "At least you and I agree on one thing."

She shoved it back into Amber's bag. "What's that?"

"We should have followed our instincts instead of adhering to the expectations of others."

They gazed into each other's eyes for what seemed like the longest, most unsettling moment Cash could remember. He thought he had complete control of his emotions but instead found himself locked into her clear, twilight-blue gaze as that old, familiar ache tugged at his soul. He suddenly wondered how things would have turned out back when they were kids if they had listened to their hearts instead of allowing others to control their destinies.

As if reading his thoughts, she let out a sigh of exhaustion. "We're wasting precious time. Let's hurry up."

He broke eye contact with her and turned away, poking his head into Amber's closet. He had no idea what to look for but hoped to find something that might aid their search.

The closet overflowed with clothes, shoes, purses, stuffed animals, and a box filled with old board games, but nothing that would give him any idea where she could have gone. He backed out of the cluttered space and straightened his spine, emitting a small groan in the process. Libby had moved rapidly, exploring the bathroom, the dressers, and now proceeded to look through the files on Amber's computer. Only one place remained to search. He dropped to his knees to look under the bed, expecting to find nothing other than a few dust bunnies.

He couldn't have been more wrong.

Libby's voice pierced the air in puzzlement. "What are you doing?"

"Looking for the floor," he answered dryly as he pulled out clothes, shoes, books, pens, and wads of crumpled notebook paper. Then he found a bowl half-full of cereal with the milk dried in the bottom and the spoon glued to it. He held it up. "I can't imagine how long this has been setting under there." Next, he pulled out a plate containing a pair of rock-hard bread crusts, an empty taco chip bag, a pizza box, and an open can of soda that he almost spilled.

He held up a tattered address book. "I've been wondering what happened to this..."

Crawling under the bed again, he saw something dark and flat propped against the wall, as though it had slipped off the backside of the bed at some point and dropped on one end to the floor. Extending his arm, he reached toward the wall and grasped it. To his surprise, he pulled out a large, thin book. He brushed the dust off it and turned it over. "What is she doing with *this*?"

At the sound of his voice, Libby swiveled in the desk chair. "What did you find?"

Cash held it up for her to observe. "It's my senior yearbook." He stood up. "I didn't know it still existed."

"I remember that. Let me see it." She extended her hand to take the black, leather-bound book. "Maybe she picked it out of a box in your basement."

"No, that's impossible. She couldn't have found it in my house. I haven't seen that book since I graduated."

"Then where did it come from?"

Cash thought for a moment. "She must have come across it at my parents' home when we were helping them clean out the house for their estate sale."

"That still doesn't make sense to me." Libby flipped through the shiny pages, perusing memories of days past. "Why would she take it without telling you? For that matter, what would she want with a dusty old tome filled with nerdy pictures of your classmates?"

She turned to a page with the corner folded. They both saw the section Amber had marked and stared at each other as realization dawned. "That's it!" They said in unison.

Todd's baritone voice boomed from the living room.

Cash stuck his head outside Amber's bedroom door. "What did you say?"

"Did you find what you were looking for?"

"That depends. We'll be right down."

*   *   *

Libby followed Cash downstairs to join the others in the living room. She knew without a doubt why Amber secretly kept the book and how Amber's discovery of certain facts contained within its ivory pages had changed the course of their lives. However, questions remained and the more she thought about it, the more upset she became. Why had someone purposely kept Amber's knowledge of the book from her? That person had some heavy explaining to do!

Todd pointed to the book nestled under Cash's arm. "What have you got there?"

Cash sat in the sofa chair next to Brian and opened up the aging volume. "It's my high school yearbook." He pointed to Brian's iPhone. "Any luck?"

"Not yet." He lay stretched out in the chair with both feet resting flat on the floor, holding his phone with both hands as he rapidly typed a text message. "I'll keep trying."

Libby took the remaining spot on the sofa. Her mouth went dry with apprehension as Cash thumbed through the pages. He found the section he wanted and held it up for the group to examine. Everyone leaned forward to gaze at a black and white picture of the sophomore class president, Medley Grant, and her cousin, Libby Cunningham in a foods class, demonstrating how to make chocolate-dipped strawberries. Under Libby's half of the picture, Libby had written a personal note to Cash, expressing her longing for the day when they would be 'together forever' and hinting with excitement over the 'secret' they shared. She'd signed the passage, added "I LOVE YOU" underneath it in capital letters, and encircled it with gold stars.

"Now I know how Amber found out about Libby," Cash announced. "What I don't know is how much more information she's acquired." He focused on Brian. "Do you have anything to say about this?"

"Amber wanted help locating someone. What's the big deal?" Brian sat up. The phone dropped into his lap as he held up his palms in defense. "I researched the information on the Internet and supplied her with the number to a beauty salon, that's all."

Just as Libby expected, the answer fell into place with startling clarity. She leaned past Todd to get a good look at the guilt on her cousin's face. "Medley, when did you plan to tell me the truth?"

Medley's face flushed deep scarlet, her eyes spilling over with new tears. "I'm sorry, Libby! I meant to tell you everything, but you kept encountering so many problems with Amber and Cash that the right time to talk about it never came along."

Libby's heart began to race. Knowing what Medley knew might have eliminated a few problems. Then again, it might have caused even more. "Don't worry about that now." She placed her hand over her cousin's trembling fingers and squeezed them. "Just tell me what happened."

"You know how much I believe in happy endings," Medley began with a catch in her voice, "especially where you're concerned. I've always believed in my heart that one day I'd help you to find your daughter. So..."

She blotted her eyes with a clump of tissue.

Todd reached over and with his thumb, cleaned off a smudge of makeup from her cheek. "Take your time, darling."

The room fell quiet as everyone waited to hear her story.

She straightened and sat forward. "One day this beautiful young girl showed up in my chair at the shop, identifying herself as Amber MacKenzie. Of course, the name sparked my interest. You know how I am. I always act nonchalant while giving people the third degree, but this time I couldn't get a word in edgewise." She sniffled loudly and wiped her rosy nose. "Instead she kept grilling *me*. She already knew my identity from the yearbook." Medley gestured toward Brian, "and the information that he supplied to her from the Internet."

"How much did she know about me?" Libby pointed at the book now lying open on the coffee table. "I mean, other than what she learned from the things I wrote."

Medley daintily cleared her throat. "Actually, she knew very little. That's why she made the appointment to see me. She got ahold of your old address out west and sent you a letter, but it came back undeliverable. She didn't know you had recently moved back here."

Cash stood up. "Before we go any farther, I want to clarify something." He stood ramrod straight, his hands gripping the waistband of his jeans. "I didn't plan to withhold information from Amber about her mother, but at the time of her adoption, my parents pressured me to wait until she turned eighteen. They were adamant about sheltering her from what happened, and truthfully, I didn't know how to explain all that to a child, anyway, so I agreed. She grew up happy and well-adjusted under the circumstances and I assumed things would go as planned. I never expected her to discover her mother's identity on her own."

"She doesn't blame you for not telling her." Brian turned to Cash. "She's always suspected something bad happened because no one in your family would talk about the past." He turned his attention to Libby. "When she saw your picture there," he pointed to the book, "she needed to find out for herself."

Libby reached over and picked up the book. "Medley, what did you tell her about me?"

Medley grabbed her purse off the floor. "Name, rank, and serial number only," she replied as she opened it and dug around inside. "Seriously, Lib, Amber asked a lot of questions and I wanted to tell her everything, but I knew she should get the story directly from you." Medley found a travel-sized pack of tissues and pulled one out. "Amber had already discovered you were her mother. She just used me to confirm it."

Libby shut the book, placed it back on the table, and stood. "All this time I've believed I had to press in for her friendship when all along she was actually pursuing me." In the back of her mind, she wondered now if Amber's phone call from detention was a calculated move to connect with her rather than a convenient escape from the weather. She reached over to pull her coat off the back of Cash's chair. "I need to find my daughter, and when I do, I will never allow anything to come between us again."

Brian jumped off his chair and pulled the coat from her hands to assist her.

"Todd," Cash said as he dug into his front jean pocket and pulled out his keys, "you and Medley can cover the university campus. Take the river road, go past the I-35W bridge and check out the parks along that way. Amber knows that area well because every summer we ride our bikes along there."

"Gotcha," Todd replied and slipped his arm around Medley's tiny waist. "We'll grab some coffee at Sleepy's and head out. Where are you going?"

"I'm probably going to cover the grid downtown."

Cash turned to Brian. "You said you wanted to help. It's your call. What area do you want to take?"

Brian guided Libby's coat over her shoulders. "I'm going to check out the caves down by the river. I also know of a couple of abandoned grain elevators that kids have broken into. Both places are popular for parties or just hanging out. If we don't find her by tomorrow, I'll keep an eye on a few pizza places and the restaurant across the street from my apartment building. I'll let you know if I get any leads on her."

That sounded like a good plan to Libby. "I'm coming with you," she said to him and grabbed her purse and keys.

"Sorry, Libby, but I'd better go alone," Brian replied as he walked to the door. "Some of the places I'm going to host a rough crowd and I'd just as soon not have to worry about watching your back, too."

"Don't fret over me," she insisted as she hurried after him. "I can take care of myself!"

"He's right." Cash caught her by the elbow and reversed her momentum, pulling her to his side. "You'd better come with me."

"See ya." Brian nodded gravely and turned away.

Cash let go of Libby and trailed Brian to the door. He extended his hand. "Thanks for stepping up and offering information about Amber. You showed real courage coming back here after I chased you off my property."

Brian listened soberly to Cash's little speech as they shook hands. "Amber's my friend and I care about her a lot, but the way things are going it's obvious she needs a big brother to look out for her. I don't mind being that guy. I don't want anything to happen to her."

"You're a good kid, Brian. Look, ah..." Cash's wide chest heaved as he drew in a deep breath and raked his hand through his thick black hair. "I need to apologize for getting rough on you earlier. I stepped out of line and said some inappropriate things. You didn't deserve to be treated that way."

Brian nodded. "There's no offense taken, Mr. MacKenzie. I'd probably act the same way if I had a teenage daughter."

"From now on, call me Cash, okay?" He opened the door, but stood with his hand on the handle, blocking the kid's way. He seemed hesitant, nervous. "Say, ah, I've got an idea. How would you like to go fishing sometime with me?"

Brian stared at him, obviously flattered by the offer, though stunned. "S-sure, but I don't have any gear."

"Don't worry about that." Cash flashed a crooked grin and stepped out of Brian's way. "I've got a boat and enough gear for both of us." He angled his head in Todd's direction. "Him, too."

"Sounds like a good time. I'd like that a lot. Thanks!"

"Good. As soon as things get back to normal around here we'll talk again."

Smiling, Brian stepped through the doorway and shut it behind him.

Libby stood off to one side, awed but relieved by Cash's change of heart toward the boy. She didn't know what had transpired between them in her absence, but it must have been quite an encounter.

She folded her arms into a tight bow, ready to get back to business. "Why didn't you want me to go with Brian?"

"He and I both know you'll be safer riding in the truck with me." Though Cash's face showed no emotion, the gruffness in his voice indicated loud and clear that he didn't favor the idea of her going into rough neighborhoods without him.

She didn't favor the idea of tramping through rough neighborhoods, either, although, striking out on her own had briefly crossed her mind. Unfortunately, she didn't know many of Amber's friends or socializing habits. She knew she'd fare better if she joined forces with someone close to her daughter.

Todd and Medley stood up to leave.

"Did Amber plan to meet me for the first time at the game?" Libby asked as she walked Medley to the door. Todd stayed behind to discuss the details of the search with Cash.

"No! Amber wanted me to talk to Cash about meeting you, but I came up with a better idea. I wanted you and her to meet by accident instead." Medley slung her purse over her shoulder and placed her hand on the doorknob. "I didn't tell her that I'd talked you into coming to the game with me. That's why she took off with Brian. She didn't know we were there." Medley paused with a smile. "You know what? I really did remember where we parked the car. I just didn't know where Amber went!" She placed her fingers over her lips to suppress a snicker. "I made you wander all over that place looking for the Focus until we ran into her so I could introduce you. I didn't expect Cash to show up at the same time!"

Libby still had one unanswered question. She followed Medley onto the lighted porch and closed the door behind them, hoping to keep their conversation private.

"I'm curious about one more thing. Did you talk Amber into planning a birthday dinner for Cash and me?"

Medley's surprised look appeared genuine. "No, honestly, I didn't. She came up with that idea on her own."

The door opened again and Todd stepped out. He gazed at Medley with the fascination of a man newly in love. "Are you ready, darling?"

"Whenever you are," she said, but turned back to Libby. "Lib, how could you even consider my involvement in something as atrocious as that meal?"

Todd gently slipped his arm around Medley's and began pulling her down the steps.

"Don't blame me for that," Medley resumed, looking back as he guided her toward the Hummer. "When she called me about it, I volunteered to pay a caterer, but she wanted to do it all herself. I told her I'd advise her on all of the details, even the invitations, but she insisted that she had everything under control. *Not!* During dinner, I saw so many things I wanted to fix that I could hardly concentrate."

Libby couldn't remember Medley noticing anything except Todd Trisco!

Medley raised her hand to signal goodbye when Todd opened the passenger door, placed his hands around Medley's tiny waist, and lifted her into the vehicle.

"I'll call you when we find her!" She waved through the windshield as he shut the door on her words.

Libby didn't know whether to laugh or cry at this new revelation about Amber and her insistence on turning down Medley's help. She didn't have time to think about it, however, for the door opened again and Cash emerged from the house. Keys jingled as he selected one and jammed it into the lock.

"We're leaving, too," he said and gestured toward his pickup.

He walked her to the vehicle and stopped at her door, but made no effort to open it and help her get in. Instead, he stared at her, a serious frown creasing his brows. "There's something we have to do before we set out."

Libby understood immediately and turned toward him.

Cash took her hands in his and bowed his head. Libby closed her eyes and opened her heart as she joined him.

"Father God," he said gravely, "we come before you in humility and repentance. Thank you for your loving kindness and your unfailing mercy. All glory and honor are yours. We praise your holy name."

Suddenly, he stirred and Libby looked up to find Cash staring at the sky.

"We've gone through difficult times in the past, Lord, but this is without a doubt the darkest night of our lives. Please guide us and give us the ability to stay in faith through this crisis while we wait for you to bring our child home." He paused for a moment and took a deep breath as if drawing the strength to continue. "She's in your loving hands."

Cash gently squeezed her fingers, silently telling her, "*It's your turn.*"

"Heavenly Father," Libby said in a thin, high pitch, her voice barely audible as she looked up to the starry heavens. "Your Word says we can call on you in trouble and you'll answer us." She swallowed hard. "We're calling on you now to place a shield of protection around our baby and keep her safe until she comes back to us. Thank you for giving your angels charge over her. In Jesus' name..."

"Amen," they said in unison.

She tried to pull away, but Cash gently tightened his grip, keeping his fingers wrapped around hers. The gesture comforted her as they stood in silence for a few moments, listening to the hum of occasional traffic crossing the Hennepin Bridge and the ever-present roar of the water rushing over St. Anthony Falls.

"Thank you," Cash said gently, "for agreeing with me in prayer."

"I needed it as much as you did."

Her eyes suddenly stung with fresh tears. "I've waited so long to get my baby back. I can't lose her now." A rock-hard lump formed in her throat. "I love her so much!"

"We both love her." He gave her fingers a little tug. "Don't worry. God is watching over her. She's going to be all right."

Her grief bubbled over. "How could God allow this to happen in the first place?"

"He didn't let it happen. We did," Cash said in a firm, but remorseful tone. "But He will keep her safe."

Her voice thinned to a bare whisper. "I don't know how I could go on if anything happened to her."

He grasped her by the shoulders and pulled her close. "Look, don't fall apart on me now. I need you to be strong. We both need to be strong to get through this."

"I'm so scared, Cash—"

She tried to pull away, but he held her fast. "Listen to me. We will find her. We're not going give up until we do."

"What if we don't?"

"We *will*."

A silvery shaft of light from the street lamp highlighted the strong planes in his lean face. She glimpsed her own desperation mirrored in his eyes.

"I promise you," he said stubbornly, "we're going to find our little girl. This time, we're going to bring Amber home—together."

Chapter 15

Cash didn't know why, but as he drove his pickup across Nicollet Island, having Libby by his side generated poignant flashbacks of when they were teens. Back then, she'd dominated his thoughts night and day. He couldn't imagine life without her. Then one day she'd disappeared without a trace, leaving him with bittersweet memories and sending him on a quest for the child she'd left behind. That girl didn't exist anymore. She'd matured, becoming a woman he barely knew.

Then why couldn't he stop thinking about her?

He stared out the side window as he downshifted and turned onto the northbound lane of Hennepin Avenue. The night sky hosted a solid blanket of clouds. Ironically, his preferred radio station had promised that Saturday would be unseasonably hot and sunny. Though he didn't have proof, he believed in the weather forecast.

Why did he need proof to believe in Libby again?

"Do you have any idea where Amber might go this time of night?" she asked, cutting into his thoughts.

"No," he confessed. "I realize now that I should have listened better when she talked about her friends and the places where they hung out. Looking back, I realize I've spent so much time building my company, I've failed to give her the attention she deserved."

He caught Libby blinking back tears before she turned away from him to stare out her window as they crossed the bridge and drove past square, brick buildings in the Old St. Anthony Historic District.

"Where are we going?" She pointed in the opposite direction to the other side of the river. "Downtown is back that way."

"I thought we'd get some burgers to hold us over until morning." His stomach rumbled, agreeing with him. He hadn't eaten a decent meal since yesterday at lunchtime. Besides, fast food ranked high on Amber's list of eating establishments. For some crazy reason, he held out hope that he'd find her sitting in the dining area of her favorite burger place, munching on fries.

The restaurant parking lot held only two other vehicles. He turned off the truck and jumped out, planning to go inside to pick up a sack of cheeseburgers and sodas while checking for Amber. To his disappointment, however, he found the doors to the dining area locked. Only the drive-through stayed open all night.

Eager to be on his way, he made a quick trip through the drive-through and then headed back downtown.

"You'd better have something to eat," he said to Libby with a mouth full of food as he deposited the warm sack in her lap. The savory aromas of juicy burgers and crisp, salted fries filled the air. "We could be on the road for a while. You need something hot and filling to sustain your energy."

She munched on a couple of fries then set the bag on the floor and dug into her coat pocket. "I'm going to try calling Amber first."

He didn't think it would do any good but refrained from commenting as she pulled out her cell phone and pressed redial. She'd been calling Amber repeatedly with no success since they'd started out.

After another disappointing try, she shoved the apparatus into her purse. "Something's wrong with Amber's phone," she said unhappily, "otherwise, she'd answer my call. She wouldn't ignore the fact that I've called so many times!"

Knowing Amber as he did, Cash figured she probably forgot to charge the battery, but he kept that piece of information to himself. He didn't want to give Libby another reason to be upset.

He turned back onto Hennepin Avenue and crossed the bridge into downtown. Hennepin cut through the heart of the entertainment district, but in the early morning hours, the towering brick and glass buildings that housed the bars, restaurants, and theaters looked eerily deserted under the bluish-white glare of the streetlights. At the Sixth Street intersection, he spied a pair of young girls, standing on a brightly lit corner in front of a bookstore. They looked younger than Amber. He estimated the shorter one to be nine or ten. At Libby's request, he pulled over to the curb.

She rolled down her window and held up Amber's most recent school picture. "Have you seen this person?"

The girls cautiously moved a couple of steps toward the vehicle, still keeping a safe distance. The oldest one, a pretty thing with freckles and long brown hair took the picture and studied it. She shook her head and handed it back.

"What are you doing out here all by yourselves?"

"We're waiting for the bus," the younger, blonde girl answered. "We're going home."

Libby leaned slightly out the window. "Does your mother know where you are?"

The older one shook her head. "She's working."

Libby placed Amber's picture on the dash with a worried frown. "Let's stick around for a little while," she whispered to him. "I can't leave until I see them safely boarded on the bus."

The younger girl shivered and rubbed her bare arms.

Cash watched in awe as Libby slipped out of her pea coat and shoved it through the open window. "Put this on," she said to the younger one. "You're going to get sick if you aren't dressed properly." Then she reached down and grabbed the sack of burgers and fries. "Take this, too. You must be hungry." The colas went next.

Minutes later, Cash and Libby watched in relief from a hundred yards away as the girls safely boarded a city bus and, hopefully, headed for home. The thought prompted him to grab his cell phone and call the house. He urgently hoped that his own daughter had come home, too.

* * *

For the next couple of hours, Libby vigilantly kept watching for Amber as they combed the streets of downtown, block after deserted block. Every time they saw someone, they pulled to the curb and spoke to the person. She always held up Amber's picture, hoping someone would recognize her. To her dismay, no one did.

By the time they stopped for breakfast, the golden October sun had begun to pierce the horizon. Libby called Stefano's and left a message for Ron, the general manager, letting him know that she needed to take the day off for personal reasons.

Cash went into the coffee shop to get something to eat. Ten minutes later, he reappeared with a cardboard beverage carrier and a box of fresh pastries.

"I bought you the Mumbo Jumbo," he said and handed her a twenty-ounce cup of black coffee. "You've got owl eyes."

He probably meant it as a friendly comment to make her laugh, but Libby didn't take it that way. She leaned against the grill of the pickup and cautiously pried the cover off the coffee. "You would too if you were as tired as I am."

She sipped the strong liquid and looked through the clear cover of the pastry box. Her mouth watered at the sight of twin giant cinnamon rolls covered with a thick layer of fluffy white frosting.

He squinted from the bright sunlight. "Then you should go home and get some rest. There's no need for you to push yourself so hard. I'll call you if something comes up."

She almost choked on her coffee. The scalding liquid burned as it rushed down her throat. "Not on your life, MacKenzie!" She squeezed her eyes shut and swallowed in pain. "I'm sticking to you like Velcro for the duration, no matter how long it takes. I have to find my daughter!"

He stared at her as though trying to figure her out. "Then let's get going, Ms. Crabby Pants. We're wasting time." He turned away and walked around to the driver's side.

"Then let's get going, Ms. Crabby Pants. We're wasting time," she parroted under her breath as she covered her coffee again and opened her door on the passenger side. What did he expect? She probably did have owl eyes, and the disposition of a pit bull, too. A person tended to get that way when she hadn't slept in twenty-four hours. Circumstances had stretched her beyond her limit.

Still, she didn't want to spend the day at odds with him.

"Let's make a deal," she said as she climbed into the truck and placed her coffee in the cup holder next to his. "I won't smart off if you'll quit telling me to go home."

He slipped on his royal blue Minnesota Twins baseball cap and grabbed his sunglasses off the dashboard. "Are you serious?"

She rolled her eyes. "No, Cash, I'm kidding."

"Ah, man," he countered with a quick sigh. "I can see this is going to be a character-building day."

Her head swam with fatigue, but she managed to clear her mind long enough to hear that he hadn't actually objected. "Hey, are you *in* or what?"

He held up his broad palm. "Sure. No problem."

She smacked palms with him and vowed to keep her lip buttoned from now on.

"What do I get if you renege?" He grinned. "Again."

She thought for a moment. "I'll buy lunch. What do I get if you renege?"

He slipped his wire-rimmed sunglasses on and stared straight ahead, as though the question posed a problem. After a moment, he angled his head toward her and said, "Let's make this interesting. If I lose, I'll let you decide what my fate will be."

She picked up her coffee and flashed him a confident smile, warmed by his sense of adventure. "You're on."

After a short stop at Cash's house, they spent the morning canvassing the city, checking out places where teens were likely to frequent on a beautiful fall day. For Libby, the drive seemed like a journey back in time. She hadn't been to any of the city's picturesque lakes since high school, including Lake Harriet, the massive body of sky-blue water situated across the street from her late father's house. Since moving to Minneapolis, she'd spent many mornings in the sunny breakfast room, gazing through the wall-to-wall windows at lush lawns and the walking trail circling the lake. The rose gardens and turn-of-the-century bandshell were also tempting, but the thought of exploring those places without her daughter always dampened her enthusiasm.

They'd started out in high spirits, but as the morning wore on, their search proved as fruitless as the night before. Tired and achy, Libby drank more coffee and tried to stay positive. However, after a couple of hours, her hope began to wane, becoming as weak as her energy flow.

They headed to Boom Island Park, along the river, to check out the paddleboats and a picnic area where Amber often hung out with friends. There, they met up with Jenny and a couple of teens that Cash knew, but they saw no sign of Amber. Discouraged, they drove to the high school and talked to kids coming to sports practice or just hanging out in the parking lot. Libby went about, introducing herself to students and showing them Cash's most recent school picture of Amber. Everyone she met either knew Amber or knew of her, but no one knew about her disappearance, much less her whereabouts.

"My feet hurt," Libby complained as they sat in the truck, taking a break. With one ankle resting on her knee, she examined her blistered toes. She cut him a sideways glance. "Don't take that the wrong way. I'm not giving up."

He gripped both hands on the steering wheel, looking as exhausted and beat up as her swollen feet. His ebony, five o'clock shadow had grown to resemble the beginning of a beard. Dark circles underscored his eyes. "We're supposed to meet Todd and Medley at the Mall of America in about ninety minutes," he stated, checking his watch. "How are we going to look for Amber at the mall when you can't even get your shoes on? The floor plan of that place probably covers more ground than a stadium."

She'd give anything for a fifteen-minute nap but knew that would be a worse mistake than trying to put her spiked-heeled sandals back on. Her head began to swirl as she sat back and let out a weary sigh. "I've got some Band-aids."

When he didn't answer, she glanced his way and found him sitting with his head tipped back, his eyes closed. After about thirty seconds of silence, she nudged his shoulder.

"Huh?" He lifted his head and groggily looked around.

"I said I'm going to cover my blisters with Band-aids."

"Uh...where are you going to get those?"

"From my medicine cabinet." She focused her attention again on her battered toes, gingerly setting her foot on the floor mat. "I've got a brand-new box stored on the top shelf. Take me home." As an afterthought, she leaned over and shoved a finger in the center of his chest. "But don't even *think* of leaving me there."

He let out a tired sigh and started the truck. "I should be so lucky."

*   *   *

Cash sat in his truck in the driveway of Libby's house and checked his watch for the umpteenth time.

"What's she doing in there, trying on every pair of shoes she owns?"

He hadn't seen any sign of her since she disappeared through the front door nearly twenty minutes ago; she'd promised him it wouldn't take longer than ten. He'd arranged to meet Todd at the Mall of America at noon sharp to search the area for Amber. The hands on his watch pointed to 11:30 am. They needed to get on the road—now!

He yawned and gazed tiredly through the windshield of his pickup at the three-story, six-bedroom Georgian Revival home Libby had inherited. The red brick building with white trim looked pretty much the same as it did seventeen years ago when she lived there with her father. Multiple dormers protruded from the gabled roof, centered between brick chimneys on each end. Tall, stately oaks shaded the front yard, their leaves turning a deep red. A realtor's 'For Sale' sign stuck out of the ground near a pair of concrete lions positioned at the end of the front sidewalk.

Even when they were teens, Libby had always forced him to wait long past their agreed time while she made herself pretty—or prettier, as the case may be—for him. He hadn't minded it back then. Given better circumstances, he might not even mind now, but he had a runaway daughter to find today. They needed to get on the road.

"She said she'd be right back," he grumbled to himself and shifted uncomfortably in his seat. Every minute he passed in idleness increased his fatigue. "If I sit here much longer, she might as well just throw a blanket over me." Losing patience, he leaned on the truck's horn.

Five minutes later, he still sat in the same spot, waiting for her and fighting to keep his eyelids from closing like a curtain after the last act. How long did it take to find a lousy pair of shoes? A movement in one of the upper windows caught his attention. He picked up his cell phone and called her. She answered just before it went to voicemail. "What are you doing in there? Are you ready to go?"

"No..." She sounded distracted.

"What's holding things up?"

"I can't—ouch! My feet are in pretty bad shape."

Throwing open the door, he slid out of the truck and marched toward an elegant portico at the front entrance. "We're way behind schedule. I'm leaving here in five minutes, so if you're planning on coming with me you'd better get a move on."

He shut off the phone and shoved it in his pocket as he reached the front entrance. The stupid door wouldn't budge, adding to his frustration. He jammed his knuckle against the doorbell.

"Okay, okay," Libby said as she swung open the door, "this entrance is always locked because I usually let myself in through the garage." She stood aside. "Come in."

He stepped onto the hardwood floor of the receiving hall, an area of dark oak woodwork and walls painted the color of fresh cream. To his amazement, nothing had changed since the last time he stood here, over sixteen years ago. The same gilded console table and matching wall mirror graced his right. Centered on the table's marble top he saw the crystal dish the senator used to hold his keys. To Cash's left, the wide stairway with dark-stained oak treads and polished oak handrail led up to the second floor. A large chandelier hung from the ceiling.

As he glanced around, poignant memories of their past engulfed him like a flood, overtaking him with so much force he had to brace his hand against the doorframe to stay upright. He meant to turn away, but the desire to see if she'd sensed it, too, prompted him to look into her eyes. She didn't say a word. She didn't have to; the way her gaze locked with his then darted away told him everything he needed to know.

She shut the door behind him and then wordlessly led the way into a room with dark-paneled walls and a box-beam ceiling...the dining room. Filtered sunlight reflected off the shiny surface of a large, square table in the center of the room. At one end, Libby had pulled out an armchair and placed a dishpan filled with soapy water on the floor in front of it. A small pink towel lay on the adjacent buffet.

"I need to soak my aching feet," she announced as she held up her hand to stop his protest. "You said I have five minutes. I'm holding to you it."

He wandered over to one of the twin French doors overlooking a private terrace and stood with his back to her, his arms folded, staring through the lace curtains. Being in this house again alone with her made him nervous. The place conjured up too many memories.

"You look like you're about to fall asleep on your feet. Why don't you help yourself to a Coke or a glass of ice water?"

The sound of her voice startled him. He spun around. "No thanks." He paused for a moment, wondering what looked different about her then realized she'd changed into another pair of jeans and a white knit shirt with blue trim. With her frosty blonde hair swept back into a ponytail and bare feet, she looked like a teenager once more. Make that one incredibly beautiful teenager. "Is that what you've been doing all this time?" he fired at her, trying to cover up the fact that he found her attractive—and that she'd caught him staring at her again. "Changing clothes?"

Ignoring his question, she sunk into the chair, rolled up her pant legs past her ankles, and slipped her pink-polished toes into the water. "Oh, that feels good." She placed her upturned wrists on the wooden arms and leaned back with her eyes closed. "I've been tearing my closets apart, looking for my tennis shoes. When you own six bedrooms that takes a while. Unfortunately, they're nowhere to be found."

"Yeah, well, there's no such thing as a woman without shoes," he remarked, unable to resist a grin. "You must have something else to wear." He checked his watch. "And you'd better find them in three minutes. That's all we've got."

"I will on one condition." She opened her eyes. "There's something I've been meaning to ask you about, but I don't want excuses this time. I want the truth."

Her serious tone put him on alert. Bracing himself for something unpleasant, he looked into her eyes, wondering what she planned to spring on him now.

"That day we met at Sandhill," she began, "I asked how you ended up with Amber and you gave me a vague answer. You said something about...getting her the old-fashioned way with a lawyer. What really happened? I mean, how did you go about it?"

"That's two questions." He looked away, resistant to delve into the past once again. "What difference does it make now? It's ancient history. We need to concentrate on our current crisis."

"That's two excuses." She sat up. "It makes a huge difference to me, Cash. I can't go back and start over, but I can learn from the past. Something has been bothering me ever since I discovered you adopted Amber." She laid her hand on the table, steadying herself as she leaned forward. "What part did my father play in all this? Did he approach you about adopting our child?"

"How much do you already know?"

"Nothing." She froze, as though his question worried her. "Nothing at all."

Cash turned back to gaze through the curtains and pondered giving her what she wanted. After all, her old man had been dead for months and his parents lived in Florida. The restrictions placed upon him years ago didn't apply any longer. Besides, given the situation they found themselves in now, what did it matter if he told her the truth?

"It's not what you think," he said, deciding to level with her. He approached the table and pulled out a side chair with ball and claw feet, straddling it. "The senator played a major part in the adoption, but I don't know if he ever realized it." The confusion on her face spurred him on. "He gave my parents ten thousand dollars toward my education in exchange for their guarantee that I would never contact you again."

Her jaw nearly hit the floor. As the truth sunk in, the pain of her father's betrayal filled her eyes.

"Hear me out first." Cash raised his hand to silence her next question. "Look, I didn't agree to it, but no one asked my opinion. My parents told me after they'd sealed the deal and taken possession of the money. When I asked them why they'd accepted it, they would only say that they considered the payment a once-in-a-lifetime opportunity for me. They justified it as a consolation for what our family had been through."

The shock on Libby's face saddened him. He hated to be the one to tell her that her father would stop at nothing to make sure his 'family values' image stayed intact. Still, she'd asked for the facts.

"I didn't use the money for college," he continued, "but I'm sure you've already concluded that." In a surge of restlessness, he stood and walked around the room, stopping at the front windows. "I came home early from class one afternoon. As I entered the back porch, I heard my mother talking on the phone. She always used the wall phone in the kitchen because that one had a long cord and she could cook or do dishes while she discussed everything from Hollywood icons to world peace with her sisters."

He parted the curtains and studied the twin cement lions positioned at the entrance of the front sidewalk. "My dad happened to call at that time. I could tell because of the serious tone of voice she always used with him. I heard her tell him that you'd just given birth to a baby girl and that you were placing the child for adoption."

He turned his head far enough to glance at her from the corner of his eye. "You can guess the rest of the story. I withdrew the senator's hush money and spent every penny of it to make Amber legally mine."

He let the curtains fall and turned around, folding his arms for something to do. "They never intended to tell me about the adoption. I guess feelings of attachment for my *love child* weren't supposed to exist, but they did. More so, it hurt to know that my own parents conspired to keep me ignorant of her future."

Libby stared at the floor for a moment, as if digesting his explanation then snatched the towel off the buffet and began to dry her feet. "I wrote to you every week and told you all about the situation. It's unfortunate that you never received the letters."

There she goes again. What letters? If she wrote as many as she claimed, what happened to them? I need to find out.

He glanced at his watch. "We should be halfway to the mall by now. Hurry up, okay? We've got to get going."

She stood and picked up the dishpan. "Here, take care of this while I get the bandages."

He took the pan to the kitchen and put it in the sink then went looking for her. He found her across the hallway in the senator's office. Three walls of the wide, square room held floor-to-ceiling bookcases filled with law books and picture frames. The fourth wall hosted a pair of large windows and at least a dozen framed awards in all sizes. The senator's massive oak desk commanded the center of the floor like a king's throne. Libby sat behind the antique structure in his worn office chair, wrapping flesh-colored bandages around her puffy toes.

Cash jammed his hands into his pockets and looked around, taking a cursory tour of the room. "You can almost feel his presence here, can't you?"

* * *

Libby tore open a bandage and looked up, amazed. "Oh, so you've noticed that, too." She pulled her knee up to her chin and positioned her heel on the edge of the chair. "From the moment I arrived, I sensed his presence throughout the house. At first, I didn't know what to make of it." She wrapped a tiny, flesh-colored bandage around the worst blister on the baby toe of her right foot. "I saw so little of Dad growing up that we barely knew each other. I felt like I'd inherited the property of a stranger."

"Did you inherit enough funds to take care of the place, too?"

She paused, caught off guard by his boldness then busied herself in her work again. "Yes. He left me more than enough to live in style for the rest of my life. Nevertheless, I took a job for something to do. I needed to stay busy to keep my mind off...everything."

"Then why are you moving?" Cash glanced around. "I noticed the 'For Sale' sign on the front lawn. Have you purchased another house?"

She shook her head. "Not until this house sells. It's been on the market for almost six months and so far, I haven't received what I'd consider a decent offer. Now that I've met Amber, I'm considering pulling it off the market and keeping it for her. After all, it's her inheritance, too." She gazed up at the books stocking the wall-to-wall shelves and sighed, dreading the thought of having to pack up all of her father's things.

"When I first moved back in, I couldn't stand to live here by myself," she said, purposely going back to the previous subject as she tackled the next blistered toe. "I felt so alone in this big house. I don't know why, but at night, I'd always end up in this room, reading or simply poking around. Everything in here is just the way Dad left it and in going through his everyday things, I've come to know Frank Cunningham as a loving, caring father; not the strict, distant man I barely remember."

She pointed to a stack of books and papers neatly arranged on the credenza under the windows, the wire-rimmed glasses and pen lying across his open appointment book. "I've been meaning to put all of that stuff into a box and store it in the basement, but I can't bring myself to part with it. Having his things around makes me feel closer to him than I ever thought possible."

She felt a sudden urgency to make Cash understand Frank's true motive for giving him money—to forget the past and start over.

"Contrary to what I've always believed, his mementos in this room prove he loved me very much and that he truly cared, in his own way, about my future." A lump formed in her throat. She swallowed it back as she made a wide sweep with her arm, encouraging him to look around. "See for yourself."

He walked around the room, glancing at dozens of the framed photos of her positioned on Frank's desk, on the credenza, and on each shelf of Frank's massive bookcases, nearly camouflaging his law books. On the wall encircling his awards were larger, more elaborately framed certificates of Libby's accomplishments.

She commenced taking care of her feet and left Cash alone to inspect Frank's personal shrine for his only child. Once finished, she stood up.

"I didn't want to move back to Minnesota, but now I thank God every day that He led me here. Though the last six months have been difficult, the journey has proven to be one of the most valuable experiences of my life. I've learned to forgive my father and be at peace with him." She placed her hand over her heart and took a deep breath. "It feels *so* good."

Cash's brows drew together. He hesitated, his lips parting as though he wanted to say something, but instead he moved toward her. "Are you ready to go?"

"Yes." She threw the empty bandage wrappers in the chrome trash can under the desk. More than anything, she wanted to hear him confess that he'd forgiven her for hurting him. His silence, however, indicated loud and clear that today didn't appear to be that day. "My purse is in the kitchen," she replied in a flat tone. "I'll grab it on the way out. We're leaving by the service door in the garage, anyway. I have to set the alarm."

She expected him to lead the way, but he made no move to depart.

"What about your shoes?"

"I've got them." She reached under the desk and pulled out a pair of orange flip-flops. "I'm wearing these."

His eyes widened in disbelief, but he kept his opinions to himself. He moved closer and took them from her hands. "You can put them on once we're on our way. It might be a little awkward trying to climb into the truck with them on and I wouldn't want you to slip." He looked up, his face positioned dangerously close to hers. Their eyes met and held. His head angled slightly.

Her pulse went from calm to erratic in two seconds. She held her breath, waiting for his next move...

"After you," he said brusquely and stepped backward, putting an arm's length between them.

Shaken, she led the way through the kitchen into the garage and punched in the alarm code before locking the service door. The few moments of friendship they'd shared in the dining room and then in Frank's office were nothing more than a fading memory now. Her mood sagged as she climbed into the truck. Fatigue began to seep into her bones.

Cash climbed into the driver's seat and slid on his sunglasses before jamming his keys into the ignition. His muscular arms, tousled black hair, and two-day beard made him look like a hockey player out of uniform.

Libby sat back and stole another glance at him. He had no idea how ruggedly handsome he looked right now. Worse than that, he had no idea how much she still loved him.

She turned quickly, pretending to look out the window before he could see her blink away her sadness.

Chapter 16

Thirty minutes later, Cash pulled into the second level of the west parking garage at the Mall of America. He shut off the truck and sat back, yawning fiercely as he rubbed his eyes with the heels of his hands. Bleary-eyed, he glanced at his watch. "We're a half-hour behind schedule."

Libby slowly slipped her orange flip-flops between her bandaged toes, concentrating on that simple task as though she hadn't heard him. "Knowing Medley, that's about right," she murmured unexpectedly.

"I told Todd we'd be here at noon. He's never late." He surveyed the parking lot through the windshield, wondering if Todd had given up on him and gone into the mall to have lunch without him and Libby. "We agreed to meet in this corner of the ramp, but I don't see the Hummer anywhere."

"That's impossible." Libby gave him a weary look. "I don't see how you can miss a glorified bulldozer with a front grill that looks like massive chrome teeth. We're probably on the wrong level."

He opened the door and slid out of the truck, shrugging at her suggestion that he had his directions mixed up. "Nope, I know my way around here. We're *not* on the wrong level."

She rested her hand on the door latch but didn't attempt to leave her seat. "Then we must be in the wrong spot because otherwise, we'd see his vehicle."

On any other day, he'd have probably agreed with her. However, on any

212

other day, he wouldn't have been dog-tired and struggling to salvage his last shred of sanity. "We're *not* in the wrong spot."

She thrust her hands upward. "Whatever you say, boss. You're driving. But when we find ourselves still sitting here this time tomorrow, maybe then you'll admit you could be wrong."

He leaned into the truck and shook his finger at her. "Hey, you keep smarting off, lady, and I'm going to—"

"—you're going to do what?" She shoved open her door. "Send me home?"

He pointed to her mummified feet. "If you weren't so crazy when it came to shoes, I might consider making you walk home."

"Me?" She eased out of the truck, grimacing as her feet touched the ground. "You're the one who insisted we cover the entire Mill District on foot. I should make you carry me home!"

"Whoa," Todd's baritone voice boomed behind Cash, "people can hear you clear across the ramp." He let out a chuckle. "Everything sounds normal between you two."

Cash leaned against the truck door for support, upset at losing control as Todd and Medley ambled toward him, holding hands. "I...we...we're just exhausted. That's all. Arguing is the only thing keeping us awake." He absently rubbed the rough stubble on his jaw. "Where did you come from?"

"Over there." Todd leisurely pointed to a corner spot one section down from where they stood. He didn't look tired at all. "That's where we agreed to meet."

So worn out he could barely think, Cash surveyed the rows on both his left and his right. They all looked alike. "Are you sure?"

"Don't you remember? We always park over there."

Libby hobbled around to the front of the truck to join them.

"Oh." He scratched his head, purposely avoiding her gaze. "Sorry, I guess I got mixed up. Have you been waiting long?"

"We've been here since eleven-thirty." Todd smiled with approval at

Medley. "My little honey didn't want to be late."

Libby's mouth gaped open so wide it almost hit the cement floor. Cash reached over and gently closed it with the tip of his finger. He agreed with her but couldn't repeat the words charging through his head. Watching the lovey-dovey stuff going on between Todd and his *little honey*, along with their irritating perkiness, drove him crazy.

Medley, the group's fashion aficionado reacted to Libby's new glow-in-the-dark footwear with a gasp. "Lib, what happened to your feet?"

Libby pursed her lips and ripped the ponytail holder out of her hair. "I ran a marathon in high-heeled sandals." She combed through her long strands with her fingers then pulled them back into a ponytail and wrapped the shiny elastic band around them again. "I think we'd better get moving. Otherwise, I'm going to fall asleep standing up."

Todd slipped his arm around Medley's tiny waist and pulled her close. She reciprocated the gesture, simultaneously lifting her face to gaze into his loving eyes. Her sunshine smile radiated pure happiness.

Cash watched their bold display of affection as that canyon-sized crater in his heart grew to the size of Alaska. Through all the years they'd been friends, he'd never known Todd to fall in love so fast with a woman before. What had happened to him?

He stuffed his hands into his jean pockets as he and Libby fell into step behind them and headed toward the mall. He didn't dare look at her, but he sensed her mutual discomfort by the stiff-sounding patter of her steps.

"I lost the bet," she whispered in a humble tone as they trekked through the noisy ramp. "I apologize for my crankiness and promise to make good on our agreement. Lunch is on me."

The remnants of Cash's petulance melted like butter at the honesty in her voice. He leaned toward her and murmured in her ear. "Hey, I messed up, too, which means you get to decide my fate." She looked into his eyes with genuine surprise and it made him realize that she spoke up first because she truly wanted to dissolve the uneasiness between them.

Deep in his heart, he did, too. He smiled, hoping his own sincerity came through his next carefully chosen words. "How about this—I apologize for instigating the argument and I'll spring for lunch, too." He held up his palm in a 'gimme five' gesture, smacking hands with her to seal the payoff.

Inside the entrance, they approached the young security guard stationed at his post. Cash produced his picture of Amber for the guard, but the young man didn't recognize her. Despite the blow to his spirits, he continued into the mall, stopping at the kiosk displaying the mall directory. Tourists and local shoppers swarmed the wide, open corridors, creating an echo of voices resembling the gathering of a small nation.

"Todd, why don't you and Medley cover the lower level and the amusement park?" Cash pointed to the mall's floor-by-floor map. "Libby and I will stay on this level and keep in touch with you by phone. When we're confident we've covered every venue, we can meet back here to check out the upper deck and the food court."

"The food court, huh? Okay." Todd flashed a toothy grin. "I can handle that."

Still clinging to one another, Todd and Medley headed for the escalator.

Cash turned to Libby. "Which way do you want to go?" She gestured to the right and they set off in the direction of Abercrombie, stopping at each store on the way to check for Amber. To Cash's relief, jostling through the noisy crowd created enough diversion to supplant conversation. About twenty minutes into their search, however, Libby began to slow down.

Cash grasped her elbow and gently pulled her to a halt. "What's the matter?" Her pallid face and sagging shoulders worried him.

She took a deep breath as she closed her eyes and massaged her forehead with her fingertips. "I'm so fatigued I can hardly think much less walk another step."

Instinctively he slipped his arm around her waist. "Does this help?"

For a moment, they froze. Cash stood stunned, unable to move as an amazing fullness of peace flooded his heart, spreading throughout his chest.

"That—that's not necessary. I can manage." She tried to pull away, but the thought of letting go and losing his fragile hold on her for even a moment sent a tremor of panic through him. Instead of releasing her, he tightened his grip.

"I'm simply trying to hold you up until we can find someplace to sit down." He'd softened his voice to show his concern. "Just relax and lean into me, okay? Let me take care of you."

Wide-eyed, she wordlessly gazed into his eyes. He accepted that as permission and pulled her closer. Her narrow, rounded shoulder fit into the cleft of his arm like the missing piece of a unique puzzle. They proceeded slowly at first, adjusting to each other. Then something amazing happened. Her muscles began to relax. She leaned into him as they ambled along, watching for Amber and an available place to rest at the same time. He relaxed his grip a little, soaking up the surge of energy that flowed through his limbs.

Around the corner from Abercrombie, they found an unoccupied bench. Cash eased her down on the seat. "I could use a nice cold bottle of water. Would you like one?" At her nod, he patted her on the shoulder. "I'll be right back."

He had more than water on his mind, however, and took off in the direction of a store they'd recently passed. A short time later, he returned, carrying two bottles of Evian water and a mid-sized plastic bag.

"I bought you something," he said, unable to suppress a smile in response to her questioning look. He handed her a bottle of Evian water and knelt in front of her. Opening the bag, he pulled out a waxed paper envelope containing two large chocolate chip cookies, still warm from the oven. "I couldn't resist. They smell so good."

"You remembered!" Wearing that special glow of the Libby from his past, she set down her water bottle and accepted the cookies.

Yes, he remembered. She loved chocolate chip cookies. He used to buy them for her all the time back in school. How could he forget?

He reached into the bag again and pulled out a pair of white socks. Lastly, he took out a shoebox and pulled off the top. A pair of white walking shoes constructed of a butter-soft fabric lay tucked inside. With utmost gentleness, he removed those ridiculous flip-flops and covered her feet with the thin, cotton socks. The shoes went on next, fitting her with perfect precision. He took Libby's hands and pulled her to a standing position.

"I guessed at your size. Well, actually, I figured that you and Amber probably wore the same size. How do they feel?"

"I feel—I mean...the shoes feel wonderful." She picked up each foot one at a time, testing the fit of each shoe. "My toes don't hurt at all."

Cash stuffed the flip-flops into the bag and tossed it into the trashcan next to the bench. As an afterthought, he dug into his pocket, pulled out the purple package, and tossed that, too.

"What did you throw away?" Libby asked.

"Nothing important," he answered quickly. "Just getting rid of some extra baggage."

* * *

Libby and Cash met up with Todd and Medley around two o'clock. As planned by phone, they'd scoured the third level and then proceeded to the food court. Cash made good on his promise to Libby to purchase lunch at a Chinese food vendor. With full trays, they went in search of an empty table and found one in a far corner, overlooking the indoor amusement park that filled the center of the complex. Down below, the rumbling of a roller coaster and the whispering waterfall of a flume ride accompanied by screams of excitement echoed through the air.

Todd and Medley joined them at the table. After blessing the food, everyone commenced eating. Libby slowly savored her chow mein, grateful for the relaxing break while Cash devoured his cashew chicken. No one had spoken since the group sat down.

"You must have been mega hungry," Cash remarked to Todd, breaking the silence. "I inhaled my food, but you've beaten me." He stared in awe at Todd's empty tray. "You hogged down an entire pizza in ten minutes."

Todd didn't answer. He sucked on his thirty-two-ounce cola and stared a hole through the ceiling. Medley gazed, tight-lipped, at the roller coaster as it sped along the perimeter of the park.

Something is going on between those two, Libby thought, wondering why Medley had barely touched her baked potato topped with bruschetta. *Did they already have an argument?* She glanced at Cash and the deep crease in his brow left no doubt in her mind that he'd sensed it, too.

She didn't know what to say to either of them, but Cash didn't have any problem broaching the subject.

"All right," he declared as he shoved his empty plate away and glared at Todd. "What's going on? What happened during the time we split up until we sat down fifteen minutes ago?" He leaned forward. "Did you learn something about Amber you haven't shared with me?"

Neither Todd nor Medley answered the questions. Expecting the worst, Libby exchanged frantic looks with Cash. From the corner of her eye, she saw Todd and Medley follow suit. What secret *were* they protecting? The tension around the table became almost unbearable.

Todd's jaw visibly tightened. He threw his shoulders back; his spine went ramrod straight as though bracing for a fight. "We're gettin' married."

What?

Libby's plastic fork made a hollow noise as it bounced on the table.

Looking equally surprised, Cash shook his head once and blinked twice. "You-you've only been together f-for one day," he stuttered. "Granted, it's been a l-o-n-g twenty-some hours, but not long enough to—"

Todd banged his monster-sized jug of cola on the table as if to slam a gavel. "Unlike you, MacKenzie, I know when I've found the right woman, so why wait?" His words, issued almost as a reprimand, boomed through the air.

Libby stared at Medley, struggling to comprehend what she'd just heard. "Medley," she whispered in astonishment, "you've always claimed you didn't believe in marriage. What has changed your mind?"

Medley smiled sugary sweet at Todd, her eyes shining with love. "Remember the night we stood outside Cash's house waiting to catch Amber sneaking out?" Her moonstruck gaze locked with Todd's shining blue eyes. "When I looked through the glass in the front door and saw him staring back," she placed her hand over her heart, "I knew I'd found the man for me."

Like emotional zombies, Libby and Cash slowly turned and gawked at each other, speechless. From what she remembered of that night, Medley's screaming and threats never indicated she'd met the man of her dreams.

Medley sobered and faced her cousin. "Well...there is something else, Libby. Remember when we had that talk about your stay at the unwed mothers' home?"

Libby frowned. "Yes, but what does..."

"I confided something to you that I've never told anyone before; how I've always harbored guilt because I grew up in a happy home with loving parents who always put me first. And you didn't."

Libby pushed her food away and clasped her hands in a death grip, waiting for the other shoe to drop. "What are you saying?"

"It hurt me so much when Mother said Uncle Frank took Amber away from you," Medley confessed. "That time we visited you at the home, I saw how deeply losing your child had devastated you, but I didn't know how to help you heal." She pushed her cold, uneaten potato toward Todd. Like an obedient servant, he picked up his fork and began to devour it.

"I've always loved you like a sister, and whatever happens to my sister, happens to me, too. So, I vowed to myself not to get married until I knew you were living happily ever after with the man that God hand-picked for you."

Cash reached over and placed his hand over Libby's, but she pulled away and brought both hands up to her face as shock and guilt burdened her soul. This couldn't be true! "Do you mean to tell me that all your talk against marriage and commitment amounted to nothing more than a charade for my sake?"

Medley nodded as moisture pooled in her eyes. Cash cleared his throat and exchanged baffled looks with Todd as they looked up from their plates. Red-faced, Todd lowered his head and went back to Medley's potato. Cash helped himself to Libby's shrimp egg roll.

"When Grandma Cunningham told my parents that she and Uncle Frank were disposing of your baby, it really upset Mother," Medley continued. "She didn't agree with their decision but knew she couldn't change the outcome." Medley reached across the table and clasped Libby's hand in hers. "In my mind, I can still see Mother sitting at the kitchen table, going through a box of tissues over losing a member of our family. She wanted to adopt Amber herself, but Grandma Cunningham told her that the baby had already been *shipped out*."

"Are you okay?" Cash placed his arm around Libby as tears streamed down her face. She nodded but couldn't talk. He reached over and gently blotted her face with a napkin.

Medley sniffled. "I stayed in contact with you through all those years you lived in Seattle because I didn't want to lose you. I knew you were being dutiful to Uncle Frank by staying away, but I held out hope that someday you'd move back home, and together we would track down your child."

"We're going to track her down and get her back," Cash tightened his arm around Libby. "We're not going to give up until we do."

Todd stood up and started throwing empty dishes on his tray. Taking the hint, everyone else stood and pushed back their chairs. By the time they'd finished clearing off the table, a happy family with two elementary-aged children and a sleeping infant in a stroller waited to take their place.

The group walked back to the parking garage in silence. Once they reached Cash's pickup, however, Libby embraced Medley with a tear-filled hug.

"Thank you, Medley, for everything you've done, and thank you for being the best sister I could ever ask for. I'm very happy for you and Todd. Maybe someday I'll find my knight in shining armor as well."

Medley smiled radiantly at Todd then turned back to her cousin. "You already have," she whispered. "You just need to acknowledge him as the one."

Cash shoved his hands into his pockets and pulled out his keys. Though he had turned away, Libby saw his eyes light up, and she knew he'd overheard. She wondered if Medley's little speech had merely amused him, or had Medley's prediction filled his heart with hope?

Her phone suddenly rang deep inside her purse.

"Hurry!" Cash's voice sounded strangled, as though his heart had catapulted to his throat. "It could be Amber!"

Sweat collected on the back of Libby's neck as she fumbled with the zipper of her bag. She pulled the phone out and when she saw the number flashing on her caller ID, she almost threw it across the parking lot.

"It's Stefano's," she sputtered with annoyance.

Cash's disappointment erupted like a volcano. "Don't answer it! You told them you needed today off for personal reasons."

She shook her head. "I'd better take the call. Something must be wrong." She swiped her finger across the screen but accidentally activated the speakerphone at the same time. Everyone could hear a sob on the other end of the line.

"Libby, *she's* here." The youthful caller's voice quavered with panic. "Ardelle showed up early for her daughter's reception and she's demanding to see you!"

Chapter 17

Stefano's buzzed with the usual frenzy of the first dinner 'push' on a Saturday night. In the lobby, Libby maneuvered her way through the hungry throng of people awaiting seating and headed down the long, wainscoted hallway, past her office to the Florentine Room. She walked into the Johnson-Hargrove reception and glanced around. The mahogany-paneled room looked beautiful with oriental rugs over wood floors, mirrors, paintings, and amber chandeliers. Thirty-two round tables were meticulously set with white linen cloths, silver-rimmed china, and crystal.

Libby had insisted Cash drop her off at the front door and wait for her somewhere in the already overflowing parking lot. She couldn't predict how long it would take to deal with Ardelle, but she'd promised to call him when she'd taken care of her business. The thought made her cringe. Of all days to miss work, this had to be the worst timing ever!

Brianna rushed into the Florentine Room, clutching a clipboard and a shrink-wrapped package of linen napkins. Her flushed cheeks matched the same hue of her soft red hair.

"I feel stupid for calling you, Libby, but I didn't know what else to do. Ardelle is fit to execute someone!"

Libby gave the worried redhead a quick hug. "You don't have to apologize, Bree. You've done a fantastic job."

She surveyed the work furiously going on around her, noting with relief that the appetizer buffet had been set up exactly as the contract stated. A duo of bakers clad in white slacks and shirts stood at a table off to the side, testing the fountain in the multi-tiered wedding cake. The florists rushed around, applying last-minute details to an arched trellis of fresh roses for the bride and groom to make their entrance. A tall pillar of peach roses with gold centers stood in the center of every other table. The alternate tables held a smaller arrangement.

In another corner, Ardelle's team of wedding planners conversed with the harpist, presumably requesting last-minute changes in the music.

Libby turned to her assistant. "You have everything under control. What's the problem?"

Brianna's large green eyes widened and her hands shook with the same frequency as her voice. "She's due back at any minute. I'm scared of what she's going to say when she finds out that I'm the one in charge tonight and not you!"

"Don't worry about it. You've got a full staff of our best people working this event." Libby took the clipboard from Brianna to double-check every item on the contract. "I'll stick around until she arrives and I'll explain the situation to her."

"Explain what?"

Libby whirled around to find a tall, stately woman in her mid-fifties standing in the doorway. Wearing an avocado suit, glittering diamonds, and the air of a queen, Ardelle Johnson's presence commanded the attention of everyone in the room.

Libby steeled herself and smiled. "Hello, Ardelle."

Ardelle's slate eyes scrutinized Libby's jeans and casual top with alarm. "Why are you dressed like that?" Don't you realize that my guests will be arriving minutes from now?"

Libby took a deep breath and displayed a poised smile. "Yes, Ardelle, I'm aware of the timeline, but I've had a family emergency so Brianna is supervising tonight."

"What are you talking about?" Ardelle shook her dark, bobbed hair in distress. "No! I forbid it! This is my only daughter's wedding reception. You can't turn this event over to a mere assistant. I demand to speak with the manager!"

Libby turned to Brianna. "Go find Ron and inform him that I need to speak with him—right away, please. Oh, and on your way back, stop into the Executive Chef's office and tell Marcello that his presence is requested as well."

Still clutching the bundle of napkins, Brianna backed away and almost ran out of the room. Determined not to be intimidated, Libby confidently turned back to Ardelle and smiled again, keeping her demeanor professional. "Please understand—I have complete faith in the proficiency of my staff. They're experienced in serving large groups, and they have successfully handled dozens of receptions this year alone. I'm confident that you'll be extremely pleased with the level of their service tonight."

To pass the time until her manager and chef arrived, Libby suggested a tour of the room, going over every detail with Ardelle and answering all of her questions. Confident that she'd satisfied Ardelle for the moment, she decided to change the subject.

"While we're waiting for Ron Calder, may I ask you something? Do you love your daughter more than anything else in your life?"

Ardelle gaped at the audacity of the question but quickly recovered. "Of course, I do. She's been the center of my life since I gave birth to her."

Libby gripped the clipboard with white knuckles. "I know exactly how you feel. My daughter means the world to me, too."

Ardelle sniffed at Libby's boldness. "What does your daughter have to do with your failure to fulfill your contractual duties for my event?"

Libby bit her lip to keep it from quivering. "If I don't find her, I may never have the chance to someday plan her wedding reception. You see, she's run away from home and I've been searching for her since last night."

This is the second time I've lost her and the second time it's brought my life to a screeching halt. This time, however, I'm not going to let her go without a fight!

Ardelle appeared genuinely shaken as she clutched the jewels at her throat with a loud gasp. "That's horrible. I'm so sorry! My heart goes out to you."

Libby swallowed back a wave of emotion. "Thank you for your understanding. This is a very difficult time for me."

Ardelle stared at the floor for a moment. "I must confess I've been through it myself." She looked up, gazing at Libby with a painful expression. "My daughter, Laura, became involved with a good-for-nothing boy and ran away twice in high school. She put my husband and me through a virtual nightmare each time. I thank God that we made it through those difficult seasons and helped her turn her life around." Ardelle wrapped her arms around Libby and refused to let her go. "My prayers are with you."

Relieved, Libby thanked Ardelle for her concern and then gestured toward the staff overseeing the setup of tables for the bridal party on the other side of the room.

"Allow me to introduce you to the banquet captains," she said politely, jumping into her professional mode once again. "They'll be at your service throughout the evening, ready to assist you with anything you need..."

*　*　*

Cash parked his truck at the far end of the lot and jerked out the keys. Taking a needed time out, he sat with his arms draped across the steering wheel and pondered the events of the past several weeks. The scheming, untrustworthy Libby Cunningham he thought he'd battled at Sandhill never existed. The woman he'd come to know since that day had turned out to be amazingly different. This Libby continually put others first, literally gave the coat off her back to strangers, and pushed herself beyond her limits, despite blistered feet and exhaustion.

He remembered Medley describing her mother's devastation over losing Amber and it caused him to wonder about his own mother. How had Maggie reacted to the news of the senator taking Libby's baby away from her? Did she mourn the loss of her son's only child? He suddenly had to know...

He extracted his phone from the clip on his belt and speed-dialed the number to her home in St. Augustine. They should have held this conversation long ago.

Maggie McKenzie answered on the third ring.

225

"Hello, Ma?" He rolled down the side window and rested his free arm on the doorframe. "It's Cash."

"Cash! What a coincidence, dear!" She sounded pleasantly surprised. "I've been thinking about you all day. How have you been?" He visualized her standing at the kitchen sink of her townhome, smiling and gazing out the window.

"I'm doing fine." *As fine as I can be in the midst of a crisis,* he thought grimly.

"And how is Amber? Doing well in school, I assume."

"You know her. She's a busy kid—always trying something new." He swallowed hard at the frightening truth in his reply. "How's Dad?"

"He never slows down." Maggie chuckled. "He's competing in a senior golf tournament today. Say, I've been meaning to call you about Thanksgiving. Why don't you and Amber fly down for the weekend? Your sisters are both coming with their families. I'll make a nice turkey dinner. We'll spend a day at Disneyworld."

"Sounds good, Ma. Well...ah..." He hesitated, not sure of the best way to introduce the subject. "Something has been on my mind lately and I'd like to put it to rest."

"What's that?"

"It's about Amber and the situation at the time of her birth. Did...ah...did the senator ever approach you about his plans for her adoption? What I mean to say is…how did you find out that Libby had decided to give her up?"

She didn't reply right away and her delay gave him the impression that she wanted to be careful about her answer. She suddenly cleared her throat. "I grilled him about his daughter and the baby when he met with us to discuss giving money toward your college fund. He presented it as a gift, but he also made it clear that he expected you to forget his daughter ever existed. Before we agreed to anything, I wanted to know what her future intentions were because I knew you'd never get over her unless she'd already gotten over you. That's when he told me about the adoption and sending his daughter to a foster home to have the baby before moving her to Seattle to finish out her education." She paused. "Does that answer your question?"

Cash looked down at his clenched fist, transparent proof of the agony overwhelming his heart. Since day one, she'd known Libby's whereabouts! "Yes, but didn't it bother you that you would never know your first grandchild?"

She groaned. "Of course, it did. We knew what we were losing and it upset us a great deal, but given the circumstances, we believed we had to protect you from bringing any more disasters in your life—like getting married too young. The statistics showed back then, and still do, that the odds of having a successful teenage marriage were stacked against you. The senator wanted his daughter to make a clean break from her mistakes and turn her life around. We wanted the same thing for you. We did what we had to do and so did he."

"Ma, I don't fault you and Dad for trying to make the best of a bad situation, but why didn't anyone consider what Libby and I wanted?"

"I just explained that to you," she stated crisply.

"End of discussion," came through loud and clear in her tone of voice, but he still had more questions.

"Did you give my senior yearbook to Amber?"

She answered with a quick laugh, visibly relieved that he'd changed the subject. "No, I haven't laid eyes on that thing in years. I don't have any idea what happened to it or any of your old yearbooks. Why do you ask?"

"Ah, never mind," he replied. "It's not important. What I really want to know is..." He flexed his cramped fingers then reached over and gripped the steering wheel. "What did you do with the letters that Libby sent to me?"

A tense silence engulfed the airwaves.

"Ma? Are you there?"

"Why do you want to know that?" Again, she laughed. This time, however, her voice sounded strange, as though the question had caught her off guard and made her extremely uncomfortable.

He let go of the steering wheel and wiped his sweaty palm on his jeans. "I talked to Libby the other day and she said that she had written to me—repeatedly. If she did, I never received any of her letters. Or did I? You've always handled the mail at your house. Do you remember those letters?"

227

Maggie let the question hang for a few moments and he wondered why. What did she have to hide?

"I need to know," he persisted.

She countered his insistence with a stern tone. "That happened so long ago. Why are you bringing up such unpleasantness now? It's over and done with."

"It's important to me." More than anything, he wanted to know for sure if Libby had told him the truth. "Did you take those letters? Did you withhold them from me?"

"Well...maybe." He heard a tinge of guilt in her voice. "There might have been one or two."

He leaned his head back and closed his eyes, absorbing the implications of her admission. "Why didn't you give them to me?"

"Have you forgotten," she shot back, her voice rising, "that Senator Cunningham threatened to put you in jail if you ever contacted his daughter again? I feared that if you read her letters you'd attempt to see her."

"Why? What did she—"

"I couldn't allow that, Cash. You had a great future ahead of you. I couldn't permit you to throw it all away over that conniving little tramp."

Cash's eyes flew open. He stared across a sea of vehicles in the parking lot, sinking into a pit of despair. All these years he'd believed a lie. His own mother had deceived him! It made him wonder if he'd merely scratched the surface.

Before today, he'd possessed no knowledge of Maggie's true feelings toward Libby. It deeply bothered him to hear her refer to the mother of his child as a *conniving little tramp* and he wondered what she'd say when she learned that Libby had become a major part of Amber's life. He hung his head, realizing that his parents, albeit well-meaning, held just as much responsibility as Frank Cunningham did in trying to keep Amber from him.

Nailing down what really happened mattered more than ever now. "What did you do with the letters?"

She couldn't remember at first and mumbled something about throwing them away. When he pressed her again, she retracted that thought, deciding that she must have returned the whole stack to Senator Cunningham. The truth punched him in the chest with more force than an exploding airbag.

Cash needed air. He opened the truck's door and slid out. Slamming the door, he leaned against the side of the pickup, struggling to catch his breath.

"I'm disappointed, Ma, that you kept such critical information from me." Stress, combined with Libby's Chinese food had turned his stomach into a knot of pain. He searched his pockets, looking for his antacids. He had a brand-new roll somewhere but couldn't find it.

"Honey," she said earnestly, "you were a hot-headed kid, harboring infatuation over a young girl who had a very powerful father. What else could I do? I couldn't stand by and watch you throw your future away over the likes of her. Senator Cunningham warned me when he gave us your tuition money that by accepting it, we were guaranteeing you'd never *ever* go near her again. When Libby's letters began arriving in the mail, I didn't know if I could trust you to make the right decision, so I made it for you."

Cash stared at the ground, sick to his stomach over the way things had turned out, but most of all, over how he'd treated Libby—criticizing her eagerness to get close to Amber and questioning her motives. She'd told the truth all along, but he'd refused to believe her. How would he ever make things right with her? He didn't want to talk about it anymore. He needed to act.

"Thanks for being straight with me, Ma."

"The years have proven that I made the right decision," she answered on a sober note. "I thank God every day that Amber isn't turning out like her mother. You've done a great job raising her."

He said goodbye, promising to come for Thanksgiving weekend, hung up, and gazed at the crimson sun hovering over the horizon.

"From the way things have turned out, Lord," he said aloud, "I've failed to do a great job at just about everything."

He closed his eyes and leaned back against the truck, turning over in his mind how he'd treated Libby, but not knowing how to rectify his actions in a meaningful way to prove to her that he truly wanted to make it up to her. After a few minutes, a thought suddenly crossed his mind...

"Forgiveness is a choice," he said solemnly, barely recognizing his own voice, "a decision you make because you know in your heart that it's right, not because you feel like it. At the end of the day, you should go to bed with a clear conscience and peace in your soul, but you can't have that if you won't give yourself permission to let go."

He'd heard that sermon in church many times, even as recent as a week ago. Why, then, hadn't it ever sunk in?

Because, he thought, *forgiveness and pride don't coexist in the same situation.*

His refusal to forgive Libby had caused him years of pain, and for the most part, the so-called *facts* had turned out to be untrue.

"So, it was all for nothing..." he said as he sighed and shook his head. "I spent years believing a lie."

Forgive me, Lord, he prayed silently, *for judging Libby unfairly. I realize she's made mistakes in the past, but I have, too, and mine are probably worse. I have no right to hold her accountable for her sins when I'm just as guilty.*

No wonder he'd come to know antacids as one of the four main food groups. He didn't need a cure for his stomach. He needed a cure for his bitterness!

The time had come to change that. He'd struggled in vain long enough. He just hoped he had enough time left.

Chapter 18

Libby opened her eyes to find herself sitting in solid darkness.

Where am I?

She bolted upright. The large blanket covering her slid off her shoulders, dropping to the floor mat in a soft puddle.

Fighting her way through a sleep-induced haze, she struggled to focus as she stared through the truck's windshield. Cash's garage came into view. Then she saw his house.

"This is Nicollet Island," she said aloud, drawn to the porch light shining brightly in the unseasonably warm, humid night. "What are we doing here? We should be searching for..."

Where did Cash go?

She dug into her purse and checked her cell phone. No one had tried to call. The digital display on the screen read 8:35 pm. Anxious to find Cash, she opened the truck door and hopped out, but before her feet hit the ground, dizziness overtook her, buckling her knees. She startled, emitting a cry of surprise as strong, gentle hands caught her from behind, steadying her.

"Easy, easy," Cash's deep tone quietly echoed in her ear.

She angled her head toward the sound of his voice. "I must have dozed off. Why didn't you wake me?"

"I thought it best to let you sleep," he said as he pivoted her toward him. "Let's go into the house." He reached out and shut the truck's door. "We need to talk."

"What's wrong?" Libby's hands flew to her face, fearing the worst. "Is it Amber?"

"No."

"Then what are we doing here, Cash? Let's get back on the road." She grabbed the door handle, intending to climb back into the truck, but he blocked her way. "Come on! We've got to find her!"

He took her hands in his and gazed into her eyes. The silvery glow of the streetlight illuminated his damp, freshly showered hair and clean-shaven face.

"Look, we've covered every area we could think of and didn't obtain even one clue as to her whereabouts. Her future is and always has been in God's hands. Don't you see that? We've done everything that the situation called for. Now it's time to stand, to stay in faith, and wait for Him to bring her home."

She leaned forward, resting her forehead against his warm, comforting shoulder. Her mental strength had completely given out. "It's so hard to be patient, Cash. I've spent half of my life waiting for her."

His fingers intertwined with her hair and gently patted the crown of her head. "Well, there is one last thing we can do. She's been gone for twenty-four hours now so I can file a police report." He took her hand and led her around the front of the truck toward the porch. "In a couple of minutes, I'm going to the station to take care of it. While I'm gone, I want you to rest. If you don't, you're going to get sick. I've stacked a pillow and a blanket for you on the sofa in my den. It's the most comfortable room in the house and if you shut the door you'll have total peace and quiet."

At the front door, he stopped under the porch light. A new glow sparkled in his eyes, his face brightened with elation. "There's something I need to share with you, though, before I leave." He placed his hands gently on her shoulders. "Olivia, I—"

Stress, disappointment and so little sleep had frayed her nerves to the breaking point. "Please, stop calling me, Olivia!" She pulled away. "I *hate* that name!"

"Hey, I'm sorry." He lifted one hand to declare a truce. "I didn't mean to upset you. Sometimes it just slips out. Why are you so sensitive about your legal name?"

She hadn't intended to get so ornery, but once she'd opened her mouth, her emotions, fueled by hurtful memories had taken over. Now she regretted it.

"I'm sorry, too, Cash," she responded wearily. "It's really not your fault. The reason I'm so touchy about hearing my name is that Grandma Cunningham used to call me *Olivia* every time I made her upset. The last time she used it, she'd disowned me for being pregnant. The things she said hurt me very much. Every time you refer to me in that way you remind me of how soiled, how worthless she still makes me feel!"

"Listen to me," Cash said and gripped her upper arms, pulling her close. "You're not soiled or worthless. Everyone makes mistakes, including your granny. Once you repent of your sins and receive forgiveness, they're gone— as far as the east is from the west. You already know that, but you need to accept it. If God can forget them, you can, too. I promise I'll never call you by that name again, but please stop beating up yourself over someone else's problem."

She gazed into his eyes, surprised by the caring and tenderness of his reply, yet bewildered by the blatant irony of the words themselves. "Then why are you still angry over your own past?"

His countenance sobered. "That's what I want to talk to you about."

Something in his purposeful tone of voice unnerved her. Her head swam with confusion and fatigue as she stepped back, bracing herself.

"Libby, I've been such a fool." He moved closer, still maintaining his grip on her arms. "All these years I've believed the lies that trusted people told me, supposedly to protect me when I should have checked them out myself. Over the past few weeks, I've seen and heard things that have made me realize I've been wrong about you, and I'm sorry—sorry for everything."

His confession stunned her. Her heart raced as she tried to make sense of the moment, afraid she'd misunderstood.

He stood so close she could barely breathe. The rich, spicy scent of his aftershave filled her lungs, making her more than aware of her desire for him. Desperate to put some distance between him and her fragile emotions she pulled away and took another step backward, but her shoulders bumped against the wood siding. With nowhere else to go, she folded her arms to provide a barrier, locking them into a tight bow.

"I've already made peace with God," he said softly, "and I want more than anything to make peace with you. I don't deserve it and I don't blame you if you refuse, but I'm asking you to forgive me for letting you down. You were right. Looking back, I realize that I *did* take the coward's way out. I *did* abandon you when you needed me the most. When you disappeared, I should have tracked you down and verified the truth instead of believing what everyone told me. I should have questioned everything. The sad part is that my personal failures cheated us both out of a lot of happiness. Will you forgive me?"

Years of grief stung the backs of her eyes, but she refused to let the tears fall. There would be plenty of time to cry—tears of joy—later on.

"Oh, Cash," she whispered unsteadily, "I forgave you years ago." She turned her head to one side to avoid his piercing stare. "What about my past? How could you ever forgive me for committing the worst offense of all—for giving up our child without your knowledge?"

"It wasn't your fault. Frank made the decision for you, just like my parents made decisions for me."

He took her chin between his thumb and forefinger and gently turned her face toward his. In the silvery shadows of the open porch, their gazes met and held. His voice dropped to a husky whisper. "I don't care about any of that stuff anymore. It's ancient history. I only care about Amber and you. In fact, *I love you*." Cupping her face in his hands, he tipped his head to one side. "Ever since that night I kissed you, I've wanted so badly to do it again." He dropped his gaze to her mouth then slowly, tenderly placed his lips on hers, as though giving her ample time to refuse.

Nothing could have been farther from her mind...

The moment they kissed, nearly seventeen years of pain melted away, leaving only her deepest desires to fill the void. Denying her fears, she wrapped her arms around his neck as long-buried passions bubbled up in her soul, suddenly energizing her and yet, giving her peace. The sheltering strength of his arms felt so good, so right!

Their lips parted then joined again.

"I love you so much, Libby," he said in a desperate tone as he pulled away. "I've never stopped loving you, even though I've spent years making myself miserable—telling myself you didn't mean a thing to me. Since that night I saw you at the game, I haven't been able to get you out of my mind—or my heart. Now I know why just thinking your name drives me crazy. I'm nothing without you and I'm never going to lose you again."

"Oh, Cash, I love you, too!" Tears stung her eyes once more, but this time she didn't have the power to hold them back. "The night you kissed me, I realized I'd never stopped loving you, either, and it frightened me beyond belief because I thought you despised me. I didn't know how I could ever face you again without letting it show. That's why I barely spoke to you after that and suggested that we plan activities with Amber separately." She squeezed her eyes shut. "I didn't trust myself."

Burying her face in the warmth of his shoulder, she collapsed against him and sobbed like a child. "I wish we could go back to the beginning and start over. We've made so many mistakes and missed out on so much."

"We need to leave what lies behind—all of it—and press on because we still have today and the rest of our lives to be together," he whispered as he wrapped his arms around her and held her close. "Whatever the future brings, for better or for worse—we'll face it together. No matter what happens, we'll always have each other."

She relaxed in his embrace, pressing her face against his shoulder until her tears subsided.

"Libby, look at me," Cash said in an urgent voice.

Startled, she pulled her tear-stained face away from his shoulder.

"I asked you this once before and you told me off. I deserved it that time because, frankly, I acted like an idiot. This time I hope you'll give me the answer we both want." He gently took her hand and went down on one knee. "Libby Cunningham, I'd be very honored if—"

His cell phone suddenly went off. They both startled then froze.

He pulled his phone out of the clip on his belt, swiped the screen, and pressed the call button, but the call suddenly broke off. The caller ID flashed 'Unknown' on the screen. He growled at the inconvenient interruption and this time slipped it into his shirt pocket.

"Hurry up! Say it!" Libby cried in a high-pitched voice.

"My darling Libby," he said, starting once more. "We've got a future to plan together and I would be most honored if you—"

The phone blared again.

"Oh, no!" She blew out an exasperated sigh but knew their moment had to wait. "Answer it, quick! It could be Amber!"

Using his free hand, he jerked the phone out of his pocket, impatiently swiping the screen at the same time. "It's that unknown number again. Must be a telemarketer."

He jammed the phone to his ear. "Can't this wait? I'm kind of *busy* right now."

Libby watched; her heart hammered with alarm as his impatient scowl morphed into wide-eyed surprise.

"Right." Tense lines bracketed his mouth. He stared at the ground then jerked his gaze upward to meet hers. "We're on our way."

"What's going on?" Libby clutched her heart, knowing it had to be something serious. "Is it about Amber?"

He shoved the phone into the clip on his belt and sprang to his feet. "Yes. Brian found her and he wants us to get down there right away."

*   *   *

Cash grabbed Libby by the hand again and jumped off the porch steps.

"Where is she?"

"At the pavilion," he hollered over his shoulder as they sprinted toward the truck.

"But...that's at the other end of the island! Has she been there all the time?"

He shrugged. "I have no idea. All I know is that she's by the river's edge."

They jumped into the truck and raced across the island. Five minutes later Cash skidded to a halt at the pavilion parking area, just missing a tall cottonwood tree. He slammed the truck into first gear and jerked out the keys. Before he even put his hand on the driver's side door, Libby had catapulted from the vehicle and hit the ground running.

He caught up to her in seconds. They neared the pavilion as Brian and Todd rounded the corner of the gray, historic building that reminded him of a massive barn.

"Where is she?" Cash burst out as they met up with the men.

Brian waved his hand in the direction he came. "She's back there, by the river. Some kids from school are there, too. They're trying to talk her into coming down. They discovered her and called me. Medley's there, too, keeping an eye on things."

Coming down? He cringed at the sound of that...

Libby clutched Brian by the arm. "Why is Medley keeping an eye on her? What's wrong?"

Even in the shadows, Cash saw Brian pale. The boy shifted nervously from foot to foot as he glanced at Libby then at him. "She's talking suicide."

"No!" Libby screamed and bolted toward the river.

Cash quickly caught up to her and locked his hand with hers. They ran past the pavilion and the amphitheater to an area where the trees grew sideways over the river. Large spotlights lighting the grounds around the pavilion cast long shadows across the water.

Brian pointed toward a sloping area along the riverbank. "She's down there."

They found Medley standing close to the water, holding a light, and hanging on to a sturdy branch for dear life. A dozen or so teenagers crowded around her, murmuring among themselves. When Cash saw Amber, his stomach lurched. She had climbed out on a wind-blown tree that grew parallel over the water. Beneath her, the cold current swirled. He slowed and pulled Libby to his side, urging her to do the same. He didn't want any sudden moves to frighten the girl.

They shone the light across the water. Amber saw him almost immediately and flinched then turned away. She wore solid black slacks and a long-sleeved tunic. Her pale face and black pencil lining her eyes made her look like a drug-induced zombie. He prayed she hadn't ingested anything that would impair her abilities. Libby stood at his side, trembling as she silently clung to him for support. He slid his arm around her as a protective gesture and pulled her closer.

Todd took the light from Medley and passed it over to Brian, then encased his large hands around Medley's tiny waist and pulled her out of the way. "I've called Pastor Greg and asked him to talk to her," he whispered in Cash's ear. "He's on his way."

"Honey bear," Cash voiced gently as he approached the tree. The teens parted to let him through. "It's Daddy." He hadn't called himself that in years, but suddenly it seemed like the right thing to say.

She bent her arm in front of her face as if to shield herself from him. "Don't come any closer!"

He halted in his tracks. "I'll stop right here. Okay?"

"What do you want..." Her monotone reply sounded listless, depressed.

"I want to take you home. You belong with me."

She responded with a distrustful glare. "Why?"

"Because you're my little girl and I love you."

"No, you don't." She hung her head. "I'm nothing but trouble to you."

"That's not true, Amber. You're Daddy's little sweetheart, remember? You're my fuzzy little honey bear."

Instead of answering, she turned away and leaned toward the water.

His heart began to break as tears flowed down his face. He couldn't lose her this way. *God, have mercy on my child*, he silently cried.

Somewhere in the distance, a police siren screamed, sounding like a death knell.

Chapter 19

Libby trembled at the sight of her daughter's depressed condition. Squaring her shoulders, she stepped out from behind Cash. "I want to talk to her."

Slowly, she stepped to the water's edge, clasping her hands on the tree in front of her. "Amber," she said softly to the girl's back, "it's Mom. May we talk?"

Without turning around, Amber shook her head. "I don't know why *you'd* want to be my mom anymore."

Libby clutched the cross at her throat. *Lord, give me the wisdom to say the right words. I have to get through to her!*

"I've wanted you since the first time I held you in my arms," she answered softly. "I still do, Amber."

Amber hung her head. "I'm a troublemaker. No one likes me."

Cash moved in behind Libby. She glanced over her shoulder at the touch of his hand on her arm. "There's more going on with her than I can address from here," she whispered. "If I could just get closer to her, maybe I could convince her to come down." She turned slightly in his direction. "I'm going to climb out there and talk to her."

"No," he said without hesitation. "I won't risk it. You could both fall in and be gone in the blink of an eye."

"That's a risk I'm willing to take."

"Let the police handle it, Libby." His hand tightened around her arm. "They're on the way now."

"She won't talk to some stranger, Cash," Libby whispered earnestly. "She wouldn't talk to Brian or her friends. I can hardly get her to talk to me. Look at her! She's deeply depressed." She pulled away from him. "Like it or not, I'm climbing out there. She's my only child and she's in danger. I'd rather die trying to save her than live without her."

Cash's eyes widened with terror. "Don't say that! I couldn't live without either of you!"

Todd approached them carrying a thick coil of nylon rope, the kind that fishermen used to secure a boat to a dock. "We don't have any life jackets, but this could work," he said calmly. "If we tied this rope around Libby's waist, she'd be protected from being swept away if she fell in. Besides that, she could hold on to Amber and possibly save Amber if the girl goes in first."

"No," Cash argued, his voice shaking. "It's too dangerous. We can't risk it."

Libby reached for the rope. "Help me secure it, Todd. I'm going to climb out there."

Cash ceased arguing and proceeded to help Todd secure the rope around her waist as he talked non-stop, bombarding her with instructions on several scenarios.

Nervous and shaking, Libby approached the leaning tree. "Amber, I'm coming out where you're sitting to talk to you."

She turned her head in Libby's direction. "No. It won't do any good."

Libby placed her foot in Todd's joined hands and gripped a branch to steady herself as Cash gave her a boost onto the base of the horizontal trunk. "I can't accept that. We've just begun to know each other. I can't let you go now."

Her foot slipped on the bark.

"Be careful!" Amber cried. "You might fall."

Libby began to crawl along the narrow trunk, stopping repeatedly to stabilize her balance in sync with the swaying of the tree. After a slow, nerve-wracking journey, she finally reached the spot where Amber sat, staring hypnotically at the water.

"What do you want?"

Libby steadied herself then settled down beside Amber. "Your dad and I have been looking all over for you. We want you to come home with us."

"Why?"

"We love you, Amber."

"You don't love *him* anymore. You did once, though, a long time ago. Didn't you?" She turned away. "It's all my fault."

"No, that's not true," Libby replied, shocked by Amber's statement. "Why do you say that?"

"I shouldn't have been born," Amber replied, her voice threaded with acute sadness. "You and Dad were in love once, but then I came along and ruined everything."

Amber's impression of the past broke Libby's heart. "Don't say that, honey. What happened isn't your fault. Having you has made us both very happy."

Amber shook her head. "Then why am I still ruining everything? I acted like such a brat that night we met at the restaurant for dinner. I get into trouble and make you cry. You'd be better off if I weren't around anymore."

Libby swallowed back the urge to let out a frustrated scream. "Amber, don't say that!"

The tree groaned under their weight.

"Libby and Amber, come down off that tree right now!" Cash called frantically.

"Why shouldn't I?" Amber cried to Libby, ignoring Cash's plea as her voice choked with tears. "You and Dad can't love each other because every time you try to talk about it, you start yelling at each other about me. If I were gone, you wouldn't have anything to fight about anymore. You could be in love again. You'd be happy like you were before I came along and caused you to break up."

As the truth unfolded, Libby realized what she had failed to see all along—the destructive family cycle of her childhood repeating itself in her daughter. Amber's life uncannily mirrored her own—the absent mother, the busy, distracted father, the handsome boy with an attitude...

Dear God, forgive me for being so utterly selfish. I've spent so much time focusing on my own issues that I've neglected the one person who needs me the most. Give me another chance to make things right!

Drawing strength from her faith, she leaned close. "What happened in the past is not your fault, Amber. It's mine. I've made bad choices that affected all three of us. I should never have agreed to let my father send you away. Please forgive me."

"I don't blame you for what happened, Mom. He *made* you sign the papers. He forced you to do it because he wanted you to move to Seattle and finish school there. That way no one would find out you'd had a baby."

Libby blinked in bewilderment, even as a huge burden lifted from her heart. Amber's understanding meant the world to her, but how did Amber know of her father's wish for her to attend a school in Seattle? "What did you say?"

Amber looked down at the water again and shrugged. "I read your letters to Dad."

"H-how did you get your hands on them?" She stared at Amber, shocked. "I mean, who gave them to you?"

"When we were moving everything out of the basement for the estate sale, I saw them lying in the bottom of Grandma MacKenzie's sewing chest so I took them. I didn't think anyone would notice if they disappeared." She shook her head. "No one did."

Libby swallowed hard, self-conscious of their personal content. "You read them? All of them?"

Amber nodded. "Uh-huh."

"What...did you do with them?"

"I hid them in my closet—in a box under some board games."

Libby glanced at Cash, standing at the water's edge. The stricken look on his face told her that he'd heard every word.

"I wish we could all be together," Amber said so softly that Libby barely heard it. "You know, like a real family. That's my dream."

Libby glanced at the activity on the riverbank and saw Pastor Greg's car pull into the parking lot. More people had gathered on the grounds—watching, waiting for the right moment to pull them to safety.

"Honey, you're *my* dream. You always have been, since you were that tiny little bundle I held in the hospital." Libby reached over to touch her, but Amber flinched and shrunk away. Determined to find common ground, she pressed on. "No matter what, the three of us will always be a family and you're the reason. Don't you see? You're the living link that connects us. You don't divide us. We love you. *I* love you more than you will ever know."

She looked up. "I love you, too, Mom. You're awesome."

"I love you both. I need you both! Let's go home and start a new life together," Cash begged, standing at the base of the tree. "We *can* be a family."

Amber shook her head. "I'll just ruin everything again."

"I'm the one who keeps ruining things," Cash said, looking chagrined. "I should have asked Libby to marry me a long time ago."

Amber perked up, raising one eyebrow. "You didn't call her Olivia. That's weird." She cut Libby a hopeful look. "She might say yes now if you asked her nice."

Cash tossed his hands into the air. "I've tried to ask her twice, but the phone rang and—"

"D-a-a-d," Amber whined, "just d-o-o-o it!" She rolled her eyes. "Sometimes he can be such a geek."

"Geek, huh? Watch this," Cash said and knelt at the base of the tree. Behind him, everyone on the scene stood motionless as he pulled his phone from the clip on his belt and threw it over his shoulder in the direction of where Todd stood. "Now," he said, looking up at them. "Libby Cunningham, will you *please* do me the honor of being my wife?"

"Well, it's about time." Libby smiled. "Yes!"

"Oh, Mom!" Amber threw her arms around Libby. The tree began to sway. Libby tried to steady herself to keep her balance, but the momentum caused them both to panic.

Screams pierced the air as they suddenly plunged into the river.

*   *   *

"N-o-o-o-o!"

The scene unfolded with the surreal quality of a black and white horror movie. Cash watched, stunned, as Libby and Amber cried out and dropped into the swirling water, disappearing before his eyes.

Without a second thought, he broke loose from the hands that struggled to hold him back and dove into the dark, icy river, frantic to save his family.

He couldn't see a thing in the frigid, inky water, but fought the current as he held his breath and pulled himself along the rope, praying that he'd locate Libby—and Amber. About twenty feet out, his hand suddenly grabbed a piece of clothing. He pulled on it as it came toward him, thrashing violently. Instinctively, he knew he'd found Amber, but he couldn't tell if she held on to Libby.

Still clutching the rope, he bobbed to the surface with her. Knowing how to handle herself in the water gave her at least a fighting chance. Cash coughed up water and gasped for air as he fought the current. He shook the water out of his eyes.

"Amber! Where are you?" he cried over the shouting and confusion as she slipped away.

"I'm over here! I'm okay, Dad!" she screamed as she swam toward a bevy of clamoring people on the riverbank with their arms outstretched.

Thank God for Amber's swimming lessons!

She quickly reached the riverbank and turned her head toward him as a half-dozen people, including Pastor Greg, pulled her to safety. "Where's Mom? Find Mom!"

Find Mom...

Without answering, he dove under again and found Libby thrashing about in panic, trying to unhook her clothing from a sunken branch. A surge of adrenaline propelled him to yank her free. Knowing she needed air *now*, he slid his arm around her ribcage and pulled her to the surface.

"I've got you," he said once they'd broken through the water. She slumped against his shoulder, coughing in between gasps for air. "We're almost there..." A sharp tug reminded him of the rope around her waist. He grabbed hold of it with one hand and tugged in response, holding on while their rescuers towed them both to shore.

They emerged from the water, falling to the ground from sheer exhaustion.

Amid the din, someone pried Libby from his arms. Someone else wrapped a blanket around him as he sat up, trying to catch his breath. Once his head cleared, Cash glanced around, looking for Libby and Amber, but he couldn't see them in the crowd surrounding him. Panicking again, he rose unsteadily to his feet. Todd suddenly appeared beside him and urged him to sit down. Instead, he broke away from his best friend and staggered through the crowd like a drunken man, desperately searching for the girls.

"Libby! Amber! Where are you?"

"We're over here, Dad!" Amber shouted behind him.

He spun in the direction of her voice, but too many people surrounded him, blocking his view. Suddenly he saw them both sitting on the ground with Pastor Greg, Medley, and Brian. Though they shared a blanket, they shivered from being cold and dripping wet—but they were unharmed! The rope idea had worked! Cash didn't know how to thank Todd for his quick thinking and a Hummer full of fishing gear, but he knew he owed his best friend more than he could ever repay.

He stumbled over to the group. "I don't know what I would have done if I'd lost either of you," he blurted hoarsely to Libby and Amber as he numbly fell to his knees.

"Mom, Dad, I'm sorry for not listening to you!" Amber cried. "If I would have come down when you told me to, this would never have happened."

"We're safe now and that's all that matters." He wrapped his blanket around both girls, pulling them into a huddle. "I just want to hold you both and never let you go. I love you both."

Libby shivered violently and moved closer into his embrace. "Say that again, Cash. I'll never get tired of hearing it."

Under the silvery glow of the pavilion's outdoor lights, he put his hand under her chin and raised her face to his. "I love you, Libby Cunningham. I always have and I always will. I promise you this time there won't be any lies, deception, or others making our decisions." He kissed her tenderly. "No one will keep us apart ever again. This time, it's forever."

Epilogue

"Blink hard!" Medley sniffled loudly as she fussed with last-minute details on Libby's hair. "Lib, Lib, we have to stop this, or both of our faces will be ruined."

Libby sat in front of a large dressing table with a sheet over her wedding dress and forced back tears of joy. She wanted to look perfect for Cash on her wedding day, but every time she and Medley made eye contact in the mirror, their happiness and excitement spilled over.

Medley had been staying at the house for two days, serving as both a wedding planner and Libby's personal attendant. Armed with her trusty clipboard of invoices, contracts, and a tightly crafted schedule, Medley had personally supervised every detail of both the ceremony and reception, leaving nothing for Libby to do but watch the transformation of her house into a yuletide wedding chapel.

"You're finished," Medley announced with a sigh of relief and reached for a can of hair spray so large she could barely wrap her fingers around it. "Cover your face!"

Libby cupped her hands over her professional makeup application, squeezing her eyes shut as a heavy shower of sticky mist enveloped her. "That's enough, Medley," she said, unable to stifle a small cough. "My hair feels so stiff I can hardly move my head."

"It's perfect." Medley set down the blue spray can and picked up a square hand mirror. "Here, take a look."

She didn't doubt Medley had performed a marvelous job, but she took the mirror and viewed her cousin's handiwork, anyway. Medley had given her a sweeping up-do of curls intertwined with tiny sprigs of white baby's breath. Wispy tendrils trailed past her temples and from the nape of her neck.

The bedroom door opened and Amber burst in wearing a red velvet dress. "Oh, Mom! You look s-o-o-o beautiful!"

Medley stepped away, rattail comb in one hand, extra hairpins in the other, radiating with personal satisfaction. "Just like a princess bride. Am I not the best makeup and hair artist in this town or what?"

"You're awesome," Amber exclaimed as she peered over Libby's shoulder into the mirror. Medley had parted Amber's French braid on the side and started the braids at her forehead, working two narrow ribbons, one red, one white, through each braid, weaving the fabric together into the thick main braid at the nape of her neck.

Medley put down the mirror and began to rearrange a tiny sprig of baby's breath wound around the elastic band at the end of Amber's braid. "What's going on downstairs?"

Amber good-naturedly pulled her hair out of Medley's grasp. "The house is full of people. It's a good thing this is a big place. So far, most of them are my cousins, aunts and uncles, and Dad's friends, but some of Mom's relatives have arrived now, too." She glanced at Libby in the mirror. "Some lady named Ardelle just showed up and a lot of your friends from Stefano's are also here."

Medley gasped. "Have the caterers arrived yet?"

Amber shook her head. "I haven't seen anyone bringing in food. They're supposed to come in the back door, right?"

"Yes." Medley tapped her red designer shoe on the carpet. She looked stunning in her red velvet bridesmaid dress. She'd colored her hair a rich mahogany hue to complement it. "Well, they'd better not be late."

The food for the reception came from Stefano's, of course, and Libby had chosen a three-tiered raspberry cake with white chocolate "buttercream" frosting from a vendor she trusted and regularly used.

Medley ruled with autonomy over everything else. She'd contracted with a rental company to erect a massive walled tent in the backyard, complete with heat, carpeting, and an enclosed walkway to the house. The house, reception tent, and grounds had been decorated with enough lights, poinsettias, and festive ornaments to rival Christmas at the White House. Libby had preferred to plan her own wedding; it definitely would have been a much simpler affair than the holiday extravaganza Medley somehow put together in a mere two months. Instead, she'd given in to Medley's shameless begging and allowed her cousin to orchestrate the entire day.

Medley couldn't have been happier—or more stressed.

Amber rested her hands on the back of Libby's white boudoir chair and stared into the mirror. "Mom?"

"What?" Libby smiled. *I'll never get tired of hearing that name.*

"Now that you and Dad are getting married..." A mischievous twinkle in Amber's eyes hinted that she wanted something. "Um...can I have a little brother?"

Libby nearly swallowed her tongue.

"Puleese!" Medley exclaimed with a chortle. "You don't put in an order for a sibling like you're sitting at the drive-up window, yelling into the microphone for a Big Mac."

"I know that." Amber danced across the bedroom and flounced upon the bed. "I'm not stupid."

"Hey!" Medley jabbed her rattail comb toward Amber like an accusing finger. "Watch the hair!"

Libby turned at the waist. "Your dad and I haven't given any thought to having another baby. We've been concentrating on the wedding and our honeymoon."

Amber stretched out, propping herself on one elbow. "But Mom, you don't want me to be an only child like you, do you?"

The words pierced Libby's heart. No, she didn't...

Amber's cocoa eyes widened with hopefulness, as though she'd read

Libby's thoughts. "Do you want another baby?"

Libby held still as Medley fixed a mascara smudge under her left eye. "I guess I'm not opposed to it, but—"

"Really?" Amber sat up. "Wow, I can't wait to tell Jenny!"

"Honey, it's a *family* decision. In other words, your father needs to be in favor of it as well."

"Then when can we talk to Dad about it?"

Libby evaded answering as a soft rapping on the door interrupted the conversation.

"May I come in?"

Medley pulled a hairpin from a curl, her hand stopping in mid-air at the unfamiliar feminine voice. "Who is it?"

The door opened slowly and an older woman of medium build with short, curly gray hair appeared wearing a tailored black suit and shimmering gold blouse.

"Of course, Maggie." Libby waved her in. "You're always welcome."

"Hi, Grandma!" Amber jumped off the bed and approached Maggie, giving her a hug. "Where's Grandpa?"

Maggie embraced her granddaughter with a chuckle. "Ray's downstairs with your aunts and uncles. Who is that young man with your father? The one with long hair." She frowned. "He's not your boyfriend, is he?"

"N-o-o-o." Amber rolled her eyes. "He's more like my brother. He hangs around with Dad and all they ever talk about is hunting, football, and that ice fishing trip they're going on after Christmas."

"How is your counseling coming along? Are you making progress?"

"Ah, it's okay." Amber shrugged. "Sometimes Mom and Dad participate in my sessions."

Maggie gave her a squeeze. "Are you excited about today?"

Amber nodded, beaming with happiness. "It's the best Christmas present—ever!"

Maggie turned to Libby. "Speaking of presents, I have a little gift for you." Though she spoke with the utmost politeness, the lack of warmth in Maggie's voice confirmed her reservations over her son's decision to marry Libby.

She has good reason to doubt me, but I intend to change that, Libby thought, determined to earn her mother-in-law's acceptance.

"Why, thank you." Libby accepted the small black velvet box. Opening the lid, she gasped with surprise at a pair of sparkling diamond earrings and a matching pendant in a yellow-gold teardrop setting. "They're beautiful!"

"I received the set from my husband on Christmas Day many years ago." Maggie clasped her hands together, as though needing something to do. "I thought you might like them."

Medley unhooked the gold cross from Libby's neck. "Wedding tradition calls for something old. Now you have it."

Amber looked puzzled. "What's that?"

Medley placed Libby's cross around Amber's neck and fastened the clasp. "It goes like this...something old, something new, something borrowed, and something blue." She began straightening one of the ribbons woven through Amber's braid. "The diamonds are old, the wedding dress is new, Libby's diamond bracelet is borrowed—from me—but I guess we still need to come up with something blue."

"That's easy." Amber slithered away from Medley's picky fingers. "Mom's eyes are blue."

Everyone laughed.

Libby slipped on the earrings. "They match nicely with my ring." She held out her left hand and examined the two-carat marquise diamond solitaire against her freshly manicured nails. "It's a bit extravagant, though."

"No, it's not!" Medley and Amber chimed together.

Maggie lifted the edge of the pale-yellow sheet covering Libby's dress. "May I see your gown?"

"I can't wait for you to see it," Libby replied, removing the sheet with a soft swish. She stood then pivoted slowly in front of Maggie.

"It's lovely." Maggie's hazel eyes took in Libby's strapless, cream silk gown with satiny crisscross ribbons around the waist. "You're going to make my son proud."

Everyone turned as a burst of laughter outside the doorway drew their attention away from the wedding discussion.

"That sounds like Cash." Medley hurried to the door and stood guard, ready to throw herself against it to protect the tradition of keeping the bride's dress a secret until the ceremony.

When the voices faded, Maggie turned back to Libby. "My son says he's going to sell his place and establish residency here."

The way she referred to Cash as *my son* made Libby uneasy. Maggie didn't approve of Cash pulling up stakes, selling his prized historic property on Nicollet Island, and moving into his wife's home.

"The plan is to keep both residences until Amber graduates then sell Cash's house." Libby hesitated at first but quickly decided she might as well tell Maggie everything. "Next summer we're going to build a lake home up north. Cash wants a place to store his boat and snowmobiles. Both of us are looking forward to getting away from the city on the weekends."

Maggie put her arm around her granddaughter. "How do you feel about that, Amber?"

"I can't wait to move in here, Grandma," Amber announced excitedly. "The rooms are gigantic. Mom's walk-in closet in the master bedroom is bigger than my whole bedroom at home. Besides, we're going to need more room, anyway." She held out her palms and looked perfectly serious. "I mean, who knows? Mom and Dad could have another baby—"

"Amber!!" Libby and Medley cut her off simultaneously.

Maggie's face blanched.

Medley gripped Amber's shoulders and gently, but firmly pushed her toward the door. "Let's go downstairs and check to see if the caterers have arrived, shall we?"

Libby and Maggie stood motionless as Amber and Medley left the room. The invisible wall between them grew with each passing second.

As soon as the door clicked shut, Libby turned to Maggie. "I apologize for Amber's outburst. Cash and I have never discussed expanding our family. It's simply wishful thinking on her part."

"That's all right, dear. You don't have to explain," Maggie said smoothly.

"Yes, I do," Libby insisted. "It's important to Cash and me, especially me, to do things right this time. We made serious mistakes in our youth and hurt many people. I'm truly sorry, Maggie, for the grief my actions caused your family and mine as well. I'd give anything for the chance to make amends with my Dad, but I can't, so I intend to honor his memory instead by conducting my life according to the Christian values he instilled in me."

Maggie's eyes widened but showed no sign of softening.

Libby blinked quickly to avoid messing up her makeup. "I thank God every day for giving Cash and me a second chance at happiness together. I'm blessed to be a part of your family."

Maggie clasped her hands together and said, "I hope you and Cash will find happiness together. He loves you very much."

Libby smiled. "Thank you, Maggie. That means a lot to me."

*　　*　　*

The chamber orchestra playing "Pachelbel Canon in D" filled the house as Medley, Amber and Libby waited at the top of the stairs for their cue to descend. They'd rehearsed this piece several times and Libby knew the exact note that signaled Medley to start the processional.

The scent of pine filled the air, courtesy of a heavy garland covering the railing of fresh boughs, gold ribbon, and red velvet bows.

The moment arrived. Medley took a deep breath, clutched her nosegay of ivory roses, and started down the stairs. Amber followed a couple of seconds behind her. Libby held back, waiting for her turn.

"Breathe," she whispered to herself when she heard her cue. She began to descend, holding on to her bouquet of red roses for dear life.

Medley reached the bottom stair and proceeded into the living-room-turned-chapel on a white carpet runner. A few moments later Amber took her place on the runner, sprinkling red rose petals behind her as she followed Medley.

Libby touched her foot on the runner and looked into the chapel. Pastor Greg stood at the altar. Cash stood next to Todd and Brian, waiting, smiling. Love and devotion shone in his eyes.

The instant their gazes met, her apprehension faded into a deep calm. She proceeded down the aisle on autopilot past rows of people but took no notice of them, even though the attention of one hundred and fifty guests rested upon her. She could only focus on Cash and the love he exuded for his bride.

She had never loved him more than at this moment.

As she reached the altar, Cash suddenly exchanged glances with Amber, imperceptibly shaking his head. As if nothing had happened, he focused upon Libby again, but this time his eye reflected a twinkle she hadn't seen before. The amused curve of his smile puzzled her. She glanced at Amber and saw her daughter suppress a giggle. Then realization dawned. That stinker had already started hounding her father about having a baby!

Libby smiled at both of them, barely able to contain her composure. Life with these two would never be dull.

But, this time, it would be forever.

The End

Thank you so much for reading this book! If you enjoyed it, please leave a review at the retailer where you purchased it. Thank you!

A note from Denise...

Parts of this book were difficult to write. Though the characters were Christians, I still wanted them to struggle with their humanity and it was hard to see them suffer! There are areas in which we all struggle with emotional issues and I wanted to show that even though our problems seem insurmountable, we can overcome them when we purpose in our hearts to forgive and move on. Thank you from the bottom of my heart. I look forward to sharing more stories with you.

Want more? Read the first chapter of each of my novels on my blog at:

https://www.deniseannette.blogspot.com

More Books by Denise Devine

Christmas Stories
Merry Christmas, Darling
A Christmas to Remember
A Merry Little Christmas
Once Upon a Christmas
A Very Merry Christmas - Hawaiian Holiday Series
~*~

Bride Books
The Encore Bride
Lisa – Beach Brides Series
Ava – Perfect Match Series
~*~

Moonshine Madness Series – Historical Suspense/Romance
The Bootlegger's Wife – Book 1
Guarding the Bootlegger's Widow – Book 2
The Bootlegger's Legacy – Book 3 - Coming Fall 2022
~*~

West Loon Bay Series – Small Town Romance
Small Town Girl – Book 1
Brown-Eyed Girl – Book 2 (September 2022)
~*~

Cozy Mystery
Unfinished Business
Dark Fortune
Shot in the Dark (August 2022)
~*~

This Time Forever - an inspirational romance
Romance and Mystery Under the Northern Lights – short stories
Northern Intrigue – an anthology of mystery stories